The man standing looking out of the window with his back to the room was not her husband, she realised that at once; this man was taller than Dick, and darker. She stopped and opened her mouth to cry out, but before she could do so, he had turned, crossed the room and taken her into his arms.

'My darling Louise, thank God I've found you!' he said. 'I've been searching all day.'

Before she could protest, he had pressed his lips to hers as if he really was glad to have found her. Taken by surprise, she did nothing at first, feeling his strength folding about her, supporting her. After the trials of the last year and the exhausting day she had had, she felt a great temptation to relax in his arms, to let him take charge of her life. But then she pulled herself together and began to struggle so that he was forced to take his mouth from hers.

'Let me alone!' she cried breathlessly, ashamed of her weakness. 'How dare you! Who do you think you are?'

'Me?' he queried, ignoring her anger and bowing slightly towards her. 'Why, Captain Paul Fourier, at your service.'

GW00337646

Although born in Singapore of a Dutch-South African father and English mother, Mary Nichols came to England when she was three and has spent most of her life in different parts of East Anglia and now lives in Ely, Cambridgeshire. She has been a radiographer, school secretary, information officer and industrial editor as well as a writer. Her writing career began in her teens with short stories and articles and more recently, novels. *In Love and War* is her first Masquerade Historical Romance.

Mary Nichols has three grown up children and three grandchildren.

IN LOVE
AND WAR
MARY NICHOLS

MILLS & BOON LIMITED
15-16 BROOK'S MEWS
LONDON W1A 1DR

First published in Great Britain 1986 by Mills & Boon Limited

© Mary Nichols 1986

*Australian copyright 1986
Philippine copyright 1987
This edition 1987*

ISBN 0 263 75669 6

*Set in Linotron Times 10 on 10 pt.
04-0287-77328*

*Typeset in Great Britain by
Associated Publishing Services
Made and printed in Great Britain by
Cox & Wyman Ltd, Reading*

CHAPTER ONE

DAWN DRIFTED ACROSS the sluggish waters of the Thames, along its muddy bank with its moored shipping, some of it bound for the Peninsular War, already two years old, over the huddle of riverside warehouses to the room at the Cross Keys where Louise Oakingham lay sleeplessly listening to the noise her husband and his gambling friends were making in the inn's parlour immediately below her.

She had been downstairs when the game began, helping the landlord as she often did in part payment for their lodgings. It was humiliating work for someone brought up as she had been in a comfortable loving home and comparative affluence, but she would not allow herself to dwell on it any more than she could help, retaining her self respect and a pride in her appearance which owed nothing to vanity in spite of her undoubted beauty.

She was small and slim, with auburn hair and clear blue eyes which sometimes flashed with a spirit nothing could quench, and a firm red mouth which could be set in a stubborn line if that was the way she felt. It angered Dick, as so many things angered him lately.

His companions she knew from earlier gambling sessions; there was a big, dark-haired man who was a costermonger by trade, when he bothered to follow it; there was Will Fletcher, a thin, bent little man with a pitted complexion; and Reuben Black, bearded, uncouth, with one eye several shades lighter than the other, which would have made him a sinister figure even in more wholesome surroundings. Louise, not normally given to strong dislikes, hated and feared him.

They had not been playing long when the costermonger dropped out; he had lost all he possessed and the stakes were beyond him. Disgusted, the others looked about for a substitute, and their eyes lit on a man sitting quietly in the corner who had been watching the game with evident interest for some time.

Dick called to him. 'You, sir! You in the corner, have you more stomach than our friend here? I'll wager you are not afraid to tempt Lady Luck. Come and make up our four.'

The stranger rose with feigned reluctance. 'I am not a gambling man, but I admit the pot is tempting.' He indicated a pile of coins in the centre of the table.

'Sit y'self down then,' said Reuben Black, indicating the chair just vacated by the costermonger. 'It's yours for the winning.'

'Your name, sir?' Dick asked, beginning to deal.

'Captain Paul Fourier of the 95th Rifles, home on sick leave.'

Louise had become aware of him much earlier in the evening, when she had served him with a tankard of ale. He was lean and muscular, with an upright bearing and proud head, topped by short dark hair which curled a little at the nape of his neck. He was bronzed as a man would be who lived most of his life out of doors in a warmer climate than England; his dark clothes were unpretentious, as if his appearance was of little importance to him, and though he appeared relaxed, he seemed wary, like a watchful cat, ready to spring as soon as its prey comes within reach of a well-aimed paw. Louise had found his demeanour disturbing, almost as if she herself were the prey. His brown eyes had looked directly into hers when she took the ale to him, and they seemed to see past the façade of indifference she had adopted, to pry into the depths of her unhappiness and size up her situation. She felt that he might somehow want to take advantage of that and though she did not see how he could, it put her on her guard.

At first Dick had insisted she stay at his side to wait on them, but she had obeyed so reluctantly, conscious that the stranger was staring at her with only half-veiled interest, that her husband, losing patience, had packed her off to bed.

'Off with you,' he had said, cuffing her in a pretence of playfulness. 'Away to your bed and your beauty sleep. I'll be with you as soon as I've relieved these fellows of their money . . .'

That had been hours and hours ago and still she could not sleep. She had started to think of home, and although she tried not to do that because it made her miserable, sometimes she could not help it; home was so far away, so unreachable, so much to be desired. Oh, if only she could turn the clock back, never to have made that fateful decision to link her life with Dick Oakingham's.

She recalled the comfortable old rectory where she had been born and brought up, the happy days of her childhood, her loving parents, now so tragically dead. Those had been golden days, full of sunshine and laughter. Lessons over, she liked nothing better than to ride her horse across hill and heath, galloping with the sun on her back and the wind loosening her hair. It was on such a ride she had first met Dick.

He was with his cousin David, out for a day's shooting, when she inadvertently rode across their line of fire.

'Hey you, girl,' he had shouted. 'Get out of the way! D'you want to be killed?'

She had reined in and turned to face them, then trotted over to where they stood on the edge of a copse of copper beech, her sixteen-year-old dignity on display. 'You are a very rude young man!'

He laughed. 'What else am I to call you, seeing I don't know your name?'

'It's Louise Topham.'

He was rather a plump young man, pink-cheeked, blue-eyed, with a shock of fair curls. His companion, a year or two older, was taller and slimmer and seemed to be the shy one of the two, content to let Dick do all the talking.

'And where do you live, Louise?'

'Miss Topham, if you please. You can't know the

area very well, or you'd know I am the daughter of
the Rector of Haleham.'

'Is that so?' He had smiled, and although she had
tried to keep a straight face, she found herself smiling
back. 'I think we shall see more of each other, my
dear Miss Topham. My parents have just bought
Haleham Manor; we shall be neighbours . . .'

'And do you usually go about shooting your
neighbours?'

He had laughed aloud. 'Not if they are as pretty as
you.'

There was no answer to that and she had cantered
away, jumping a gate just to show off, but when she
was safely out of sight and range of their sporting
guns, she slowed the horse to a walk. What a silly
she was! She had not even asked his name, and
Mama was sure to want to know it.

But, as it happened, her mother knew more about
their new neighbours than she did. Lady Oakingham
had already called at the rectory and been invited in
to take tea.

'Sir Richard is very well thought of in society,'
Mama had said. 'He is very wealthy, I believe, and
his wife is a charming lady. I'm sure we're all going
to be great friends.'

A few days later they had attended a supper party
at the Manor, and Louise met Dick and his young
cousin again. Under the watchful eye of his parents
he behaved perfectly, and she came to the conclusion
she had misjudged him, that his forwardness at their
earlier meeting had been due to his concern for her
safety.

The Oakinghams did not live permanently in the
country, but divided their time between Haleham and
London and the boys went away to Oxford, so that it
was three years before she spoke to either of them
again. In three years Dick had grown into a tall, slim,
handsome man with an easy charm, and she had
become quite a lady, her tomboy days behind her.

He began to call on her, bowling her over with his
attentions and, before long, his protestations of
undying love, a love she had accepted and returned,

feeding his vanity with her silliness. It was not as if he were the only man in her life: other young men had called at the rectory, shy, serious young men, among them Dick's cousin David, who had become a lawyer and had his own modest home in London. She had turned them all away, because the heart rules the head when it comes to falling in love, and for her there was only Dick.

When her parents had been killed in a dreadful coaching accident leaving her, at nineteen, suddenly and devastatingly alone in the world, it was to Dick she turned. He supported her through the ordeal, stood beside her at the grave, offered her his love and protection and, after the funeral, when she was at her most vulnerable, asked her to marry him.

'But I am in mourning,' she had demurred. 'Ask me again in another year.'

'Oh, my love,' he had said. 'I don't think I can wait that long.' He had smiled and kissed her with every appearance of fondness, adding, 'And what will you do in the meantime? You have no family and you can't stay here alone; Haleham will have another rector, and he will need this house.'

'But it would be unseemly to marry so soon.'

'Oh, to blazes with convention!' He had exploded into anger, an anger she was to come to know so well, but then checked himself and spoke softly. 'We could marry in secret and move to London. Oh, say you will, my love.'

'What will your family say? I'm sure they won't approve.'

'We needn't tell them, not immediately. When the period of mourning has passed . . .'

Why had she allowed herself to be persuaded? It was the most terrible decision of her young life.

They were married at a small church about twenty miles from Haleham, where the parson had been bribed to keep their secret. There were only two witnesses, complete strangers to Louise, and she guessed Dick had never met them before that day either; they had been paid to do the job and she had never seen them again. It was far from the wedding of her dreams, but Dick had made it seem like a great adventure and promised her a proper wedding when the mourning was over and his parents had been told. Afterwards they took a coach to London.

She had always looked forward to going there; she had imagined it would be so gay and happy, an endless round of balls and receptions, carriage rides in the park with Dick beside her, shopping excursions, a nice home to furnish and people coming to dine. How different the reality had been!

It had not been long before she discovered Dick had no money of his own, but, until his twenty-fifth birthday, still two years away, relied on an allowance from his father which was less than adequate for a married man and which, in any case, he gambled away.

In the last year she had endured the loss of her own money, the pawning of her jewels, the move from house to apartment, from apartment to furnished room, one room, then another, each smaller and more sordid than the last. She had endured because there had been no choice; she could not go back, there was nowhere to go back to, and besides, she still loved him.

There was very little left now, but still he gambled; it was like a disease, contagious, incurable, eating into his soul. No matter what the game was—horse-racing, cards, dice, cock-fighting, rat-catching—'I'll wager' was the most frequent phrase he used. She knew she could never stop him and had given up protests which fell on deaf ears, and because he was bitterly disappointed that her inheritance was smaller than he had hoped, he somehow managed to lay the blame for their troubles at her feet.

She raised her head from the pillow as an extra loud gust of laughter carried up from the room below, then died and was replaced by angry words. Though she could not hear what was being said, it was almost certainly a quarrel about money, no doubt Dick had lost, and could not pay; it was always something of the sort and usually meant another sacrifice on her part, a brooch, a ring, even her clothes. Her fashionable diaphanous gowns with their high waists and full sleeves, the heavily embroidered tunics, fur-lined coats, warm boots, flower trimmed bonnets, all had gone. She dressed like the working-class woman she had become, in skirts and blouses and shawls. But none of that would have mattered if she could be sure he still loved her.

In spite of the chill of early spring, the room was airless; she got out of bed and padded across the floor in her bare feet and pushed open the casement. Day was growing; she could see the broad stretch of the river, gleaming like pewter, the hulls and masts of half-loaded ships, the dockyard warehouses, the neighbouring buildings, stark against the skyline. She could smell the dank odour of the river, wet coal, rotting vegetation, fish, sewage. Soon people would begin moving about on their daily business, but now all was quiet except for the noisy group in the parlour, whose voices drifted up to her through the open window.

'Of course I'll pay, have I ever let you down? Honest Dick, that's me, and a gambling debt is a debt of honour.' Her husband attempted to laugh, but it died in his throat.

'And how, pray?' Reuben Black asked. 'Has that pretty little wife of yours anything left for the popshop?'

'And what makes you suppose I'm dependent on her?' Dick's voice was boastful. 'She's only a plaything I've tired of.'

'Meaning you've bled her dry.'

There was a pause before Paul Fourier said quietly, 'Well, sir, how do you propose to pay?'

'My father . . .'

This was greeted by laughter from Black and Fletcher, justifiable derision, Louise decided; Dick's father had cut off his allowance and threatened to disinherit him if he asked for a penny more to pay gambling debts. He still had not been informed of his son's marriage, though Louise had asked Dick repeatedly to tell him.

'You may laugh, but my dear papa has come

forward with a solution to my problems that I've a mind to go along with . . .'

'And what is that?' The Captain's voice was still quiet, but its tone was far more menacing than the loud threats of the other two.

'Marry into money. He has been busy on my behalf and found a suitable wealthy match.'

'But you're already married,' Will said. 'Are you thinking of chancing the bigamy stakes?'

'Mebbe.'

'And how do you propose to accomplish it? It'd have to be a society wedding and all that caper. D'you suppose little Miss Louise will keep her mouth shut and let you do it?'

Louise was almost hanging out of the upper window, intent on catching every word. It was the sort of fantasy her husband would indulge in: he lived in a world of his own imagining, one in which his every wish was indulged and everyone accepted whatever he said, however preposterous. But bigamy! That was going too far; surely he did not expect them to believe he meant it? But whether they did or not, she knew from experience what the outcome would be. Somehow he would convince them he meant to pay, and they would agree to return for their winnings at a later date. As soon as they had gone, he would bound up the stairs and tell her to pack. She might as well begin doing it now, it was a course of action so familiar to her.

But she stayed at the window when she heard Reuben Black say, 'The Thames is wide, and in the middle it's very deep, and accidents happen all the time.' No one answered him and, after a pause, he added, ''Tis no different from putting down a clutch of kittens. And who is there to mourn her or even notice her passing?'

'You'd do it?' Will Fletcher asked.

'If it were the only way to collect our dues.'

Louise held her breath, waiting for Dick to laugh and protest he had only been jesting, but he remained silent. She wondered what he was thinking, tried to picture the scene—the two ruffians, the quietly-spoken

Captain, the cards spread on the table, the pile of coins, and Dick, looking from one to the other with a slight smile on his handsome face, trying to bluff his way out of trouble with a story so wild that it was almost funny.

''Twould be a pity to end such a pretty young life.' Paul Fourier's voice was a drawl. 'It would be a crying shame . . .'

'Ain't you wasted a few young lives y'self?' demanded Will. 'You're a soldier—killin's your game.'

'It's no game, I can assure you.'

'But you wouldn't hesitate if it was necessary?'

'No.'

'And women are the spoils of war, ain't that so? The dark-eyed Spanish wenches, are they not game?'

'We are not at war with Spain.'

'And what has that to do with Oakingham's debt?' Reuben Black said impatiently. 'I want to know when I'm to be paid, and that won't be 'til Dick gets hisself a new meal ticket, or I miss my guess. If that's so, it's up to us to help him get it . . . For a price, o' course.'

'Meaning?' Paul Fourier's voice was almost too low for Louise to hear.

'Like I said, we do the deed and get paid out o' the new dowry . . . with interest, naturally.'

Louise gasped aloud; Dick might have been joking, but the others clearly were not, they were deadly serious. Surely he could see that? He must put a stop to the dangerous game they were playing before it went too far. But he did not; he said nothing. 'Please!' she whispered. 'Please stop them talking like that. If you love me, if you ever loved me, stop them now.'

But she pleaded in vain. It was the Captain who spoke. 'I'll make you a proposition, Oakingham. Double or quits, winner takes the girl . . .'

Louise could not believe she was not having a nightmare, and shifted her position at the window; it squeaked ominously and she was afraid they would hear it, but no one came to the lower casement and the conversation continued.

'That won't serve,' Black said. 'If she lives, she can call her husband to book at any time the fancy takes her, and where will he be then? High and dry, that's where . . .'

'Once you've been paid, will that be any concern of yours?' the Captain asked.

Both Black and Fletcher let out a loud guffaw of laughter, and Will said, 'You're right there, ol' mate. But what will you do with the little beauty? She'll not be much use as a bed-warmer . . . cold as charity, she is, and haughty with it, and she ain't much good at real work neither, not bein' used to it.'

'I'll break her in, you can be sure.' There was amusement in Paul Fourier's voice. 'I'll take her away where she won't trouble you again.'

Dick spoke at last, but his words cut like a knife into her heart. 'Where do you propose to take her?'

She pushed her fist into her mouth to stop herself crying out, staring out across the riverside buildings to the river itself, seeing it through a mist of tears. Surely he was not contemplating taking up the challenge and gambling his own wife? He couldn't, he couldn't, treat her like a piece of furniture to be handed over to a stranger to use as he pleased—not even Dick, whose capacity to hurt her seemed unending, could be so monstrously wicked. It was unbelievable. He had been driven into a corner by the others, that was it, and the best thing she could do was to make it impossible for him to honour the debt if he lost.

'Does it matter?' the Captain asked. 'If I win, I take her and you never hear of her again. If I lose, your debt is cleared and you may do with the wench what you please.'

Louise did not wait to hear Dick's reply, but turned back into the room and hurried across the bare boards to scramble into some clothes, a petticoat, skirt and blouse, topped by a woollen shawl, nothing too cumbersome; then, gathering up her few valuables into a small canvas bag, she went to the door.

Stealthily she opened it, pausing to listen as it creaked, but the men in the room downstairs, busily dealing cards, did not hear and there was no one else about. She crept down the stairs slowly, standing to listen on each step, her heart thumping. At the bottom she paused; the door to the parlour was only inches away and she could hear the chink of glasses as they toasted this new, outrageous gamble. She fumbled with the bolts of the outer door, taking what seemed ages to draw them and open it, but at last a gust of cool air fanned her face and she was out in the open. She shut the door quietly behind her and crept away, her only thought to escape, to put herself out of reach of those barbaric men.

Convinced she was being followed, she hurried along the wet streets, turning this way and that, trying to shake off her pursuers and, by doing so, became completely lost. Not that she had any idea where she wanted to go, but the area in which she found herself was so dreadful she wanted only to leave it. At every turn she seemed to be getting deeper into the slums and rookeries of the city; she had heard about them and believed she had already seen the worst in the area around the Cross Keys, but that was evidently not so, for here was filth and squalor she had never dreamed existed, and the people were staring at her in a way that thoroughly frightened her. Then, just as she was ready to sink to the ground in despair, she found herself approaching Covent Garden.

It was not particularly clean, but noisy with people, ordinary people going about their business. Donkey carts and costermongers' barrows lined the road, while brawny women porters, their heads piled high with baskets, moved sure-footed in and out, overtopping the hordes of ill-clad, half-starved children who swarmed thicker than flies, running alongside the carts and scrambling among the clopping hooves when anything was thrown to them. The noise was deafening as vendor and purchaser alike tried to shout each other down.

'Oranges, three a penny.'

'Rosy apples, come on, the best in the market! See for yerself, rosy apples, ha'penny a pound.'

Louise did not think she was still being followed, perhaps there never had been anyone at her heels, but that did not help her to decide where to go, what to do. She knew that not far away were wider, cleaner thoroughfares where there were respectable well-dressed people, that if she kept her back to the river, she would find Oxford Street. Before the day was out she had to find some employment which included bed and board, and she did not care what it was so long as it was enough to feed and clothe her and give her independence from her impossible husband.

She wrote a good hand and had enough education to teach a small child, but looking down at her clothes, now grown shabby and rather damp from the drizzle, she realised that might be a little too ambitious, especially as she had no recommendation to support her application. There was nothing for it but to swallow her pride and try to find domestic work.

Asking directions at frequent intervals, she made her way to an employment agency at the Oxford Street end of Drury Lane which her father had sometimes used when he wanted domestic staff. They listened with scant interest to her request for a position, any position, where she could live in.

'You haven't done a day's work in your life, miss, just look at your hands. You've got yourself into trouble, that's what, and you've only yourself to blame for it! Our clients expect decent respectable girls to be sent to them; we've a reputation to think of. That ring won't fool anyone.'

She turned and stumbled down the steps to the street, her eyes filled with tears of humiliation. Now what was she to do?

Earlier in the day, she had seen a small dressmaking establishment which had a card in the window advertising for a seamstress, and it was in that direction she turned, even though it meant retracing her steps towards where she had left her husband and the arrogant man who thought he could win her with a hand of cards. As if she would acquiesce in that!

He had been a strange man: socially, she guessed, almost on a par with Dick, but not so fiery-tempered; in fact he had been decidedly cool and she wondered what sort of life she would have had if she had stayed long enough to see him win the game. She shuddered at the thought. Better a life of drudgery than slavery or worse, if drudgery meant she kept her self-respect. The other possibility, a watery grave, she would not even contemplate.

She found the place at last and, taking a deep breath to compose herself, went in and offered herself for the vacancy.

She was interviewed by a thin sharp-faced woman in a black bombazine gown, tight-waisted, full-skirted; on her wrist she wore a pincushion and round her neck a measuring tape.

'Can you begin right away?' she asked. 'I've a big order to finish.'

'Yes, if you wish.'

'Show me your hands. I can't have girls with rough hands; the fabrics we use are very fine.'

Louise held out her hands, palms downwards. The woman took them in both her own and turned them over. 'You're not used to hard work, are you?' She stroked the girl's left forefinger with her thumb, feeling its smoothness. 'Your fingers would be full of needle-holes if you'd sat at it all day.'

'I use a thimble and I'm a good needlewoman.'

'So you may be when you sew for your own pleasure, but you've never had to sew for your livelihood, have you?'

'No,' Louise admitted, looking her straight in the eye. 'But I'm prepared to.'

The woman shifted her gaze to Louise's third finger. 'Where is your husband?'

'Dead,' she said, promptly, deciding that was how she would think of Dick in future.

'And left you destitute, is that it? Now you have to fend for yourself?'

'Something of the sort,' said Louise, then added, 'I'll work very hard, I promise you.'

'I'm very busy, so I'll give you a trial. Come down

to the sewing-room and I'll find something for you to
work on, then we shall see . . .'

They had been talking in a room on the ground
floor, a carpeted, well-furnished front to the business,
but now her new employer led Louise through a
curtained doorway at the back and down some bare,
ill-lit stairs to the basement. Here a dozen girls were
at work, some plying their needles by the light of
candles, others pressing garments on padded tables
with heavy black flat-irons, sending up clouds of
steam. Another, better dressed and obviously a
supervisor, stood at another table cutting a shape
from a length of blue silk.

'Sit there,' the woman said, indicating a chair at a
bench where the girls were sewing. 'Susie will show
you what to do.' She turned to one of the girls. 'This
is Louise Oakingham. Put her on the underskirts of
Mrs Tyler's day gown, she can't hurt that. And look
lively, or you'll be at it all night.'

'Yes, Mrs Robson.'

The mention of night reminded Louise, as if she
could have forgotten it for long, that she also needed
somewhere to sleep.

'I need lodgings,' she said, almost diffidently,
anxious not to put obstacles in the way of her
employment.

'You can sleep upstairs with the others,' she was
told, crisply. 'That is, if I find your work satisfactory
and decide to take you on. Bed and board come out
of your wages, you understand?' She did not wait for
Louise to reply, but turned and went back upstairs.

'Here,' said the girl called Susie. 'Here's the stuff
and here's the thread and take yer pick from the
needles in this case. Got yer own thimble, have yer?'

'I'm afraid I haven't brought all my things with
me.'

'Use one o' mine til yer can fetch them.'

Louise smiled at the irony of it; she could not fetch
her things, she could never go back to the Cross Keys
because if Reuben Black or Will Fletcher saw her,
they would throw her in the Thames whether Dick
had won or lost the game, and she would be washed

up on the mud, just another poor wretch who had
drowned, a nameless body, unrecognisable flotsam of
the river. The alternative, a life as the chattel of Paul
Fourier, was equally unthinkable. What sort of man
was it who gambled on people's lives, who thought
she would go willingly with him just because he was
lucky at cards?

She was weary beyond imagining, but determined
to survive, to be mistress of her own fate, and so she
sat uncomfortably hunched over her sewing, stitching
away in the feeble light of the candles, supplemented
by what little daylight filtered through the grimy
basement window on the level of the street.

Mrs Robson seemed to have plenty of orders and
she came down at frequent intervals to bully the girls
into greater effort, working them without a break for
hours on end. Louise wondered if the customers who
came to that comfortable upper room realised what
was going on beneath their feet as they ordered their
fine dresses, their delicate underwear, their warm
coats. She could hear the bell on the outer door
tinkling from time to time as they came and went.

It was after one of these, that Mrs Robson came
down and, from the bottom step of the stairs, called
'Louise!' in an imperious voice which made the girl
shake in her shoes. Her employer's brows were drawn
together in annoyance and Louise wondered what
had angered her, as far as she could tell, her
work was perfectly satisfactory, she had even been
complimented on it.

'You told me your husband was dead,' Mrs Robson
said. 'I do not like liars, nor do I employ runaway
wives . . .'

'Husband,' whispered Louise. 'Did you say
husband?'

'I did. He is upstairs, waiting to take you home
and I never saw anyone looking less dead.'

So she had been followed after all, and now Dick
had come for her. Her first reaction was one of joy;
her husband had talked his way out of his predicament,
as usual, and come to fetch her home. But could
their life together, their love for each other, ever be

the same again? Could she trust him never to repeat the experiment? She wanted time to think.

'Please,' she begged. 'Please let me stay . . .'

'I should think not. Whatever do you think I am?'

'Please . . . He . . . He doesn't love me.'

'What nonsense! You are an ungrateful wretch to treat such a real gentleman in that cruel way.'

'Please don't make me go!'

'I most certainly shall, deceitful little minx that you are, making me feel sorry for you, when all you've done is run away from a loving husband.' She moved off the stairs to allow Louise to precede her. 'Up you go, girl, and no more buts.'

Trembling, Louise climbed the stairs, with Mrs Robson behind her, and silently parted the curtains in the doorway of the reception-room. She stumbled momentarily, but her pride reasserted itself and she stood upright, ready to defy him.

The man standing looking out of the window with his back to the room was not her husband, she realised that at once; this man was taller than Dick, and darker. She stopped and opened her mouth to cry out, but before she could do so, he had turned, crossed the room and taken her into his arms.

'My darling Louise, thank God I've found you!' he said. 'I've been searching all day.'

Before she could protest, he had pressed his lips to hers as if he really was glad to have found her. Taken by surprise, she did nothing at first, feeling his strength folding about her. After the trials of the last year and the exhausting day she had had, she felt a great temptation to relax in his arms, to let him take charge of her life. But then she pulled herself together and began to struggle so that he was forced to take his mouth from hers.

'Let me alone!' she cried breathlessly, ashamed of her weakness. 'How dare you!'

He put his finger over her lips to silence her, and smiled easily. 'Come, my love, Mrs Robson doesn't want to hear our family squabbles! All is forgiven and forgotten. Come home where you belong. We shall kiss and make up in private.'

He smiled at Mrs Robson, who hovered behind Louise and could not see the expression on the girl's face, picked up his tall hat from a table and, taking Louise firmly by the arm, led her from the room and out to a waiting carriage.

CHAPTER TWO

His grip on her arm did not relax until they were both in the carriage and it had started to move; then he shifted his position to the opposite seat so that he was facing her. She noticed for the first time that when he smiled, his brown eyes held a light which she found most confusing. Was it humour or triumph?

'How dare you!' she said, trying vainly to remain calm and in charge of herself. 'How dare you abduct me in that fashion. Who do you think you are?'

'Me?' he queried, ignoring her anger and bowing slightly towards her. 'Why, Captain Paul Fourier, at your service.'

'I am aware of your name,' she said coldly. 'I want to know where you are taking me, and why. I am assuming you won that ridiculous wager you had with my husband.'

'I did indeed. As to where I am taking you, I must fulfil my part of the bargain, and as you seem to have eavesdropped on the proceedings, you will know what that is.'

'To take me out of the way, so that Dick can commit bigamy. It's a pity no one thought to ask me what I thought about it first!'

'And would you have consented?'

'Certainly not! You are the last person I would want to go away with. The very last!'

He laughed aloud, and she noticed his firm jaw and white teeth and the sparkle of amusement in his dark eyes. It was most disarming, and she looked out of the window to hide her confusion. They were bowling along a wide thoroughfare with tall white houses set in well-kept gardens on either side, and she realised they had left the slums behind and were heading towards open country at a speed which would make it suicidal to try and jump out.

'Even when the alternative is death?' he asked quietly.

She turned to look at him again. 'Don't be silly! Dick would never harm me; it was just a foolish game he was playing to placate the other two and gain time. He didn't mean to hold you to it.'

'You don't think so? I wish I could be so sure.'

'Why? Why should you concern yourself?

'My concern, my dear Mrs Oakingham, is to save a young life, nothing more.'

'Very commendable,' she snapped. 'Now, if you would be so good as to ask the driver to turn round, you can take me back to where you found me.'

'I can't do that, it would be condemning you to certain death. Besides, a gambling debt is a debt of honour, and the bargain was that I should take you with me.'

'Honour!' she scoffed. 'How can your behaviour possibly be classed as honourable? If you think I'll be content to be a camp-follower, trailing from one battlefield to another, mixing with that sort of company, you have sadly misjudged me. I have a mind of my own. Now turn round at once, please.'

He ignored her request and in desperation she reached for the door handle, but before she could open it, he had taken her hand and pulled her round to face him.

'Now, sit still,' he commanded, no longer smiling; indeed, his tone had an edge to it that frightened her. 'I shall do you no harm—on the contrary, I wish you nothing but good—nor will I ask you to trudge in the wake of an army. Such women go willingly and face death bravely . . . I have nothing but admiration for them.'

'And none for me!' she cried, before she could stop herself.

'I did not say that. I am filled with admiration for your pluck and spirit, but that is all, and if I could find a way of fulfilling my obligations without holding you against your will, I would.'

'I am an embarrassment to you?'

'At the moment, I am afraid you are.'

'If that's so, why have you been following me all day? Why couldn't you leave me to make my own way?'

'You are mistaken, Mrs Oakingham. I have not been following you all day. When we found, after the game, that you had disappeared, I was prepared to let you go, assuming you had found friends to protect you. I am not so wanting in feminine company that I need to take a lady against her will. There are others . . .' He smiled faintly as if at a memory, then added, 'I saw you going into Mrs Robson's when I was on my way back to my quarters, and you looked so wet and bedraggled that I realised you were not as safe as I had imagined. I had to make certain arrangements first, but I decided to return for you . . . For your own good.'

'Take me back at once!'

'To your husband?' There was a hint of amusement in his voice.

'Yes. Where is he?'

'I'm afraid I do not know. He left the Cross Keys by himself almost immediately we found you missing.'

'He is no doubt looking for me. We must find him.'

'I think not.'

'Then take me back to Mrs Robson's.'

'And do you suppose she will re-employ you?'

Louise had to admit that it was unlikely, and the thought that she would have to begin looking for work all over again made her want to cry, but she would not let him see her in tears. She blinked and straightened her back, holding her head high.

'I neither want you nor need you, so why can't you let me be?'

He sighed. 'We've been through all that before. But, tell me, what makes you think you were followed?'

'I don't know, perhaps it was my imagination, but I felt it all morning, particularly down near the river. I thought it was you . . .'

'I can assure you it was not, but it confirms my own fear that your life is in danger.'

'I refuse to believe it! And, in any case, you won the game, did you not? If Dick honours his debts, he will not come after me . . .'

'It is not your husband who concerns me but the other two, particularly the bearded one. There is no honour there.'

They rode on in silence for some time, while she digested the implications of what he had said, and although she was firmly convinced Dick would not harm her, she was inclined to agree with the Captain about Black and Fletcher, particularly Reuben Black, who seemed to have no scruples at all.

She looked up suddenly to see him leaning back against the squabs, regarding her with his head on one side as if sizing up the bargain he had made. She found herself colouring.

'What are you going to do with me?'

He laughed lightly. 'I'm danged if I know. For the moment, I am taking you home; we'll decide later.'

'Home?'

'Yes, we're nearly there. But I must ask you, when you talk to my mother, not to tell her how we came to meet. I shall introduce you as a dear friend. She will jump to quite the wrong conclusion, but no matter.'

'But I know nothing about you at all. How can you say I am a friend?'

'You need only know that I am unmarried, thirty years old, a captain in the 95th Rifles, home on leave from the Peninsular campaign. You will also be relieved to hear that I am shortly to rejoin my regiment; all I am waiting for is news of a ship.'

Louise had a sudden feeling of regret that they were soon to part and there would be no time to get to know each other any better, and it took her by surprise. She checked herself sharply; whatever was she thinking of?

'And your parents, who are they? Where is home?' she asked.

'Home is on the northern outskirts of Edgware,' he

said, unperturbed by her questions. 'My father owns a small estate and breeds horses, mainly for the cavalry, or he did before a serious fall left him an invalid. Now he leaves it to the men. Do you ride, Mrs Oakingham?'

'I used to.' Louise sounded a little wistful, remembering the happy rides of her childhood.

'Perhaps we'll ride together,' he said. 'It will put some colour in your cheeks. You are far too pale and I abhor pale women; they seem so lifeless, like little wax dolls.'

Louise bridled at the familiarity—he seemed to think because he had won her in a game of cards he could say what he liked. 'And how do you propose to explain me to your parents?' she asked, deciding not to comment on his outspokenness. 'My clothes, my lack of luggage, it's all highly suspicious, especially as I am a married woman . . .'

'We'll have to think of a plausible story.'

'I'll not be party to lies.'

'Then it will have to be the truth. I have rescued you from a wicked husband bent on murder . . .'

'That's not true, either!'

'Very well. You are a friend of a friend and you have been ill; the physician has recommended some country air.'

Louise did not answer because they had turned into a wide gravel drive and were passing through a wooded park and, in spite of herself, she was curious for the first glimpse of his home.

It was an imposing building, standing four-square on a slight hill, surrounded by neat gardens and beyond that rolling parkland, where horses grazed.

They drew up at the front door and the Captain jumped out to hand her down, but her feet had hardly touched the ground when a small middle-aged woman came hurrying down the steps to greet them.

'Paul! Paul! *Quelle surprise!*' The voice had a strong French accent.

He turned and smiled, kissing the woman's cheek. '*Maman, chérie*, this is Mrs Oakingham, and we've come to ask you a favour . . .'

'Oh, is that all? I might 'ave known there would be a reason for your veezit—not just wanting to see me.'

'Of course I always want to see you, that goes without saying,' he said, as Louise bobbed a curtsy. 'But Mrs Oakingham has been advised to rest . . .'

The woman smiled at her. 'Welcome, *ma chère*. Have you been ill?'

'A little tired, that's all,' Louise said, hating the thought of deceiving Madame Fourier.

'And she had such an adventure yesterday,' Paul went on, smiling. 'The coach she was travelling in overturned and she was lucky to escape with her life. A passing stage brought her on to London, but unfortunately, in the confusion, all her luggage has disappeared.' He sighed heavily. 'You can't trust anyone these days. She had to borrow what she is wearing . . .'

'Oh, *ma chère*, 'ow terrible for you! I do 'ope you were not 'urt?' Madame Fourier was full of sympathy and Louise felt worse than ever. She wished the Captain had not chosen an overturned coach as the reason for her being in the state she was in; it reminded her of her parents. But, on the other hand, taken to its logical beginning, it was not so far from the truth.

'No, just shaken,' Louise said, looking meaningfully at Paul and realising, as his eyes met hers, that he was laughing inside.

She was furious with him and decided, there and then, to tell his mother the truth and insist on returning to London on the hired coach which had brought them. But before she could do so, Paul had turned to pay the coachman and dismiss him, and she realised that if it went, she would be left stranded.

'Don't let the carriage go,' she cried. 'I must go back!'

'Why, child, what is wrong?' asked Madame Fourier.

'I must go back . . . I must.' Louise broke away and began to run after the vehicle, fast disappearing down the curved drive.

She heard Paul say, 'She is distraught, the shock,

you know . . .' and then his footsteps behind her. He
took her arm, stopping her, and spoke in low tones
so that his mother could not hear. 'You will not
embarrass me in front of my mother or throw her
hospitality back in her face in that fashion. I brought
you here for your own good. Remember, your life is
in my hands.'

'I won't accept that.'

'You have no alternative.' He put his arm about
her shoulders to lead her back to where his mother
stood at the door, looking towards them in concern.
Suddenly it was all too much for her and she burst
into tears, great sobs of anguish she could not control.

He pulled a fine linen handkerchief from his pocket
and handed it to her, as Madame Fourier ran towards
them.

'*Ma pauvre!*' she cried. 'It must 'ave been a very
trying ordeal for you. Come inside and rest. Tomorrow
will be soon enough to worry about your lost baggage.'
She was full of sympathy, and Louise, unable to say
much without compounding the lies Paul had told,
was silent and allowed herself to be led indoors.

She was pale and uncommunicative all through an
excellent supper which she had very little appetite
for, and almost immediately afterwards retired to the
room she had been given, pleading tiredness, so that
she would not have to stay and make conversation or
answer awkward questions.

The large room was warm and well furnished, the
feather-bed comfortable, but she could not sleep; the
events of that extraordinary day crowded in on her
mind and she found herself going over everything
again, trying to make sense of it, trying to find a
logical pattern. What had Dick done when he found
she had gone? Had he shrugged his shoulders and
dismissed her from his mind, as just one more wager
lost? Perhaps it really was a joke and Paul Fourier
was part of it, but if that was so, it was in very poor
taste. Somehow she could not bring herself to believe
it, any more than she could believe her husband
would condone her murder.

As for Paul Fourier, she did not know what to

make of him. What sort of man would make such a preposterous wager, even in fun? Why did he do it? They had never met before, and it was not as if he knew anything about her. And having won the game, which she assumed he had, why had he gone to such lengths to try and honour his undertaking? He treated her like an inanimate object, a chattel to be owned; and, owning her, thought he had a right to govern her life. He seemed to have no amorous designs on her, although for one brief moment, when he had kissed her in Mrs Robson's shop, she had wondered, had almost, in spite of her anger, been flattered. But nothing he had said or done since had reinforced that, and she had come to the conclusion he had no interest in her as a woman. Well, the feeling was mutual, she had no feelings for him, none whatsoever; in fact, she was sure she would never love or trust another man again, however long she lived.

Exhausted, mentally and physically, she fell asleep at last and woke only when a maid brought a breakfast tray at nine o'clock next morning and drew back the heavy green curtains.

This was a new day, a new beginning; her mind had been made up while she slept. She would go to her parents-in-law and confront them—Dick, too, if he was there. He would have to acknowledge her as his wife, and it might be that if they talked things over calmly and rationally, they might be able to re-discover their love for each other. Ever the optimist, the thought cheered her; she sat up and took the tray on her lap, realising suddenly just how hungry she was.

She had barely begun eating when there was a knock at the door and Madame Fourier came in, smiling a greeting.

'Did you sleep well, *ma chère*?' she asked, seating herself on the edge of the bed and eyeing the girl with interest.

'Yes, thank you.'

'What shall we do today?'

'Do?' Louise repeated, taken by surprise.

'Yes. Paul said I was to entertain you until 'e
returns.'

'He has gone away?'

'Yes, but only until this evening. I expect 'e 'as
gone to see if 'e can recover your lost baggage.' She
smiled suddenly. 'Now, that would make you more
'appy, would it not?'

'Oh, yes,' said Louise, wishing it were true.

'So,' Madame Fourier went on, 'I 'ave found some
clothes for you. Oh, don't look so alarmed, they are
not mine, I do not expect you to dress in my dull
clothes. These once belonged to Jeannette. Jeannette
was my niece; she lived with us after we came to
England. Her mama and papa were guillotined in the
troubles . . . We would 'ave been too, if we 'ad not
fled. Paul was only an *enfant* at the time—that is why
he 'as learned English without an accent, but me, I
will never master it.' And although she sighed, Louise
felt sure she did not really regret her fascinating
accent. 'Jeannette died two years ago, from a
congestion of the lungs.'

'Oh', was all Louise could manage to say before
her hostess went on, 'Paul was very un'appy, we all
were. We survived terrible 'ardships to come to
England and we thought our troubles were over, but
then to lose Jeannette like that, it was almost more
than we could bear . . .'

She paused for breath, and Louise murmured, 'I'm
so sorry.'

'But there, life must go on, must it not? We are a
military family. Monsieur Fourier was in the French
cavalry, you know, in the days before Napoleon,
that's why Paul chose the army. Besides it kept him
busy at a time when I feared he would brood over
the loss of his cousin. Now, of course, England is at
war with France, and that is a terrible state of affairs,
especially for people like us.' She stood up suddenly
and smoothed the coverlet where she had been sitting.
'I 'ave talked too long and you 'ave not finished your
breakfast. My own maid is pressing the gown for you;
she will bring it directly, and then you must come
and meet my 'usband. 'E is an invalid, you know,

that is why you did not see 'im last night. Come to the morning-room when you are ready.'

She left the room, wafting expensive perfume in her wake, leaving Louise to digest the information about Captain Paul Fourier which she refused to admit she found fascinating. He was not poor, in spite of his severely simple clothes, and he knew what it was to love and lose that love, and he had chosen the military life to help him get over it. But his life was a life of violence without the softening influence of feminine company and, to him, it was cheap, which might account for the fact that he thought it could be won or lost at the turn of a card.

Two maids arrived soon after Madame Fourier's departure, one bearing the newly-pressed gown, the other a bowl of hot water, which was left on a table against a wall. Towels and soap and a hairbrush were found for her and the two left, taking with them the breakfast tray and the grubby clothes she had worn the day before.

For a moment Louise lay back against the soft pillows and shut her eyes, relaxing in the pleasure of such lovely surroundings, being waited on as she had been as a young girl. She was tempted to allow herself to luxuriate, to dream, to make impossible wishes, but the feeling did not last; she had no right to accept the Fouriers' hospitality, she was there under a cloud of deception and it troubled her. She must leave and she must do it before Paul returned, because when he did, he would have made plans for her future and she had no intention of waiting to find out what those were.

She left the bed, washed and dressed in the simple blue silk dress with its high waistline and softly falling skirt, topped with a darker wool pelisse for warmth, then brushed her hair and tied it back with a single ribbon, allowing a few short curls to fall about her ears, surveying herself in the oval gilt-framed mirror which hung on the wall near the window. She was certainly not the fashionable lady-about-town, but she looked infinitely better than she had the day before, something more like the beautiful girl she had once been and that made her feel more cheerful, ready to face anything, even her husband.

She went downstairs to find her hostess in the morning-room, a cheerful, sunny room with a bright fire in the grate beneath a marble fireplace, and comfortable chairs with soft cushions scattered on them. A french window overlooked a stone terrace and steps leading down to a large lawn. Between the trees of the park, Louise could see a distant church spire.

'There you are, *ma chère*,' said Madame Fourier. 'And very *charmante* you look, too! Come and sit by me and tell me all about yourself.'

Louise obeyed, saying, 'There isn't much to tell.'

'Come, don't be shy.' She laughed suddenly. 'You won't offend me if you tell me Paul has been less than honest. It would not surprise me in the least if you said there 'ad been no overturned coach . . .'

'Oh, but there was,' Louise broke in. 'But perhaps not the way your son explained it.'

'I knew it!' Madame Fourier cried, her eyes alight with excitement. 'I knew there was a mystery. Now, tell me all about it.'

'I'm afraid it would take too long,' said Louise. 'And I must beg you to let me go. I must return to London at once.'

'*Ma chère*, I do not wish to 'old you against your will and I can understand your concern for your possessions, but Paul will arrange everything . . .'

'No, I really must go myself. Is there a stage?'

'There is a mail-coach which calls at the village inn about noon. You could take that,' the woman said, doubtfully. 'But Paul will not like you to travel alone . . .'

'I am quite used to it,' Louise assured her. 'I'll come to no harm. How far is it to the inn?'

'Three miles; but one of our coachmen will take you, if you insist on going. I do not know what Paul will say.'

'He will understand,' said Louise quickly, praying the Captain would not come back before she had left.

'If you could send for my clothes, I shall return the
ones I am wearing.'

'Goodness, no, you keep them. I'll find you a
warm cloak, too. The coach will doubtless be very
draughty and the wind is bitter at this time of year.'

She left her chair to pull the bell-rope and then
issued clear instructions to the servant who came in
response to her summons; Louise was to be provided
with a cloak and have her own clothes packed, then
Charles was to drive her to the village in time to
catch the coach.

There was still more than an hour before she need
leave and, containing her impatience, Louise allowed
herself to be shown round the lovely old house,
before being taken to be introduced to Paul's father.

He had been a colonel, she discovered, and even in
a wheelchair, his upright bearing and proud head
proclaimed him a military man. He was like an older
version of his son, but unlike Paul, his manners were
impeccable, and when his wife left them alone to
talk, Louise found herself telling him all her troubles,
knowing he would understand.

'Paul is impetuous and sometimes a little insensitive,'
he murmured, with only the faintest hint of an accent.
'It comes with spending so much time at war, I
suppose. In other circumstances I would beg you to
stay and come to know us better, but I agree your
place is by your husband's side.' He sighed. 'We all
have our crosses to bear. Mine is to be confined to
this chair, never to ride a horse again, yours is a
loveless marriage; at this moment it is difficult to say
which is worse. But you are young, who knows what
lies in the future for you, all may yet be well.' He
looked towards the door as his wife came to tell them
that the carriage was ready to take Louise to the inn.

As Louise stood up, he grasped both her hands in
his. 'God speed you, my child. I will remember you
in my prayers.'

'Thank you,' she said, simply. 'Thank you for
everything.'

Madame Fourier went to the front door to see her
off. 'Goodbye, *ma chère*. I will explain to Paul why

you left, he will understand. Your things have been
put on the seat.' She turned and took a long blue
cloak from a waiting servant and draped it round the
girl's shoulders, before stretching to kiss her cheek.
'Goodbye, and God bless you. Perhaps we will meet
again soon. I will ask Paul to bring you . . .'

Louise had no answer to that, but thanked her
hostess and said goodbye, before climbing into the
carriage. As it bowled away, she leaned back against
the squabs and sighed with relief. She had escaped;
her destiny was in her own hands again. Though she
did not really know what she had escaped from, or
what lay ahead of her, she was determined to stay
cheerful.

The wait at the village inn for the stage and the
subsequent journey seemed interminable, and at any
minute she expected to hear a horse coming up fast
behind them and the driver being commanded to stop
just like an old-fashioned highway robbery, but
nothing happened. As they jolted over the rough
roads on the outskirts of London, past the Tyburn
gibbet towards Charing Cross, her heart began to
beat uncomfortably fast at the thought of what she
had to do. It was late afternoon when the passengers
were set down at the Golden Cross and she found
herself once more on foot. Almost reluctantly she
turned her steps towards Piccadilly and the Oakingham
mansion.

It was dark by the time she reached it, a tall white
house standing in a wide road just off that great
thoroughfare. All its windows were ablaze with light,
and the drive was cluttered with empty carriages and
patient, tethered horses. There was evidently a
reception or party taking place, and she stood back
uncertainly as more vehicles arrived and a group of
elegantly dressed people descended and were welco-
med into the house.

Her sudden appearance would cause a great stir
and embarrass Sir Richard. It would certainly not
create a good impression, but she was reluctant to
turn and leave, now she had come so far. Perhaps
she should go to the back entrance and send a servant

with a message to Sir Richard asking him to come to her, but he would hardly obey such a summons unless he knew the reason, and she did not want to tell the messenger or commit it to paper; it had to be done face to face. Perhaps she should wait until everyone had gone home, but that might not be for hours.

While she stood undecided near the gate, she suddenly felt herself pulled backwards and a large, heavy hand was clapped over her mouth. She struggled vainly as a canvas bag was pulled down over her head and her hands were tied in front of her. Then she was propelled, still struggling, to a waiting carriage.

'Get in.' The voice was gruff.

She could not find the step in her blindness and was lifted unceremoniously and dumped on the seat, like a parcel. Then the vehicle moved off. For a moment she thought she was alone, but someone moved forward and pulled the bag from her head. She found herself looking into the grinning face of Reuben Black.

'There you are, me beauty!' he said. 'Thought you'd give us the slip, did you? Thought you'd put a spoke in the wheel, did you? Well, we ain't so easily fooled, you may be sure.'

'I don't know what you mean,' she retorted, trying to remain calm; it would do no good to panic. 'Kindly release me at once!'

He laughed, showing blackened uneven teeth. 'Oh, no, me beauty, we can't have you spoiling the betrothal party, now can we?'

'Betrothal party?' Then as understanding dawned, she said, 'You mean Dick . . .'

'I do indeed. The announcement is being made tonight.'

'That's not possible,' Louise gasped. 'Why, it was only yesterday . . .'

He grinned. 'There has been no time since the wager to propose to the young lady in question and arrange such a grand gathering, is that what you were about to say?'

'Yes. It's just an ordinary reception.'

'Had it not occurred to you that your husband's

plans were a little more advanced than he led us to believe?'

'That's nonsense. I would have known.'

'Would you?' He put his face close to hers and she shrank back from his gaze. 'Would you?'

'He is my husband . . .'

He laughed. 'He no longer thinks so.'

Louise could not, would not, believe what he was saying; it was all a nightmare and she would wake up soon and find herself in her own bed and Dick beside her, snoring gently. She turned her head so that she did not have to look into those odd eyes.

'Dick will make her a fine husband,' he added, softly. 'After all, she can afford to pay for his gambling and so long as that happens, he will be good to her . . .'

'And what about me? Am I to countenance that and say nothing? Because, if that's what you think . . .'

'I'm not such a fool! You are the dangerous one. On the other hand, you could be useful.'

'What are you going to do with me?' Although her voice remained calm, inside she was shaking and felt decidedly sick, and if he put his ugly face any nearer to hers, she really would be ill.

'Me? Nothing, for the moment, though I fancy your dear husband might be pleased to know you have been found.'

'Why? If what you say is true, he thinks himself well rid of me.'

'So he will, so he will, when he *is* rid of you, that is.'

'Are you taking me to him?'

'Later . . . Later, when we've come to terms.'

He was goading her with little bits of information, aware that she would not be able to stop herself asking more questions, and it amused him to see the fear in her eyes, knowing he had put it there.

'Terms?' she repeated, wishing she could deprive him of that satisfaction.

'We need to know if you're worth more alive than dead, don't we?' He laughed mirthlessly. 'Not that it

matters one jot to me either way; I'd as lief sling you
in the Thames and be done with it.'

'Then where are you taking me?'

'Why, home. Where else? Home to wait for Will to
come back from Dick's.'

'And then?'

'We shall see. Now, be silent, for I'm tired of
answering questions.'

She did not need to ask where home was; it was
the room at the Cross Keys from which she had fled
the day before, and he would make sure she did not
escape again. Neither spoke again until the carriage
stopped in the street outside the inn. If she had any
thoughts about trying to escape when they arrived
there, they were banished when he lifted her bodily
and carried her indoors and up the stairs to her old
room. Her struggles had no more effect than the
squirming of a recalcitrant child, and she was thrown
on the bed.

He lit a candle on the bedside table and then, feet
apart, stood grinning down at her. For one terrible
moment, she thought he was going to rape her, and
prepared herself for the struggle of her life, but then
he laughed and turned on his heel.

'Later, later,' he murmured. 'First things first.'
Then he was gone, and she heard the key turn in the
lock.

In an instant she was up and moving to the window,
intending to shout for help, even though such shouts
were likely to be ignored in that neighbourhood
where domestic quarrels were noisy and often violent
and certainly nobody else's business. There was no
one in the street and she returned, dispirited, to the
bed. She looked round for a way of loosening her
bonds, but there was nothing. She tried rubbing the
rope against the bedpost, but that made her arms
ache and her wrists sore; it had little impression on
the rope. She roamed the room looking for inspiration
and, finding none, sank again on the bed and lay
staring at the uneven ceiling.

She wished Dick would come back—he would
surely put an end to this nonsense. It was all

nonsense, wasn't it? She was just having a bad dream.
But the rope binding her wrists was real and the
locked door was real. Tears ran down her cheeks on
to the pillow as the stump of candle flickered once,
twice, then went out, and she was in darkness.

Sir Richard Oakingham stood beside his elegantly
gowned and coiffured wife and surveyed the scene
with satisfaction. The large reception-room was ablaze
with light from a myriad of chandeliers; the air was
filled with the sound of music from the small orchestra
and the chatter and laughter of his guests. They were
all dressed for the occasion, the women with their
open gowns revealing lavishly decorated petticoats,
the men in tight trousers and ornate waistcoats. Some
were dancing, others strolling about the room. Dozens
of footmen, most of them specially hired for the
occasion, in livery and powdered wigs, scurried to
and fro with enormous trays laden with glasses. In
the next room, glimpsed through the open doors,
long tables sagged under the weight of the food they
held. It had cost him a small fortune, but he hoped it
would be worth it.

Dick had got himself into one scrape after another
since coming down from Oxford; he had gambled and
lost vast sums of money and expected his father to
pay; he had played with the affections of so many
young ladies that there had been a queue of irate
fathers at the door, all demanding marriage or money,
and Dick had always opted to pay them off. It was a
mercy there had been no gentlewomen among them.
It might have been the same with the rector's daughter
at Haleham if the Reverend Topham hadn't been
killed so tragically and the girl vanished, and that
would have caused no end of scandal. As it was, the
gossip was confined to the girl and did not reflect on
the Oakingham family name. All the same, it had
been a near thing.

Now Dick had fallen quite happily into the
plans being made for his marriage, the betrothal
announcement had been made amid general rejoicing,
and Sir Richard had spent all he was going to spend

on his erring son. Angela Trent was a comely girl, healthy and very rich; what was more, her father was very keen for her to have the title Dick would one day inherit and was prepared to pay handsomely for it in the form of a dowry. What more could a man ask? The wedding over, perhaps Dick would settle down and he could stop worrying over him. Sir Richard beamed his smile round the assembled company and allowed himself to relax.

David Marriott had attended the function because he did not want to give offence to his aunt and uncle, not because he held his cousin in any high esteem. He considered him shallow and ill-mannered, and his opinion was not altered by seeing the expression of indifference, almost boredom, on Dick's face; surely an insult to the lovely girl he had asked to be his wife?

It had been the same with Louise, who seemed to worship him most when he was behaving at his worst. The ways of women mystified him, and he was glad he had remained single. He had often wondered what had become of the rector's daughter, and earlier in the day had been reminded of her by the sight of a girl hurrying along on the other side of the road near Covent Garden. From the back, she looked just like Louise—she had the same slim figure, the same auburn hair, the same way of carrying her proud head—but before he could cross the road and go after her, she had disappeared. It couldn't have been Louise, he realised that, but it set him thinking about her again.

Why had she disappeared so suddenly? Could anyone have seduced her? It seemed incredible, because he could have sworn she was in love with Dick. But Dick had strenuously denied any such involvement, and besides, he returned home from time to time and gave every appearance of being a bachelor still, and Louise was not the sort of girl to countenance an alliance without marriage.

Now Dick was standing alone drinking punch instead of paying court to his intended bride. Was

that the behaviour of a man in love? Were they
marrying for love?

'Your coming nuptials seem to give you little
pleasure,' David commented drily, when he found
himself standing next to his cousin later in the
evening.

'Unlike you, my dear cousin, I do not wear my
heart on my sleeve.' Dick's mocking tone was meant
to goad him into an angry reaction, but David
continued to smile pleasantly if a little fixedly.

'You think I wear my heart on my sleeve?'

'You're still pining for the parson's daughter, aren't
you?' When David did not answer, he added, 'Can't
think why. Colourless little mouse if ever I saw one!'

'Colourless! Why, she's beautiful, and she has . . .
had spirit and character quite lacking in most young
ladies nowadays. I can't believe she's the heartless
minx everyone in Haleham said she was . . .'

'Ran off with a secret lover, they say,' Dick said,
with a light laugh. 'I must say I find it difficult to
believe she had that kind of spark in her.'

'What spark?'

'Why the spark to rouse a man's desires.' He
laughed aloud. 'But then there's no accounting for
taste.'

'When did you last see her?'

Dick pretended to consider. 'Now, let me see,
when was it she disappeared? It must be over a year
ago . . .'

'I thought I saw her today.'

Dick's eyes narrowed and he turned to look into
David's face for the first time, but his tone remained
one of studied indifference. 'Did you now? Where
was that?'

'Early this morning, near Covent Garden.'

'What were you doing there at that time, or
shouldn't I ask?'

'You may ask; I have nothing to hide. I woke at
daybreak and couldn't go back to sleep, so I decided
to go for a walk. I thought I saw her in the crowd,
but I might have been mistaken.'

'She's probably gone abroad or dead by now,' said

Dick. 'We'd have heard something otherwise; people don't just disappear . . .'

'Yes, they do, all the time.'

'Not gentry, not well-brought-up young ladies.'

'Perhaps she was forced into it?'

Dick laughed. 'Who would do that, and why? My dear fellow, your imagination is running away with you. Now, you must excuse me, I can see my father beckoning. Our guests are leaving.' And with that he strolled over to where his parents, his betrothed and her parents stood by the door bidding goodbye to their guests.

He stood beside them while their carriages were sent for and the departing guests filed past, thanking their hosts with little bows and curtsies, or offering cheeks to be kissed. When the last one had gone, he turned and held out his arm to Angela and escorted her down the steps to her coach. He kissed her cheek lightly, then moved aside to allow her parents to get in beside her, and afterwards stood and watched the vehicle turn in the drive and rumble away. He smiled to himself as he went back indoors, thoroughly satisfied with the way the evening had gone, unaware that he was being watched by more than one interested party.

He went to the library to pour himself some brandy and smoke a cigar before going to bed, and it was there, after everyone else had retired, that one of the footmen found him.

'Begging your pardon, sir, there's a man at the door asking for you.'

'At this time of night? It's near four o'clock.'

'He is most insistent, sir. He said to give you this.'

Dick took the piece of paper held out to him and unfolded it. Written in an untidy scrawl, the message read: *The bigamy stakes are high and getting higher. L. is alive and in good health.*

He screwed it up in his hand, clenching his fist over it, his eyes angrily bright, his face pale.

'Are you not well, sir?'

'Of course I'm well,' Dick snapped. 'You had

better show the fellow in here, but make sure you disturb no one.'

The servant left and soon returned accompanied by Will Fletcher, looking unkempt and dirty.

'What is the meaning of this intrusion?' Dick demanded, as soon as the footman had left and shut the door. 'Why have you come here? What do you want?'

'Not so fast, me young mate,' Will said, spreadeagling himself in one of Sir Richard's comfortable chairs. 'I've waited a hellish long time out in the cold and near froze like a stone, so a little of something to warm me wouldn't go amiss.'

Dick poured a glass of brandy and handed it to him, watching silently as the other gulped it down, holding the glass in both hands.

'Like I said,' he began, setting the glass on a table and wiping his mouth with the back of his hand. 'The bigamy stakes is high . . .'

'How high?'

'Five thousand pounds high.'

Dick laughed, a crazy, croaking laugh. 'That's ten times my debt to you. Where d'you suppose I can find that amount of money?'

'Your new wife is wealthy.'

'You are premature. She is not yet my wife! When she is, I shall honour my gambling debt, no more.'

'I've a mind to attend the ceremony.'

'No need for that; all will go well.'

'Are you sure? You don't know where the fair Louise is, do you? You couldn't lay a hand on her right at this moment?'

'I don't need to. The gallant Captain will honour his side of the bargain . . .'

'And if he doesn't? She could be what you might call an impediment.'

'Where is she?' Dick's façade of complacency was crumbling, and the other knew it.

'Ne'er you mind.'

'It is in your interests to tell me where she is,' Dick said, recovering a little. 'No marriage, no money . . .'

'I am aware of that, Mr Oakingham, well aware of

it. But, as I said before, the stakes are getting higher, five thousand pounds higher.'

Dick laughed, but it was an empty nervous sound. 'It's impossible, certainly not until after the wedding . . .'

'Do you want to be haunted by Louise? She would make a very substantial ghost, unless we arrange it otherwise.' He spoke menacingly and slowly, and Dick was left in no doubt of what he meant. He began to feel the panic rising in his throat, making his hands shake and his mouth dry.

'No. The Captain will take her . . .'

'The Captain has no more idea where she is than you have. She has run away from him.'

'You know where she is?'

'Of course.' He paused, then went on levelly, 'Five thousand pounds . . . For that paltry figure I could ensure the wedding goes without a hitch, no nasty scandal, no ghosts. Of course, it would have to be paid in advance; there's no credit in this game.'

Dick drained his glass and stood smiling silkily at the other man, who was still sprawled in the armchair, grinning confidently. He was smaller than Dick and certainly older and weaker, so what had he to smile about?

'Can you do it without repercussions? Without trace?'

'Guaranteed, me ol' mate.' He stood up and held out his hand as if expecting the money to be put into it there and then.

'It might be worth it, at that.' Dick turned towards a small escritoire by the window. 'But I want a receipt, just a precaution, you understand . . .'

Fletcher looked down at the quill Dick was offering and laughed. 'Do you take me for a fool?'

'Did you suppose I was one?'

'The money, or I spill the beans.'

Realising at last that his usual powers of persuasion would not avail him, and he could not talk his way out of his predicament, Dick grabbed the man by the collar and shook him until his blackened teeth rattled. 'Out!' he hissed, not shouting because to do so would alert the sleeping household, and even he did not want to do that. 'Get out! You will be paid what I owe, and no more. And you will be paid when I see fit. Do you understand?' He flung the man away from him. 'And if you do not leave this instant, not even then.'

Fletcher fell against the writing table and his hand closed over a paper-knife that lay there. Thus armed, he moved forward. They circled one other silently like two prowling cats; no longer able to think rationally, they were driven by hate and greed, locked in a struggle that only the death of one of them would end.

CHAPTER THREE

LOUISE WOKE SUDDENLY to the sound of a door banging. Instantly alert, she scrambled to her feet and went to the window, and in the cold light of a new dawn, saw Reuben Black and the innkeeper's wife, basket on arm, leave the inn and hurry up the road and round the corner. She guessed the landlord himself was still asleep.

Now was the time to shout for help, but the road was deserted and the mudlarks, paddling about in the mud of the river, were too far away to hear her. She watched them as they collected lumps of coal, pieces of driftwood and anything else they considered useful or valuable and piled them into baskets. They were only children, ragged and barefoot, their faces and limbs caked with grey slimy mud. One of them had actually swum out to a barge and climbed aboard, where he hurled lumps of coal into the water for his companions to retrieve. They were shouting and laughing at each other, oblivious of the cold, as they gathered up their spoils. Did they sometimes find bodies in the débris they sifted so carefully, she wondered, and what did they do at such times? Did they run home to their mothers with the news? Did they have homes to go to, loving mothers, hot dinners? But they were free as air, and she was not.

If only she could untie the rope imprisoning her wrists, she could perhaps escape again, lower herself from the window on a sheet or something like that. But instead of going to Sir Richard, she would find David Marriott. He was a lawyer, and would know what to do.

She remembered the young man with affection, wondering what he had been doing since she left

Haleham. Was he successful in his calling? Had he married? If he had, would he be disconcerted by her sudden appearance on his doorstep? He might have forgotten her, might not want to remember, and besides, what legal advice could he give her except to go back to her husband where she belonged? He certainly would not believe that Dick, or anyone else, meant to kill her; he might even think she had gone mad and have her put away. No, it was no good hoping for help from that quarter; she had to face up to reality.

And the reality was that her hands were still tied and the door of her room still locked. She moved over and rattled the latch to confirm this, and then, awkwardly because of her hands, made an effort to wash and tidy herself. Reuben Black would return with Will Fletcher before long, and what would happen then, she hardly dared speculate. She imagined herself being washed up at the feet of those mudlarks, so busy salvaging the flotsam and jetsam of the river. She had to get away before they came.

She swung round suddenly as she heard someone outside the door, catching her breath in fear; it was already too late, they were back. But when the door was flung open, it was not Reuben Black who stood there, but Paul Fourier.

He had changed into the green jacket and trousers of the 95th Rifles with its shiny black leather belt over an officer's red sash. It emphasised his lean, muscular frame and straight back. There never was a more welcome sight, and she darted forward with a cry of pleasure and relief. He was her salvation; she had already forgotten telling him he was the last person she would want to go away with. Escaping from him again might prove easier than freeing herself from the clutches of Reuben Black, and she was ready to go willingly, just to get away from her present prison.

'Thank God you've come! I think they mean to use me ill . . .'

He did not return her smile, and his expression was grim as he cut her bonds with a knife he had picked up from the kitchen on his way through, and then, without giving her time to rub the circulation back into her hands or pick up her belongings, he took her arm and almost pulled her out of the room and down the stairs.

He spoke only two words. 'Be silent.'

She did not want to wake the innkeeper any more than he did, and so obeyed him, following as he led the way along a passage and out of the back door, where a black stallion stood in the yard, saddled and ready. He mounted and then, bending over to grasp her round the waist, swung her easily up behind him.

She held on tight as he set the horse at a walk. Half afraid of the future and even more terrified of what lay behind her, she put her head against his broad back and felt the strength of it and the warmth transferring itself to her, so that she felt comforted. Desperately tired, she dared not relax for fear of slipping, and her senses remained alert to every jolt, every movement of his muscles. She did not try to speak until they were well clear of the inn and crossing Blackfriars Bridge, where the mudlarks looked up and laughed at them as they passed.

'Thank you,' she said, as they reached the southern bank. 'You can stop and put me down now.'

He ignored her, and she repeated her request. 'Put me down, please.'

'No, we're not safe yet.'

'Where are we going? If you're taking me home again, this is a strange way to go.'

'I'm not. There isn't time. You should have stayed there and saved me a great deal of trouble.'

'Set me down, and I shall be no more trouble.'

He did not answer, but put a hand over hers as if to reassure himself that she was still holding tight, then dug his heels in the horse's flank and it changed into a canter. It took all her concentration to maintain her balance, and she did not speak again. Just when she felt she could hold on no longer, he pulled the horse up outside an inn and she slid, exhausted, to the ground.

He jumped down beside her, threw the reins to a

long-aproned potboy who came out to meet them and put a hand under her elbow to steady her, for her legs felt weak and trembly.

'Come,' he said gently, so gently that she was taken by surprise and found herself obeying. 'Let's go inside. We can eat, and rest here for a spell.'

'Where are we? And where are you taking me?'

'We're on the outskirts of Dartford,' he said. 'And we have to make Deal by four o'clock; but there's time to rest and eat.'

'Deal?' she repeated. 'You mean Deal on the Kentish coast? And all that way riding double?'

He chuckled, and the grip on her elbow tightened slightly. 'No, I shall forgo the pleasure of having your arms around me for the rest of the journey.'

She coloured and shrugged off his hand, preferring to walk into the inn ahead of him with her head in the air. He laughed and followed, stopping to speak to the innkeeper to order breakfast.

It was not until they were settled in the parlour, one on either side of a small table near a good fire, that she assembled her thoughts coherently enough to speak. 'This is the second time you have abducted me,' she said, speaking as calmly as she could. 'What reason are you going to give this time?'

'The same as before,' he said, confidently. 'You are mine by right of conquest.'

'Conquest!' she exclaimed. 'You mean the turn of a card . . .'

He inclined his head in a mock bow. 'As you wish . . .'

'It is not as I wish. I wish . . .' She paused, unable to go on.

'Well, what do you wish?' He leaned back as the innkeeper's wife came and set bread, butter, fried eggs and ham on the table. 'Do you wish to return to the Cross Keys, bound and locked up, at the mercy of those felons?'

'No, of course not, and I thank you for rescuing me, but now I wish to be free to go my own way.'

'And how long do you suppose you will remain free?'

'I shall go to Sir Richard.'

'You will never reach him alive.'

'Oh, that's nonsense,' she said, wishing she could believe it.

'Is it?' His smile was mocking. 'Were you of that mind last night when Reuben Black trussed you up? Did you think so this morning just before I arrived? Were you not glad to see me?'

She blushed at the memory. 'Of course! I've already thanked you.'

He leaned forward, so that he was looking directly into her face, watching her expression. 'Mrs Oakingham, I don't think you realise the precariousness of your position. Dick cannot risk leaving you alive and free to expose him . . .'

'It's a jest . . .'

'A very grim one. When I returned home and my father told me you had left and meant to go back to your husband, I went to the Oakingham house myself.'

'Why? To reclaim your winnings, I suppose.'

He shrugged. 'If you like. At any rate I soon discovered there was a reception taking place to announce the betrothal of your husband to Miss Angela Trent.'

Louise gasped. So it was true—Dick must have been planning it for some time; Reuben Black had not lied. The full implication of that was hard to grasp. 'I never thought Dick meant it,' she said. 'Not even when that dreadful man told me it was happening.'

'And I was equally sure he did; it was the only way out of the fix he was in. Why do you suppose I took you to Edgware? To protect you in spite of your own foolish optimism. You would have been safe there, at least until I could have made other arrangements. But you seem determined to get yourself murdered.'

'He . . . They . . . wouldn't dare.'

'No? One murder has already been committed; it's the talk of London this morning.'

'Who has been murdered?' Louise could hardly believe her ears.

'The other fellow in our little card game—Will Fletcher, I think his name was.'

'Who did it?'

He shrugged. 'It was done in the early hours of this morning in Sir Richard's library. And Dick Oakingham has disappeared.'

'What are you suggesting? That Dick . . . No, I refuse to believe it. There must be some mistake!'

'You may believe it or not, as you wish,' he said crisply. 'But one thing is certain—you cannot, you will not, return to London.'

She sat looking down at her hands, her food untouched. What he was saying just could not be true. Dick had treated her disgracefully and she did not think she could ever feel the same about him again, but he would not kill anyone, not even that vile Fletcher. But in the last two days she had discovered so much she had not known about her husband that he had become a stranger to her, almost as much of a stranger as the man opposite her, and she knew not what to believe.

'I can't let you go,' he said, picking up his knife and fork and attacking his food with every appearance of enjoyment. 'You must trust me.'

'Why? Why should I? You are no better than those fiends you gamble with.'

He laughed lightly. 'No? Perhaps not. But you are mine, to do with as I please. Why don't you accept the inevitable? I am not an ogre, your life will be quite pleasant if you behave yourself.'

'And if I don't?'

His smile did not waver. 'It could become quite unpleasant.'

'And for how long must I endure this?'

'The pleasantness or the unpleasantness?' He was teasing, and it angered her.

'Either . . . Being with you at all.'

'The future is something I cannot predict,' he said easily. 'I wish I could, but make no mistake, the bonds which hold you to me are stronger than the rope Reuben Black used to secure you last night, stronger even than marriage vows, for without them you die . . .'

'No!'

'Oh yes.' He paused, and pointed to her plate. 'Come now, eat something, my dear, we have a long journey ahead of us.'

'To Deal?'

He smiled, and this time his smile was gentle; it softened his features so that she realised he was quite handsome, but then chided herself for thinking such thoughts in the midst of her distress.

'That's only the start,' he said. 'It's our point of departure. We're bound for Lisbon.'

'Lisbon? You can't mean it!'

'Indeed I do. It's ironic that the safest place for you at this moment is in the middle of a war.'

'I won't go.'

Before he could answer, they both heard the sound of a coach arriving and he stood up quickly and went to the window, while she sat, unable to move, convinced Reuben Black had come to fetch her back. Paul Fourier's company was infinitely preferable to that and she began to look at him, once more, as her protector. He seemed tense, as if expecting trouble, and that increased her fear, but then, watching his back, she saw his shoulders relax and when he turned to face her again, he was smiling.

A minute later the door was opened and a soldier of his own regiment came in and stood to attention.

'Sir, the coach is ready and we've brought the things you ordered.' He inclined his head slightly so that Louise became aware of a young woman standing behind him, who was almost hidden behind the pile of clothes she carried.

'Good,' Paul said, called the innkeeper and then turned to Louise, surveying her from top to toe as though it were the first time he had noticed what she was wearing. She had not taken off her clothes since putting them on at Edgware the previous morning; the cloak was crumpled and travel-stained, the hem of her dress was torn and her stockings in holes, and there was nothing she could do to disguise the fact.

'There is a room upstairs where you can change,' he said at last. 'Rifleman Pringle's wife will help you.' Then he pointed to the clothes she was wearing, the cloak and gown his mother had given her. 'Bring those down again. I want them.'

Louise supposed he was annoyed to see her wearing something once worn by the girl he had loved; but it was not her fault if he was upset by that, she had never expected to see him again and they had been a gift. Unsure of whether to obey him or not, she hesitated, while the girl in the doorway hopped impatiently from foot to foot, but did not speak.

'Begging your pardon, ma'am,' the Rifleman said. 'Please hurry, the draw's at three o'clock and my Hetty don' want to miss that.'

'Don't worry about the draw,' Paul said crisply. 'Mrs Oakingham will need a maid, and I'll see your wife gets on board.'

The girl's rather sullen features lit up and her large grey eyes looked up at Paul with something akin to adoration. She bobbed a curtsy, maintaining the precarious balance of the clothes in her arms. 'Thank you, Captain.'

'All the same, there's no time to waste.' He turned back to Louise. 'Off you go and change, as quickly as you can.'

Her immediate reaction was to object to being ordered what to do, but she thought better of it. Her protests would serve no purpose except to antagonise him; she must bide her time. She followed the girl from the room, and the innkeeper, who had been hovering in the background, showed them up to a bedroom where a jug of hot water had already been placed on the washstand for her.

As soon as the door had closed on him, Hetty bustled about helping her to wash and choose a serviceable gown from among the many she had brought.

'It'll be cold at sea,' she said. 'You'll need something warm.' She held up a blue wool dress with a high neckline and long leg o' mutton sleeves; its only

decoration was a ribbon around the high waistline
and a frill at the neck. 'How about this?'

Louise slipped it on, and was surprised to find it
fitted perfectly. 'Whose clothes are they?'

'Why, yours, ma'am.'

'Mine?'

'Yes, bought for you by the Captain. He told us
how you lost all your luggage after the coach accident.'

Louise could not help smiling; so he was sticking to
that story, was he? Well, she supposed it was as good
as any, but it left her wondering how he had explained
why she was accompanying him to Lisbon. But
perhaps explanations were not necessary; perhaps
army officers habitually took their mistresses on
campaign with them. After all, the men had their
camp-followers. But she was not his mistress, and she
would take good care not to become one.

'How did he know what size I am?' she asked, as
she pulled a matching tunic over her head.

The girl laughed. 'Men always know how big their
women are . . . If they love them, that is. Jamie
knows he can get his hands round my waist.' Louise
was about to retort that the Captain had never had
his hands round her waist, but realised, with a sense
of shock, that he most certainly had. And he had
kissed her too. She blushed at the memory.

'And is that enough?' she asked, keeping her voice
light.

'P'raps not, but he said you were the same size as
me, and I do believe you are.'

'Then I have you to thank.'

'It were a pleasure, ma'am! I liked trying the things
on, made me feel a real lady.' She began packing the
rest of the clothes—dresses, underwear, stockings,
nightclothes, pelisses, tunics and fur-edged cloaks—
into a travelling basket.

'Best hurry, ma'am! The Captain don' like to be
kept waiting.'

'Oh, doesn't he?' Louise said mischievously, sitting
before the mirror. 'I am afraid he will have to contain
his impatience until I get the knots out of my hair.'

Hetty took the hairbrush from her and began

pulling it through Louise's tangled locks, as if to hurry her.

'What did your husband mean about the draw?' Louise asked her.

'It's for the wives to go with their husbands,' the girl said. 'There's only six allowed with each company, and they draw lots, "To go" or "Not to go".'

'And if you draw to go?'

'Why then you're on the strength and allowed half rations, and you can earn a few coppers cooking and washing for the men. And you stay with your man in barracks or billets, whichever.'

'What happens when he goes off to fight?'

The girl looked surprised at the question. 'Why, you goes too.'

'Into battle?'

'Yes. You never know when he might be wounded, and you'd be needed then, wouldn't you?'

'Aren't you afraid?'

Hetty shrugged. 'Mostly you are, but you don' have time to think about it.'

'What about the officers' wives?'

'Depends. Usually they stay back where it's safe.'

Hetty was not used to dressing a lady's hair; having brushed it until it shone, she was at a loss to know what to do with it. Louise took over and quickly knotted it up and secured it with the ribbon she had worn earlier, finishing it off by pulling short curls forward to hang on her cheeks.

'There,' she said. 'See how easy it is?'

'Yes, ma'am.'. The girl looked worried, her blue eyes troubled and her mouth turned down.

Louise looked up at her. 'It doesn't matter; I'm quite used to doing my own hair, you know.'

'You won't tell the Captain I couldn't do it, will you?'

'Not if you don't want me to, but why?'

'If I'm no good as a maid, he won't do as he said and get me on board. I'll have to go in the draw.'

'And what happens if you draw not to go?'

'Then I must either stay behind and make me own

way and, like as not, never see me man again, or I
get meself smuggled aboard with the baggage.'

'What happens if you're caught?'

'If you can stay hid 'til they've set sail, you're safe;
cep, o' course, you don' get no rations.'

'None at all?'

'No, lessen one o' the other wives dies and you
take her place . . .'

'It's inhuman!' Louise exploded.

The girl shrugged. 'It's the way.'

'And what about the officers' wives?'

'Oh they're nice and cosy; their husbands can
afford to pay.' She took the hairbrush from Louise's
hand, put it in the travelling basket, picked that up,
together with the discarded dress and cloak, and
turned to the door. 'Come, ma'am, they'll be waiting.'

Louise realised that any further delaying tactics
would only antagonise the girl, whose whole mind
was concentrated on accompanying her husband
wherever he was sent; she would do better to make a
friend of her. With a sigh of resignation, she followed
her from the room.

Paul stood at the foot of the stairs looking up at
her, and she became very conscious that it was the
first time he had seen her looking anything like
elegant and that the difference in her appearance
must be remarkable. There was a light of amusement,
almost triumph, in his eyes, as though he took credit
for the change; reluctantly she had to admit the truth
of that.

He gave her a mock bow, turned to Hetty and
took the discarded clothes from her. For a fleeting
moment, as he handled them, his look softened, but
then he bundled them up and gave them to Rifleman
Pringle.

'Take my horse and go and drop these in the river
where the tide will take them upstream. Make sure
no one sees you, and then ride to catch us up.'

'Yes, sir.'

The man left, and a moment later they heard the
horse clatter away. Paul turned to the two women.
'Come, into the carriage with you.'

Louise, as she obeyed, was not sure if his haste was because he thought they were being followed or from his eagerness to rejoin his regiment. Either way, they lost no time as the driver obeyed his instructions to make for Deal with all speed.

They had not been travelling long when Rifleman Pringle caught up with them. Paul leaned across Louise to address him through the open window. 'All's well?'

'Yes, sir, done as you said.'

'You may ride on ahead if you wish.'

'If it's all the same to you, sir, I'd rather not. I ain't cut out to be a cavalry man, I'd as lief walk.'

Paul laughed, for the man did look decidedly uncomfortable on the big horse. 'Very well. Tell the coachman to stop, and then you may dismount.'

The Rifleman obeyed with obvious relief and Paul and he changed places, then they set off again, with the Captain riding alongside, looking as if he had been born in the saddle, so easily he rode.

'What will happen to the stallion when we reach Deal?' Louise asked the young soldier.

'It'll be taken on board. The Captain don' move far without his mount.'

'But you're not a cavalry regiment?'

'No, thank the Lord, but the Captain needs his horse, bein' on special duties an' all that . . .'

'What special duties?'

'Dunno. An' if I did, I wouldn't say. I'm his personal servant, an' that's how I want to keep it.'

Louise felt that she had been very firmly put in her place, and they journeyed on in silence until Paul called a halt at a wayside inn, where they ate a light meal and then set off again as before.

The scene, when they arrived at the quayside at Deal, was one of ordered confusion. More than a thousand soldiers stood about in groups or sat on their packs while the baggage was being loaded on to two waiting frigates. There were mountains of it, together with horses, carts, cows, goats, chickens, cooking-pans, guns, limbers, rifles in boxes, muskets, ammunition. Most of the men were in the red jackets and white trousers of foot soldiers, their regimental numbers emblazoned on their shakos, but there were a handful of the élite Rifle Corps in the same green uniform as Paul. They gave scant attention to the carriage as it drew up, but when it stopped and Rifleman Pringle jumped down, they became instantly alert and full of curiosity.

'My, look who's here,' one called. 'Reporting for duty in a hired carriage, would you believe! Come into a fortune, have yer, Jamie, me ol' mate?'

Rifleman Pringle grinned but did not answer as he let down the step and handed Louise down, followed by his wife.

Louise looked about her for Paul, but he seemed to have disappeared and she suddenly felt very alone and frightened. It must have shown on her face, because the Rifleman smiled reassuringly. 'He's gone to the commissary to make the arrangements,' he said, then throwing out a hand to encompass the handful of green uniformed men, added by way of explanation, 'We don't belong to them over there.' He nodded towards the red-coated infantry. 'We're going back after sick leave, most on us, and the Captain's gone to see if there's room on board.'

'And if there isn't?' Her spirits lifted; if they could not go on board, perhaps he would release her, although she had not formulated a plan of what she would do if he did; she had no money for food, lodgings or transport back to London.

'Oh, there'll be room,' the Rifleman said cheerily, fetching her luggage from the coach. 'The Captain has a way with him. We shall go, make no mistake.'

A little way off, an officer came out of a quayside building and was immediately surrounded by dozens of women who pushed their way towards him. They were dressed in an extraordinary assortment of clothes—odd skirts and blouses, overlarge coats, many of them old uniform jackets with the shining buttons and braid removed. Some had felt hats, while others draped shawls over their heads. On the fringe of the crowd, the children swarmed, smaller, grubbier versions of their mothers.

Louise, looking from them to Hetty, realised that
the girl was much neater and cleaner in her dress
than they were and obviously took a pride in her
appearance. It would be good to have her as a
companion and she felt she was going to need one if
they did get on board.

Hetty was looking anxiously towards the women
who had become silent, grouped round the officer,
who held a bucket and was shaking pieces of paper in
it. Pringle, following his wife's gaze, said, 'The
Captain said he'd get you aboard, didn't he? If we
go, you go, so stop frettin'.'

Hetty turned her attention to Louise's basket which
her husband had set on the cobbles, but she still
glanced in the direction of the draw, as if she could
not believe her luck.

A bugle sounded, and the red-coated foot soldiers
donned their shakos and packs and fell in, their backs
ramrod stiff, their heads erect. Louise, knowing they
had only recently returned from a punishing campaign
in Belgium, was impressed by their discipline as they
drilled and formed up ready to embark and go to war
again.

Suddenly there was a shriek from the direction of
the women. Louise watched as one detached herself
with shouts of glee. 'I'm to go. I'm to go.' Then she
picked up a bundle from the roadside, grabbed a
toddler by the hand and ran towards one of the ships.
Some of the women screamed, some fainted, some
just stood looking down at the slip of paper in their
hands as if unable to believe what was written there.
One or two more gathered up their belongings and
followed the first woman on board. One ran out and
chased after the ranks of men, to pull on the sleeve
of one of them.

'Jack! Jack! I'm not to go. Stay here with me!'

The soldier hesitated for a split second, then tried
to shrug her off. The column marched on. She tried
again, tugging at his hand, trying to make him break
ranks. 'Jack, don't leave me! Don't leave me!'

Paul, returning on foot, saw what was happening

and pulled the woman bodily from the column. 'Off you go,' he said. 'Leave your man to do his duty.'

She turned on him and pummelled his chest with her clenched fists. 'It's all right for you!' she shouted. 'It's all right for you . . . and her . . .' And she turned and spat on the ground at Louise's feet. 'What's to become of me?'

Paul held her firmly, then, looking round, beckoned to one of the other disappointed women who was taking the news more stoically. 'Take her away and comfort her,' he said, giving them a sovereign. Then he turned to Louise. 'Come.'

'Is that all you're going to do for that poor woman?' she asked. 'Can you salve your conscience with money?'

'I have no conscience on that score,' he said. 'She knows the rules.'

'Isn't any provision made for the wives who can't go?'

'No.'

'Why not?'

'The ships are needed for men and supplies, not prattling women.'

'I assume you have made arrangements for me to go on board. Let her take my place.'

'Now you are talking nonsense,' he said. 'Please try not to be an embarrassment to me.'

'If you want to rid yourself of embarrassment, you know what to do,' she retorted.

'Please be silent!' He strode over to where Rifleman Pringle stood talking to his comrades, and detailed a sergeant to bring them to attention and march them on board behind the foot soldiers. Louise heard him say, 'And I want no rivalry, do you hear; no brawling, friendly or otherwise. We know we are the best, we do not have to prove it. Save your aggression for the real enemy.' Louise thought she detected a look of pride in his eyes as he watched them go, then he turned back to her.

'Come, Mrs Oakingham, we set sail directly.'

She followed him with Hetty trailing behind carrying her basket, the last to embark.

There was hardly an inch to spare on deck as the
men found their quarters, the baggage was stowed,
and the ship's crew prepared for sea. The noise of
orders being shouted, people crying goodbye to those
still on shore, boxes being humped about, ropes
hissing, sails clapping, filled her ears and set her
senses reeling. She stood confused and overwhelmed,
unable to believe she was not having some extraordinary dream. She would wake up soon and find herself
back . . . Where? With Dick at the Cross Keys? At
Haleham Rectory?

Paul took her elbow, and his grip was real and
warm. She turned towards him, focusing her eyes on
his face, noticing, not for the first time, how tanned it
was and how it suited him.

'I'll show you to your cabin,' he said, leading her
to the companionway, retaining his hold on her
elbow, ready to catch her if she slipped. Once below
deck, they made their way along a narrow passage,
made narrower because this part of the ship had been
divided into sections with rough boards—each section,
barely six feet square, being what was euphemistically
called a cabin. He opened the door of one and
ushered her inside.

It contained two bunks, one above the other, a tiny
chest with a jug of water on it and a bucket below it,
a chair and a narrow bench fastened to the bulkhead
for use as a table. She looked round it in distaste; it
was worse than any accommodation she had had to
endure with Dick, cramped and airless. But it was
too late to make any sort of protest or attempt to
leave, as the deck beneath her feet began to tremble,
and she looked up at him in alarm.

'Come up top and let us say goodbye to the land,'
he said.

Bemused, she followed him back up the companionway and stood beside him at the rail as they cast off
from the shore and the sails filled. She shivered as
they found the open sea and the wind got up and
filled more sail, making the ship cut through the
water, leaving a wake of white foam; Dick and her

life with him were left behind, before her the future stretched, unknown, unguessable.

He turned towards her, and now seemed relaxed and at ease. 'Cold?' he asked.

'A little.'

He turned the hood of her cloak up over her head and held it against her cheeks, and his touch was gentle. She felt a sudden shock course through her body, making her fingers and toes tingle. Ashamed of herself, she stepped away.

'I . . . I think I would like to retire.'

He dropped his hands and bowed slightly from the waist, his manner formal. 'As you wish. If you wait a moment while I order some food to be brought down, I shall escort you.'

'There's no need. I can find my own way, and I don't want anything to eat, thank you.'

Before he could protest, she left him, walking unsteadily, clinging hold of the rail until she was opposite the companionway, and then waiting for the ship to steady before taking the two or three steps across the deck to reach it. She felt very shaky—in fact, decidedly ill—and food was the last thing she wanted.

'I'm going to be seasick,' she said to herself, as if the thought had come as a great surprise to her. 'But at least it will keep him at bay a little longer . . .'

CHAPTER FOUR

LOUISE REMAINED in her bunk while they were buffeted down the Channel and across the Bay of Biscay, with every timber creaking and groaning until she thought the ship would fall apart. Her bunk was the only stable thing in a shifting world and she longed for the end of the torment.

Hetty tried to persuade her to go on deck where the fresh air might revive her. 'The air in this cabin is foul,' she said, not mincing her words. 'How you can breathe it, I don't know. Can't you open a port?'

'The sea comes in,' murmured Louise.

Hetty laughed. 'A bucketful of spray won't harm you! Those poor beggars cooped up between decks would give an arm for it. Come now, up on deck and walk a bit.'

Louise gingerly raised herself on her elbow, but her head began to swim again and her stomach heaved. She sank back on the pillow. 'Will this damned voyage never be done?'

If Hetty was shocked by language better fitting a common soldier than the daughter of a clergyman, she did not show it. 'Shall I go and find the Captain to help you?'

'No. No!' Louise said vehemently, knowing she meant Paul and not the captain of the ship. The longer he stayed away the better and, besides, she was in no fit state to be seen by a gentleman, her face was ghostly white and her hair in knots and she was not even properly dressed. He might think . . . She did not know what he might think, but she still had enough pride not to let him see her in that condition.

On the fourth day, they sailed into calmer water,

and on the fifth, just to show how contrary the weather could be, they were becalmed. The sea became like a great lake and the sails flapped uselessly. Louise, feeling better, sat up and sent Hetty scurrying for water, and half an hour later, washed and dressed in one of the gowns Paul had bought for her, topped by a warm cloak, she ventured on deck.

It was crowded with soldiers taking their ease while they could, sailors occupying themselves mending sails and making knots, for there was little else to do until the wind freshened. Some of the army officers, impatient to be in the fighting, paced the deck restlessly. Louise caught sight of Paul in earnest conversation with a captain of the 71st, but before he could acknowledge her, she turned away to scan the empty horizon as if searching for something. It was nearer than she had expected it to be, for fog was rolling in. In a matter of an hour or so they were enveloped so completely that the other frigate, which had been almost within hailing distance, was lost to sight. At the same time, a breeze got up and they began to make headway again, inching their way southward, following the line of the Portuguese coast, until on the evening of the sixth day they passed a magnificent tower with ornate turrets and domes, which seemed to rise out of the water; then they entered the lagoon-like expanse of water formed by the estuary of the River Tagus, and there dropped anchor to await the dawn and the lifting of the fog.

Louise was surprised but thankful that Paul Fourier had left her entirely alone during the voyage, or so she told herself, refusing to admit that she thought it very off-hand of him to ignore her so completely, although, according to Hetty, he had asked after her more than once.

'He's most concerned for you,' the girl said. 'He asked after you every day, and told me to take good care of you.'

'Did he?' Louise had replied tonelessly, thinking that he would look after his assets, wouldn't he? But if she were an asset, how did he mean to realise it? Sell her back to her husband? Hold her to ransom?

But that was silly, there was no one to pay it. She gave up the riddle; she would learn the answer soon enough.

Next morning the fog lifted slightly, and the army officers, intent on joining their regiments, ordered their men into the ship's boats to be rowed ashore, a shore which was dimly discernible through the mist as a low ridge of land. Louise stood at the rail and watched the boats coming and going all morning, threading their way between lateen-sailed frigates bringing in merchandise from all over the world, and the workaday fishing smacks with their red and brown sails. At midday she went to her cabin where she and Hetty ate a light meal before returning on deck to see the last boat being filled.

'Well, shall we join them?'

She had not heard him come up behind her, and jumped a little at the sound of his voice against her ear. She turned to face him, inclining her head. 'If you wish.'

He smiled easily. 'Is it not also what you wish?'

'Oh, yes,' she admitted. 'I am a poor sailor.'

'So I heard, I hope you are feeling better.'

'Yes, thank you.'

This stiff exchange of politeness seemed unreal, as the voyage had seemed unreal. It seemed to be not Louise Oakingham who stood there, but some other person with her face and figure, yes, but different in a way she did not understand. She allowed him to lead her to one of the boats, where places were found for them.

'Hetty?' she asked, turning towards the girl, who remained on deck.

'She will follow with the baggage later,' he said. 'She knows where to find us.'

Louise fell against him as the boat was winched over the side, where it hung precariously before being lowered into the calm waters of the bay, the Sea of Straw, as she had heard it called. He put his arm round her shoulder to steady her, and there it remained even when they were being rowed powerfully and safely towards the city of Lisbon, which loomed

out of the mist as they approached. Rather than draw
attention to herself, she concentrated on the view of
the towers, church belfries, mansions and houses that
spread upwards over the semicircle of hills on which
the town had been built.

'But I thought Lisbon was a very ancient place,'
she said. 'It all looks new and sparkling.'

'That's because it is new and sparkling—or, at
least, the part we are approaching is,' said Paul. 'Just
as the Great Fire destroyed much of London, which
had to be rebuilt, so an earthquake followed by a
tidal wave destroyed the low-lying parts of Lisbon.
Most of what you can see near the water has been
built in the last fifty years.' He pointed to a great
square surrounded on three sides by pink and green
colonnaded buildings; the fourth was open to the
river. 'We'll land there, at the Terreiro do Paço, the
Grounds of the Palace, though the palace has gone.
The soldiers call it Black Horse Square, because of
the statue in the middle.'

'It's magnificent! Who is it?'

'Joseph I, the king who ordered the rebuilding.'

They had reached a wide marble staircase which
led from the quay down to the water's edge and the
sailors shipped their oars for everyone to disembark.
Louise, feeling the flagging of the wharf beneath her
feet again, found that her legs were weak and she
could not walk properly. Although she tried to
disguise it, he noticed and, smiling in that rather
mocking way of his, took her arm to guide her.

'There will be a carriage for hire somewhere,' he
said. 'There usually is when a ship comes in.'

'Where are we going?' She was unable to contain
her curiosity, although she had promised herself she
would not question him.

'To my quarters.'

Her heart sank; for a moment she had almost
forgotten she was his prisoner and now she was
forcefully reminded of it. She could no longer plead
seasickness as an excuse for avoiding him, and would
have to think of something else. On the other hand,
she did not want to be parted from him; he was the

only one she could turn to in this foreign land where
she knew nothing of the customs and the language.

She made no protest as he called to a sun-tanned
man leaning against a dilapidated carriage a few yards
away.

'Do you speak Portuguese?' she asked, as he helped
her to climb up and got in beside her.

'Only a smattering, but I find many of the people
understand a little French.' He laughed suddenly.
'Not that it is a good thing to advertise my ancestry.
It invites murderous looks, if nothing more!'

'That's hardly surprising,' she said, as they bowled
along the wide streets which criss-crossed the new
city at right angles to each other. The buildings
seemed to have been made from a single mould, all
with identical dormer windows, wrought-iron balconies
and lanterns hanging at their doors. 'If Napoleon has
his way, the whole country will be occupied.'

'Do you think Napoleon will have his way?'
he asked mildly. 'Don't you share your fellow-
countrymen's faith in old Hooknose to drive him
out?'

'I know little of war, or of politics, but I heard it
said we had retreated almost into the sea.'

Leaving the geometrical new streets behind, they
crossed another large open space, dramatically tiled
in black and white mosaic, which Paul told her was
the Rossio, the main square of Lisbon. It teemed
with life, not only the life of the inhabitants going
about their daily business, but the life of a great
army. Black-skirted women gossiped as they waited
in line to fill their pitchers at the fountain or scrubbed
out their fish baskets; peddlars sold figs, oranges,
dried fish, fresh sardines, wines; and the air was
redolent with the bitter-sweet fragrance of the fruit
and the salty tang of the fish. Knife-grinders played
small reed pipes as they plied their trade, sharpening
not only knives but the swords and bayonets of the
soldiers.

Everywhere were off-duty soldiers, most of them
British, but some Portuguese and Spanish and a few
German, all united in their determination to push

Napoleon out of the Iberian Peninsula and back across the Pyrenees to France itself.

'An ordered withdrawal is not a retreat,' he said. 'And a retreat is not necessarily a defeat. Don't make the same mistake as the ignorant people in England who think we should always be advancing with drums beating and colours flying; war is not like that.'

'I didn't suppose it was,' she murmured, while admitting to herself she had never really given it much thought. Why should she have? Brought up in the shelter of a quiet English village where news of foreign campaigns, when it did reach there, was old and far removed from her daily life; they had no meaning. But what she saw now was real: the marching and parading, this rumble of loaded carts, neighing of horses, men lounging about waiting, eating, drinking, squabbling.

'Are they preparing to fight again?' she asked, nodding towards them.

'Of course. An army always prepares.'

'I mean very soon.'

'Possibly,' he said, and she looked up to see his jaw tighten and his eyes narrow. 'We await orders.' Then he looked down and saw her watching him, and smiled. 'But that needn't concern you. You are safe while you stay behind the Lines of Torres Vedras. Wellington has seen to that.'

'I am not afraid,' she said suddenly.

He grinned. 'No, I don't believe you are, but you have seen nothing yet to be afraid of. Here we are all well-fed and clothed because our ships command the sea and because we are behind the fortifications we have been making all winter, and Masséna fumes on the other side, six hundred miles from home, with his supply lines stretched to their utmost. It will be a very different story when we advance and it is our supplies that have to get through.' He paused as the carriage slowed to negotiate a corner by a monastery and then began to climb a steep hill where the houses were older and more widely spaced on either side of the narrow street. 'Enough of that! Let us talk of more pleasant things.'

'Such as?' she asked, her smiled fixed.

'A little social life is what we need, a little mixing with others like ourselves. It will help you relax.'

'I am perfectly relaxed.'

He inclined his head a mock bow. 'My error, ma'am. All the same, there is plenty going on, and it won't hurt us to join in a little harmless amusement. I have been told there is to be a reception this evening with dancing; we shall go to that.'

'And how will you explain my presence? Or perhaps you don't intend to; maybe you are content to let people think what they will . . .'

He looked down at her with a light of amusement in his eye, which annoyed her. 'Do you care what people think?'

'No,' she said quickly, and then more slowly added, 'Yes. I wouldn't like people to think . . .' She stopped in confusion.

He laughed aloud but did not answer because they had stopped outside a large building of pinkish stone with a coat of arms set above the door—a great oak door—and, more unusual, the house had a myriad of windows, all reflecting the sun which had broken through and lifted the mist entirely. It was already warmer than a summer's day in England. The house had a garden of semi-tropical plants, palm trees, jacaranda and acacia, a small grove of orange trees and one or two ancient gnarled olives, and, unexpectedly, rose bushes and a lawn of very green grass.

He handed her down and paid off the driver before escorting her inside. She found herself in a marble-floored hall with rows of doors opening from it. A wide staircase curved up to the next floor and, all the way up, the walls were lined with portraits. At the far end of the hall, a shaded courtyard could be glimpsed through an open door.

'Your quarters?' she said in surprise, for she had expected a single room at an inn or something similar.

'Not just mine,' he said. 'It's shared by several officers when in Lisbon.'

'You have commandeered it from its owner?'

'Yes.'

'Poor man.'

'He does not mind. He is paid, and just as anxious to see the end of the tyranny as everyone else; he judges it a small inconvenience.'

'He must be wealthy.'

'By Portuguese standards, he is, and he retains a suite of rooms on the upper floor for himself and his wife.'

'What about the officers' . . .' she paused before adding, 'wives?'

'There is room for all.'

An officer dressed in the red jacketed uniform of the 71st Highlanders came out of one of the doors and, catching sight of them, moved forward with a smile which Louise felt was somewhat less than genuine, though his words were cordial.

'Why, Fourier, back already? Are you fully recovered?' He clapped Paul on the shoulder while eyeing Louise from top to toe. 'No need to ask if you enjoyed yourself.'

Paul turned to Louise. 'Mrs Oakingham, allow me to present Major Humphrey Barton.' Then, turning to the officer, 'Humphrey, this is Mrs Louise Oakingham, who has come to Portugal to look for her husband. He was reported missing after the Busaco affair last year and feared dead, but there have been reports that he has been seen alive, though in sad straits. He might have lost his memory or something of the sort.'

Louise was amazed at the ease with which he was able to lie and turned towards the Major to see what his reaction had been, but she came to the conclusion he had hardly been listening. He was smiling at her in a way that conveyed far more than words what he was thinking, and she knew she would have to watch out for him if they were to meet very often.

'He must surely be in a bad way if he could forget he had such a charming wife waiting for him,' he said, proving that he could put his mind to two things at once.

She smiled briefly, acknowledging the compliment

with a stiff inclination of the head, but did not speak.
To have done so would have condoned Paul's lies,
and yet she could not bring herself to contradict him.
His explanation for her presence was better than
allowing everyone to assume she was his mistress,
and if it meant he would behave with a certain
amount of circumspection, so much the better.

'Excuse us, please,' Paul said. 'I must arrange for
Mrs Oakingham's accommodation.'

He took Louise's arm and led her along the
corridor, leaving the other officer to continue with
whatever business he had been engaged in when they
arrived. He showed her into a large room which had
once been an elegant withdrawing-room, where
Persian rugs covered the tiled floor, the furniture was
intricately carved and gilded, the tapestries were very
fine and huge vases stood empty in the corners. But
now it was untidy with the untidiness of a large and
not particularly caring family. Books and pamphlets
were scattered about, a uniform jacket hung over a
chair, ash spilled from the grate on the hearth, where
stood a pair of boots, one upright, one on its side.
There was an empty cup on the mantelshelf and a
tray of unwashed glasses on the sideboard.

'Wait here,' he said. 'I'll not be long.'

Unable to settle, she paced the room, admitting to
herself that if she had really been desperate to escape,
she would have made use of the several opportunities
which had occurred during the last week. She could
have told her story to the ship's captain, she could
have run away on the quay, she could have blurted
out her problem to Major Barton, she could go now,
no one was guarding the door. Why didn't she? And
why was he so confident she wouldn't?

Her cool logic told her to wait until such time as
she knew the country better, until she met someone
in authority in whom she could confide; that if she
walked out now, without a plan, he would soon find
her again. None of the arguments abated her feeling
that she had betrayed herself, her own independence,
that she ought, at least, to make a token dash for

freedom. She moved towards the door just as he returned.

'Come,' he said. 'I have arranged a room for you.'

Meekly she followed him, berating herself for a coward, knowing that cowardice was something above all else he would not tolerate.

He guided her up the main stairs and along the landing to a door at the far end, which he held open for her. 'Please make yourself comfortable. I shall send Hetty up when she arrives. I shall call for you this evening and later I'll introduce you the the other ladies.'

Then he was gone and she was left wondering who and what the other ladies were, wives or whores? Whichever they were she did not want to meet them; she would stay in her room.

It was a resolution difficult to keep. Although the room was large and beautifully furnished, the garden, viewed from the window, looked inviting and the sun was shining. She obeyed its warm invitation, found her way downstairs and out of the back door into the courtyard. From there she ventured into the garden.

She was strolling slowly along a path when she heard a woman's voice on the other side of a rose-laurel, whose heavy scent filled her nostrils.

'He's back.' The voice was young and cultured. 'Now we shall see if he's guilty or no. If the betrayal is resumed . . .'

'It will prove nothing.' The other woman's English, though correct, was laced with an accent Louise did not recognise, a soft sibilance. 'He has to be caught . . . how do you say? . . . in the act.'

'How do we do that?'

'Set a trap for him.'

'How?' The younger woman's voice was slightly petulant.

'I do not know, yet. We shall think of something, or perhaps Eduardo . . .'

'Oh, please don't involve your husband, Christina, let's keep it to ourselves . . .'

The older woman laughed lightly. 'Alicia, you are still a little in love with him, I do believe.'

'Nonsense. I hate him!' The protest, even to Louise's ears, was unconvincing. 'Besides, he has found someone else . . .'

'Tell me, do you hate him because he has hurt you or because he has betrayed his country?'

'Both.' The retort was sharp and immediate. 'When I think of Humphrey and all his men walking into an ambush . . .'

'My dear, a month before, you would have been delighted at the prospect of becoming an attractive widow.'

'Christina, how could you say such a thing! Humphrey is my husband.'

'And you would do well to remember it.'

'How dare you!' Alicia exclaimed, while Louise peered this way and that through the foliage, trying to see the two women without being seen herself.

'I dare because I am your friend and because I am Portuguese and I have more than a passing interest in this war.' The women's voices faded as they moved away, and Louise gave up her attempts to catch a glimpse of them and returned to her room, mulling over the conversation she had just heard. She was curious, curious enough to forget she had decided she did not want to meet the others in the house.

Hetty had arrived in her absence and was busy unpacking, smoothing out the creases and hanging her clothes in the wardrobe.

'What do ladies here wear in the evenings?' she asked her. 'I mean if they go to a reception or something like that.'

'I've never been to one,' said Hetty, stating the obvious. 'But I s'pose it depends on how grand it is. Same as back home.'

'The Captain wants me to meet the other ladies tonight.'

Hetty looked up in surprise. 'Tonight?'

'Yes. Why not? Did you think he would hide me away?'

'No, no, it isn't that . . .' The girl hesitated. 'It's just that I heard we was to move at first light.'

'Move?'

'There's a rumour the army marches tomorrow.'

'Where to?'

Hetty shrugged and took down a gown from its hook in the cupboard and laid it on the bed. 'This should do; you haven't got many to choose from, have you?'

'I have enough, and I wouldn't have had them if it hadn't been for the Captain.' Louise paused. 'What do you mean, "we"?'

'Why, everyone.'

'The women too? Me?'

'That's up to you. You can stay here, if you like; some do, but when my man marches, I go too.'

The news brought Louise up with a jolt. She did not know if Hetty's information was correct, or if Paul was leaving too, but she assumed that he was. His regiment was not in Lisbon, and the handful of men who, like him, had returned to the capital after sick leave were all anxious to rejoin their comrades.

In that case, what was expected of her? Go or stay? The prospect of marching with an army did not appeal to her, but neither did the thought of being left behind. She knew no one in the town, no one at all, she did not speak the language and she had no money, either English or Portuguese.

'Are you sure it's true?' she asked.

Hetty laughed. 'One thing you can be sure of in this war is that you can't be sure of anything. Orders get changed, rumours get started . . . sometimes on purpose.'

'On purpose?'

'On purpose to confuse the enemy. There are spies all round . . .'

'Here? In Lisbon?'

'Oh, yes, and not just in Lisbon . . . Here in this house, I shouldn't wonder.'

'You can't mean it! Who would do such a thing?'

Hetty shrugged. 'Who can tell? Funny things happen.' She finished laying out the rest of Louise's evening wear and poured water from a jug into a basin for her to wash. 'If you don't mind, miss, I'll go

back to my Jamie. I don't want to be absent when
the men muster.'

Louise let her go and then sat on the edge of the
bed for several minutes before rousing herself and
changing into the dress Hetty had laid out for her.

Paul was late in fetching her and she began to
wonder if, after all, Hetty had been right and he had
left without a word. She walked up and down
impatiently, turning towards the door whenever she
heard someone in the corridor outside her room. She
was behaving like a lovesick child, she chided herself,
which was silly; she was an adult, a sensible, no-
nonsense woman—her life with Dick had seen to
that—and if she were left to herself she would soon
find someone to help her, some way of earning
enough to take her back to England.

He arrived at last, dressed magnificently in full-
dress uniform complete with long curved sword in its
scabbard at his side. He bowed slightly and offered
his arm. 'My apologies. Duty comes before pleasure,
I'm afraid.' He smiled easily. 'Now I am all yours,
and I don't think we will have missed very much.'

She returned his smile without answering, and he
escorted her to the same dilapidated coach that had
brought them to the house earlier in the day, then
they set off through the city, exchanging no more
than pleasantries by way of conversation. They seemed
to have nothing to say to each other, and Louise
spent the time wondering what he was thinking, yet
not daring to ask. Was she afraid of him? But that
was silly . . . He had said and done nothing to make
her fear him. So why was she shaking?

The reception-room was already crowded when
they arrived. The incongruity of dancing in the great
hall of a one-time convent did not seem to bother the
guests, who were noisy and bent on enjoying
themselves. Louise found it difficult to believe she
was not in the centre of fashionable London: the
glitter, the gaiety, the gowns were much the same,
and the scene was made even more colourful by the
dress uniforms of the men with their braid trimming,
fancy buttons and broad sashes. And the orchestra,

though not particularly tuneful, was playing with a great deal of verve.

'There you are, Captain! We began to think you were not coming.'

Louise recognised the voice of the younger woman in the garden, and turned from handing her cloak to a footman, to face her. She was about the same age as Louise, perhaps a year or two older, with a pale complexion and fair curls, pretty in a doll-like way, with a neat figure beneath her elaborate gown. She was hurrying towards them, pulling the reluctant Humphrey Barton by the hand, and although her words were addressed to Paul, her gaze was on Louise, taking in the simple dress and her even simpler hairstyle. It was in sharp contrast to the heavily embroidered, panniered court dress of most of the ladies, and the huge wigs, now so out of fashion except for formal occasions. Fancy taking the trouble to pack such finery when following your husband to war, Louise thought. Surely the space in the ship's hold could be better used for food, medicine, blankets and necessary things like that.

'Mrs Barton,' Paul said, bowing over the girl's hand. 'May I present Mrs Louise Oakingham?'

The two women acknowledged each other briefly, and then Alicia seized Paul's arm. 'Come, you promised me a dance . . .' And she whirled him away, leaving Louise with Humphrey Barton. They stood facing each other while he slowly appraised her, head on one side, eyebrow lifted, before asking her to dance.

'I heard you are marching tomorrow,' Louise said, by way of conversation, as they joined a gavotte.

'Where did you hear that?'

'Why, from one of the women.'

'There are always rumours.'

'So I heard. Some of them false, to confuse the French, I'm told.'

He laughed. 'You seem to have learned quite a lot in a short time. What else do you know?'

She looked round before whispering mischievously. 'There are French spies everywhere.'

'And do you by any chance know their names?' He was teasing, but at least he was no longer eyeing her in the way which had made her so uncomfortable a moment or two before.

'No.' She laughed lightly. 'Do you?'

'No,' he said, and his voice became grim. 'If I did, I would seek them out and cut them into a thousand pieces and feed them to the wolves.'

She shuddered. 'How bloodthirsty!'

''Tis no more than they deserve. If you had seen your company walk into an ambush as I have, if you had seen men, and women too, butchered unmercifully, their own guns turned on them as they fled, you would not hesitate either.'

'That happened?'

'It did.'

'And it was the work of a spy?'

'It had to be. Our marching orders were kept secret until the very last moment, and we moved under cover of darkness. They were waiting for us.' His grip on her hand tightened, as they followed the couple in front of them. 'I have sworn revenge.'

'On the whole French army?'

'No, on the spy.'

'That sort of thing is bound to happen in a war, is it not? Don't they say "All's fair in love and war"?'

'It's obvious you don't understand,' he said. 'Ask Paul to explain it to you; he knows more than most . . .' His voice was heavy with innuendo and his expression grim; she was unsure whether his hate was directed at the unknown spy, or at Paul. Perhaps both, if he knew of his wife's love for the Captain.

She could not ask him what he meant because the music had suddenly ceased as an officer strode into the room and silenced the orchestra. Everyone stopped dancing and silently turned towards him.

'We march at dawn, gentlemen,' he said. 'Please rejoin your men.'

There was a concerted cry of dismay from the women, and then a general movement of red and green towards the door.

'It seems that you were better informed than the

rest of us,' Humphrey said under his breath to Louise. 'Now, I wonder . . .'

The tone of his voice made her look at him sharply. Surely he did not think she was a spy? The idea was preposterous, and he must have realised it, because his face broke into a grin, and he said, 'Perhaps you are clairvoyant! If so, we could do with someone like you to tell us what Johnny will be up to next.'

Paul detached himself from Alicia and rejoined her. 'Come,' he said. 'let's make haste.' He took her arm and led her into the vestibule where two footmen were trying to sort out the ladies' cloaks and the officers' swords and calling their carriages. Everyone was crowding round the door and there was a great deal of confusion.

''Twould be quicker it we shared,' Humphrey said at Paul's elbow. 'I sent my coach away.'

They emerged at last, and Paul found the old carriage and its driver and they set off at what seemed breakneck speed.

'Did you know that Mrs Oakingham knew we were moving tomorrow?' Humphrey asked Paul, with some asperity. 'Did you tell her? If you did, it was an exceedingly foolish thing to do; she could have passed the news on to anyone . . . Quite innocently, of course,' he added, smiling at Louise; she could see the whiteness of his teeth in the darkness.

'Well, I didn't.' She defended herself. 'I have spoken to no one but you and Hetty.'

'And it was Hetty who told you,' Paul said, and laughed. 'Pringle has a way of being first with any news. 'I don't know how he does it. I think he is friendly with the Colonel's servant.'

'It should be stopped,' Humphrey said. 'God in heaven, we do not need French spies when there are such loose tongues about!'

Alicia, who had been silent since leaving the convent, said suddenly, 'Perhaps Rifleman Pringle has some connection with the French spy . . .'

Paul chuckled. 'Pringle! Oh, my dear Alicia, you could never meet anyone more fiercely loyal than Pringle.'

'But loyal to whom?' Alicia persisted.

'Why, to King and Country, to the Colours, to me . . .'

'And can he be loyal to all three at once?'

Paul did not appear to notice the innuendo, but whether that was deliberate, Louise could not tell. 'I can see no conflict of loyalty,' he said evenly.

'Alicia,' Humphrey said, 'you have been an officer's wife long enough to know he must have the unquestioning loyalty of his servant, no matter what.'

'And one who knows how to keep a still tongue,' she answered sharply.

'He told only Hetty, and she told me,' Louise said, discomfited by the way the two men seemed to be making an issue out of something that seemed perfectly innocent to her, scoring points off each other and using her to do it. 'I would not have mentioned it, if I'd known there was going to be a fuss . . .'

'You'll know better next time, then, won't you?' Paul said, as the vehicle drew up outside the mansion that had become their quarters. 'No more need be said.'

Alicia started to laugh, almost hysterically. 'So that's how Paul is always one step ahead of the rest. He knows when and where we are going before any of us.'

'Oh, stop it, Alicia,' Humphrey snapped. 'You are making a mountain out of a molehill.' He jumped to the ground and turned to hand the ladies down. 'Come inside and help me to get ready.'

Alicia was silent, and Louise guessed that Humphrey would be on the receiving end of her sharp tongue as soon as they were alone together, although she was too much the lady to begin quarrelling with her husband in front of others.

They said goodnight, and Paul escorted Louise to the door of her room, pausing with his hand on the latch. 'This move has come sooner than I expected, in spite of what the Major's wife said, I've had no time to make arrangements for you.'

'I don't need anyone to make arrangements for me.'

He smiled. 'Perhaps not. But you can stay in this house until I return. I'll send Hetty to you.'

'She won't come, and I don't blame her.'

'Why not?'

'You, above all people, should know she won't be parted from her husband.'

'Then I'll find someone else.'

'There is no need. I became quite used to looking after myself when I was with Dick.'

She realised, with a start, that it was the first time in days she had thought of her husband; it was almost as if that part of her life had never happened. And yet, she reminded herself, it was why she was in Portugal; why she was under the protection, if you could call it protection, of the man who stood smiling at her now. Just how serious had been the threat to her life? It all seemed so far away, like a dream, and she had reacted with foolhardy impulsiveness. If she had been cooler or cleverer, would it have all blown over? And if she had stayed with Dick, where would she be now? In some seedy boarding establishment somewhere, trying to eke out her dwindling resources? Was Paul Fourier her jailer or her saviour? She could not decide.

'What deep thoughts are going through your mind now?' he asked, breaking the silence. 'You haven't heard a word I said.'

She pulled herself together. 'Oh yes, I have,' she lied, conscious that he had been giving her instructions of some sort, which she had no intention of obeying.

'Stay with Alicia; you'll be company for each other.' He opened the top button of his jacket and felt for the cord about his neck which held a small leather pouch. It jingled as he took it off and put it into her hand. Then he pressed the hand lightly to his lips. 'Goodnight, my dear Mrs Oakingham. Rest assured, I shall return.'

He opened the door and ushered her in, and the next moment it had closed again and she heard his

footsteps echoing along the corridor as he went to his
own room.

The urge to run after him was so strong that she
had her hand on the latch of the door before she
pulled herself together and turned back.

Slowly she began preparing for bed. Tomorrow she
would find some high-ranking officer and tell him of
her plight; she would go to the Duke himself if no
one else would listen . . . Sir Richard's name should
guarantee her a hearing. So why did she feel so
uneasy, almost as if turning her back on someone
who needed her? It was ridiculous; Paul didn't need
her, and she certainly didn't need him . . .

Reuben Black spread the bundle of ruined clothes
over the table. the dress was of blue silk and had
once been very fine, but after prolonged immersion
in the Thames and being quarrelled over by the
mudlarks, it was hardly recognisable as a gown at all.
But he had recognised it, given the boys a few
coppers and carried it triumphantly home, where he
dried it and kept it until the time should be right to
produce it.

It had taken longer than he expected to find Dick,
who had gone to ground in a hovel on the edge of
the Essex marshes, and when he did find him, the
young man was in no state to resume a life in society.
He was unshaven and filthy, half-starved and ill-
tempered. He had given up the will to live, the self-
confidence he had hitherto displayed.

He had looked up like a startled hare when Black
entered, but realising who it was, relaxed and resumed
gazing into the flames of the fire in a kind of lethargy.

'Oh, it's you,' he said, by way of greeting.

'It is that,' said Black cheerfully. 'And lucky
'tweren't anyone else. If I can find you, so can
others.'

'Then I must move on.' Dick looked up again.
'Have you got any food there? I haven't had a bite in
days except a few oysters, and precious little
nourishment they gave.'

Black dropped a canvas bag on to the table.

'There's vittels in there.' He watched as the young man delved into it and pulled out bread, meat pie and plum pudding, all solid stuff aimed at sticking the young fellow's crumbling guts together again. He felt in his pocket and withdrew a bottle. 'Here's something to wash it down.'

'Reuben, my dear fellow,' said Dick, feeling better already. 'You are the salt of the earth! Remind me to thank you some time.'

'You can thank me by listening to what I have to say.'

'Later. Later. Have you brought money? With money I can cross the water. There's a boat leaves Romney regular—I think it's a smuggler, but no matter, I'm not particular as to that . . .'

'No, I haven't brought money, knowing full well what you would do with it.'

Dick looked up from wolfing the food, his eyebrows raised in a question.

'You'd find a gaming table, that's what,' said Black. 'And just lately I've come to the conclusion that gambling's not for you, you're not good enough at it.'

'But it's the only thing I am good at!' Dick protested. 'It's the only thing will fetch us out of this mess.'

'Us?' Black repeated. 'Us? I'm in no mess! In truth I don't know why I bother with you at all.'

'Why do you?'

'You owe me, and I mean to be paid.'

'Sorry, old man, but there I can't help you.'

'Yes, you can. I've a mind to use you for a meal ticket.'

Dick laughed. 'Then you'll starve, for I can't stir from this place. If I do . . .' He drew his hand across his throat. 'Am I not being searched for?'

'Yes, indeed, but only by your grieving parents, a heartbroken young lady and a constable who will be easy to convince of your innocence.'

Dick laughed again and took a swig of the wine from the bottle. 'Is there a reward for my capture?'

'Of course.'

'Why don't you collect it?'

'I've my mind fastened on a greater reward.'

Dick wiped his mouth with the back of his hand and bent to stir the fire with a stick that lay in the hearth. 'Let's hear it, then. Let's hear what you've got to say.'

It was then that Black produced the dress and laid it on the table. 'Do you know what this is?'

'Looks like a rag . . . A gown once, I fancy.'

'Your wife's gown.'

'There you're wrong! I never saw her in anything like it.'

'I did. She was wearing it, this very one, when she disappeared.'

'Where did she get it?'

'From that army fellow who won the game.'

'She ran away from him, didn't she?'

'So she did, but he caught her again and took her home and dressed her up in this finery.' He looked at the clothing contemplatively. 'It was good once.'

'How did it get like that? It looks as though it's been very wet.'

Black laughed harshly. 'It got very wet indeed, having spent a week in the Thames.' He fingered the material thoughtfully. 'Your darling Louise is dead,' he said. 'The mudlarks took this off a corpse . . .' It was not strictly true, the gown had been found floating, but he needed to convince Dick he was safe.

Dick had gone very white. 'Are you sure?'

'Yes. And don't tell me you're grieved, 'cos I won't believe it.'

Dick gazed into the fire for some time before answering rather wistfully, 'No, but she was a pretty little thing, you've got to admit, and so trusting, with those big cornflower-blue eyes . . .'

'Miss Trent has blue eyes,' Black reminded him. 'And she is alive and heartbroken by your disappearance.' He paused. 'What's more, she's very rich, very rich indeed.'

Dick's eyes lit up with sudden hope and he half rose from his chair, then sank back again. 'I can't go back home . . . There's Fletcher . . .'

'I've thought of that,' said Black. 'There is a way.'

CHAPTER FIVE

ALICIA BARTON believed Paul was a spy. Louise was sure that was what the conversation in the garden had been about, and the girl had made veiled references to Paul's inside knowledge while they had been driving home. Was Alicia imagining things? Was there some truth in it?

Sleepless, Louise tossed and turned, wondering how the two women could set a trap to prove he was a spy. But was he? Could they harm him if he were innocent? She did not know enough about him or the situation in Portugal even to hazard a guess, but the feeling of unease would not leave her, and telling herself that it was no business of hers, and that her own priority was to return to England and prevent Dick doing anything foolish, made no difference at all.

She rose and dressed long before the rosy pink of dawn lightened the sky, and found her way down to the deserted kitchen. The officers had obviously taken their last meal there before leaving, and the plates had not been cleared from the table. She helped herself to bread, cold sausage and rough wine from a jug, and then left the house, carrying a few essentials for her toilet and a change of clothes in her shawl.

When she arrived at the Rossio which the day before had been so busy, she found it almost deserted. A few early-rising townsfolk glanced at her without interest, but that was all. At the Terreiro do Paço, it was the same. The equestrian statue looked down on an empty square; there was a broken limber leaning against a wall, a single spur glinted where it had fallen, small mounds of horse-droppings steamed in the early morning haze. If the inhabitants had come

out to see the men go, they had since returned to
their homes to catch up on their lost sleep. The
shutters were closed and no one stirred.

She turned this way and that, wondering which way
the army had gone; obviously inland, so she stood
with her back to the harbour and the ships anchored
there and faced the hills. Crossing the Rossio again,
she walked towards the castle, but found herself in
streets so narrow that there was hardly room for two
mules to pass, let alone a column of marching men.
The alleys were overshadowed by balconies trailing
red geraniums and blue plumbago; fishing nets and
wicker baskets hung on the walls; somewhere, out of
her sight, a dove cooed, breaking the silence and
reminding her of her need for haste. She turned to
retrace her steps.

She had not gone far when she heard the sound of
angry voices from one of the little houses on her
right. The next moment the door was flung open and
a young girl hurtled out, landing on hands and knees
almost at Louise's feet. She was bending to help her
when a man, dressed only in grubby trousers, came
to the door and continued shouting at the girl. Louise
did not understand a word he was saying, but he was
obviously very angry and was hurling abuse and
invective, pointing to the hills above the town.

'Are you hurt?' Louise asked, as the girl scrambled
to her feet, turned on her abuser and gave as good as
she had received. Windows near-by were flung open
and heads came out, yelling at the pair to be quiet.
The man shrugged his shoulders and, with a last
sentence in voluble Portuguese, turned and went
inside, slamming the door behind him. The spectators,
realising there was nothing more to be seen or heard,
retreated behind their shutters and the road was once
more deserted, except for Louise and the girl.

She was beautiful in an olive-skinned way, with
shining dark hair and almost black eyes. She stood
muttering at the closed door and shaking the dust
from her colourfully embroidered skirt.

Louise touched her arm and said again, 'Are you
hurt? What was he shouting about?'

The girl turned to her at last and spoke in heavily accented English, with a lilt that Louise found very attractive. 'He is angry because I go with an English soldier.'

'He is your husband?'

'No, my brother, but he thinks he can rule me and tell me what I must do. But he is wrong . . .'

'The English soldier is your husband, then?'

The girl threw back her head and laughed. 'No, we have not talked of marriage. My brother would not allow it, so there is no need to talk of it.'

'Oh, I see.' Louise thought she was beginning to understand.

'He is angry because I did not ask Tommy for 'scudos before he left. He says if I behave like an English whore, then I must follow the army like a whore . . .'

'He threw you out?'

'Yes, but he will change his mind.' The girl was philosophical.

'Are you going to join the march?'

'Yes. I will find my Tommy and he will give me 'scudos.'

'Do you know where they have gone?'

'Sim.' The girl pointed. 'That way.'

'How do you know?'

She laughed. 'Tommy and me, we have no secrets.'

Louise was reminded of the conversation in the coach the night before; how could one person be blamed for information leaking out, when the soldiers mixed freely with the local people and there appeared to be no restraints.

'I want to find them, too,' she said. 'Will you take me?'

The girl shrugged, eyeing Louise up and down, obviously drawing her own conclusions about why she wanted to find the men. 'If that is what you want,' she said.

'How long will it take to catch them up?'

'We will not catch them, we will go over the hills and be in Casavienti before them, then we will wait.'

'Can you find horses for us?' Louise asked and looked puzzled as the girl's laughter pealed out.

'Horses! There are no horses—the soldiers have taken them all, and all the mules, and all the carts. They took our food and our wine, slept in our beds, made whores of our women . . .'

'How dreadful!' said Louise. 'But surely they are not all like that?'

'All but my Tommy,' the girl said. 'My Tommy is a good man, but João does not understand . . .'

'Your brother?'

'*Sim.*' The girl gave one backward glance at the closed door of the house and set off up the street at a good pace, with Louise beside her.

'What's your name?' Louise asked.

'Maria. And you?'

'Louise. You speak very good English.'

'Tommy taught me. We have been together two years, since he came to my country.' She turned to Louise and looked her up and down as they walked. 'And you, why do you want to find the soldiers?'

Louise smiled to herself as she answered. 'For exactly the same reason as you do.'

'But your man is not called Tommy?' There was laughter in her voice.

Louise smiled as she answered again, 'No, his name is Paul.'

Once they had left the city behind, they were in a land of market gardens and orchards, a land of neat pink- and blue-fronted cottages, and windmills whose strange triangular sails, with their clay pots swinging, whistled as they turned. A few miles later they found themselves looking down on desolation. Every house, every wall, had been demolished, every tree uprooted; ditches had been filled in, holes dug where there had been none before, parapets and palisades had been raised where the ground had hitherto been flat. Anything which could give cover to an advancing army had gone, replaced by hidden defensive positions.

'See,' said Maria, pointing. 'That is what your army has done to my country.'

'But, surely, only to defend the city?'

The girl was angry; it showed in her eyes. 'It is like that everywhere. The land will never be the same again.'

'Would you rather the French conquered your country?'

'It would be no worse.'

Louise said no more: there was no point in arguing and, in any case, she did not feel qualified to argue. It was not her native land and she had set foot on it only the day before.

They walked on in silence, leaving the Lines of Torres Vedras behind them to their left, skirted a cork-oak forest and began climbing again, picking their way over a rocky terrain, until in the middle of the afternoon they topped the brow of a hill and stopped to rest.

The heat was intense, and up among the rocks and scrub of the hillside there was very little shade. Louise could feel her clothes clinging to her and the hair on the nape of her neck was wet. She was continually putting her hand under it to lift it away from her skin. The air was still and the only sound was the sudden, almost human, cry of a hare as a hovering hawk swooped and seized it. Far below they could see the white road, which twisted and turned, hidden here and there by olive groves, dark green against the creamy whiteness of the hills.

'They come along there,' Maria said, pointing. 'Soon.'

'You are sure?'

'I am sure.'

'Shall we go down to them?'

'No, we go along this path and down to the *casa*. We will be there before them.'

A distant sound came to them, faintly at first, but then more strongly, the beat of drums, the noise of wheels and horses. The girls moved to the edge of the hill and looked down on the road. They saw the dust first, a great cloud of it, then the flash of steel reflecting the sun, and then the column itself came into view, three miles long. It was led by officers on horseback, followed by the King's Colour and then the regimental colours. There were gloriously uniformed Spaniards with their colours, bigger than anyone else's, Portuguese, sombrely dressed and poorly equipped, marching beside their English allies. And the English! Louise, remembering regimental parades through the streets at home, the immaculate recruiting sergeants and the finery of the officers, found it difficult to believe that this raggle-taggle crocodile of men was an English battalion. They marched with a discipline which had been drilled into them, but their clothing and equipment were worn and shabby; it was almost impossible to tell red from green jackets, so grubby and sun-bleached were they. Was this the army Wellington was going to lead to victory?

Behind them, pulled by huge plodding horses, came the heavy guns, with smoke-blackened barrels, their limbers jolting and sliding on the uneven road, then the supply wagons, loaded with ammunition, food and equipment, and at the end, straggling raggedly, the women, plodding stoically behind their men to war.

Maria shaded her eyes with her hand and looked along the column. 'I cannot see him. From here, he is the same as all the others.'

Louise, too, scanned the lines. And then she saw Paul on his magnificent horse, riding up and down beside the small section of men he commanded, and suddenly her heart began to pound and she wanted to run down the slope, shouting his name.

She was suddenly aware that Maria had spoken to her. 'You see your man?'

'Yes. The officer on the black horse at the back of the column.'

'Why, that is Captain Fourier.'

'You know him?'

'Everyone knows him. He is so 'andsome,' Maria said, and laughed. 'Besides, Tommy is one of his men.'

'And Tommy told you where they were going today?' asked Louise, reminded of the stories of the

spy and Humphrey's disapproval of gossip and
rumour-spreading.

The girl did not answer but pointed silently to a
huddle of rocks to their right, where a movement had
caught her eye.

Louise looked along the line of her pointing finger
and gasped as a small band of French cavalry picked
their way along the path ahead of them, watching the
unsuspecting column. They were led by a tall,
immaculately-uniformed officer, whose upright bearing
and the way he sat his horse reminded her a little of
Paul, and she could easily imagine Paul in that
beautiful uniform instead of the dark green of the
95th. It was a disloyal thought, and she thrust it from
her.

'We must warn our people,' Louise whispered.
'Will they hear if we shout?'

'Yes, but so will the Bluecoats, and I do not want
to be hacked to pieces by their swords.'

'But we must do something.'

'Why? The Frenchies will not attack, there are not
enough of them and they are a long way behind the
English lines. They are only watching . . .'

'But they could go back to their friends and report
our positions!'

Maria shrugged, as if it did not matter. 'You cannot
keep any march a secret; they are only keeping
watch, there will be no fighting, not today. When
they have gone, we will go on.'

All through the rest of the day, as she allowed
Maria to lead her, Louise was tormented by doubt.
The girl knew the terrain very well and picked her
way along the ridge of the hill, scrambling round
boulders and crossing streams where they meandered
down towards the Tagus, not so many miles away.
The water was cool to their feet, and Louise bent to
splash her face and neck before dutifully following
her guide.

By early evening, when the sun began to drop
behind the peaks, they became as cold as they had
previously been hot, and she was glad when the

narrow path they were on took a downward turn and they began the descent into a small village.

Maria took her to the local bakery, which was run by a cousin, and here they were made welcome, given food and drink and plied with questions that Louise did not understand, but which Maria answered at great length. It seemed that she was giving her account of how her brother had thrown her out, and it must have been a convincing story because the family of husband, wife and half a dozen children smiled and nodded and clucked sympathetically.

'What are they saying?' Louise asked.

'That we are welcome to stay here tonight.'

'But I thought we were going to join the column?'

'Tomorrow. Tonight we sleep in a real bed.'

'Do they know where the soldiers are?'

'They are camped outside the village. The headman has been to speak to their commander; he will not let the men come into the village . . .'

'Why not?'

'Because they take everything, food, wine, clothes, women . . .'

'Is it always like that?'

'Most times. But our people have promised to give them food and wine if they stay outside, so . . .' She smiled serenely. 'We sleep undisturbed tonight. Tomorrow—well, tomorrow will bring its own troubles, we do not need to think of them.'

It did not take a practised eye to see that the villagers were very short of food, but Louise guessed that it had been a wise move on the part of the local dignitaries to offer provisions in exchange for remaining unmolested. If the men were allowed free rein, they would ransack the place, taking what they wanted and ruining what they had no use for; in this way the villagers would be able to keep a little back for themselves, at least until the next marauding party arrived, be it English, French or Spanish *guerrilleros*.

The trouble was compounded, Louise learned from her hosts, through Maria as interpreter, by the scorched earth policy of the Duke of Wellington the year before. He had not been a duke then, of course, just Sir Arthur Wellesley, but as commander of the British troops in the Peninsula, he had decreed that food stocks and crops should be destroyed as the army retreated so that the French, with their supply-lines stretched to the limit, would not be able to live off the land in the usual way. It had far-reaching repercussions: the populace, with no growing crops and no corn seed because they had been forced to eat it, and half the men away fighting, were left to fend for themselves. And those who, like the baker, had managed to hang on to some of their grain were continually harried by the soldiers who invaded their homes. Louise was reluctant to eat and deprive them of even a mouthful more, but they insisted and she was hungry, so she ate heartily, although Maria continued to grumble.

Afterwards she and Maria shared a bed in an upstairs room. Her limbs were stiff from unaccustomed hill-walking and her eyelids heavy, and she fell almost immediately into a dreamless sleep. When she awoke, Maria's place beside her was empty.

She rose, still feeling stiff, dressed and went down to the living-room to ask where the girl had gone. The cousin at last understood what she was asking and answered her at great length, not a word of which she understood. She thanked the family, and left.

The sun was already high and the day promised to be as warm as the one before. She stood a moment to find her bearings, and then crossed the tiny village square and passed down a narrow street between small squat houses and found herself on a narrow stone bridge, over what she guessed must be a tributary of the Tagus. She crossed it and made towards a grove of olives, where she could see smoke rising above the trees and could hear the sounds of people and horses.

Here she found the men taking their ease. Some slept, some cleaned their weapons and equipment, others sat with blistered feet in the cool water of the river. The smell of cooking and tobacco drifted on the air. Near by, the horses were tethered, and

Louise looked along their lines, trying to pick out the big black stallion. She moved forward, but her path was immediately blocked by a sentry, who seemed to appear from nowhere.

'Where are you going?' he demanded, musket at the ready. 'The women's camp is down the road.' He jerked his head sideways to where a second, smaller camp had been established. Here there was more activity and lines of washing strung between the trees. Louise gave it a cursory glance and turned back to the sentry.

'I wish to speak to Captain Fourier.'

'He is not here.'

'He was with you yesterday.'

'Yesterday was yesterday, today is today.'

'Do you know where I might find him?'

'That I don't.'

She realised he would not tell her, even if he did know. 'Major Barton, then, of the 71st.'

The sentry called to someone behind him without looking round, and another soldier joined him.

'What's up, Danny?'

'This woman wanted Captain Fourier and when I said he wasn't here, she asked for Major Barton.'

'I must see one of them,' Louise said. 'It's important.'

'Wait here; I'll fetch him.'

Louise stood, not daring to move for fear of the sentry whose finger seemed to want to stray towards the trigger, and waited until Humphrey came along the path.

He smiled broadly when he saw her. 'Why, Mrs Oakingham, what are you doing here?'

Louise suddenly realised she had not rehearsed an answer to that question, and the truth would seem lame and foolish. 'I have something to tell . . . Captain Fourier,' she said. 'But I'm told he's not here.'

'He left with a patrol before daybreak.'

'A small patrol?' she asked, her heart in her mouth.

'Yes, I believe so.'

'Where has he gone?'

He smiled indulgently. 'Now, Mrs Oakingham, you know my feelings on divulging information! You surely don't expect me to tell you.'

'But he could be in danger . . . You could all be in danger . . . There are Frenchmen up in those hills . . .'

He let out a great guffaw of laughter, while the sentry barely managed to hide his grin. Discomfited, she blushed scarlet and added angrily, 'I don't see what you find so funny.'

'My dear Mrs Oakingham,' he said, taking her arm and leading her back along the path. 'I should be very surprised if there were not Frenchmen in the hills. That's what patrols and skirmishers are for, to flush them out. We shall fight when we are ready, and we shall choose the ground. And it is not here.'

'Why stay here, then?'

He stopped talking to turn to face her. 'There's no need to worry your pretty little head with strategy. Now, we must make you comfortable.'

'But I want to speak to Captain Fourier.'

'So you shall, dear lady, so you shall, just as soon as he returns. But, in the meantime, may I escort you to the village? You will be safe there . . .'

'Safe? Safe from whom?' she asked with some asperity.

'Why Monsieur Johnny Bluecoat, my dear, whom else?'

'But I thought you said there was no danger?'

'There is always danger, and I know Paul would not want you to mix with the other women.'

'Why not? Besides, how can you take me to the village? Soldiers are not supposed to go there.'

He laughed. 'Officers are not considered soldiers in that sense,' he said. 'I have a room there, where you can stay until Paul comes back.'

'Is your wife with you?' She was beginning to feel distinctly uncomfortable with him, though she could not say exactly why; perhaps his smile was a little too confident, his grip on her elbow a little too tight.

'Alicia? No, my dear wife is too fond of her comforts. She will stay in Lisbon until I return, which is what you should have done, if you don't mind my

saying so. Paul will be none too pleased to see you.'
He halted in his tracks and grinned down at her. 'I
don't know, though, perhaps he will be delighted, as
I am.'

They were entering the square and she realised
that, after all, he was not the only soldier in the
village; a group of them were erecting an upright
wooden triangle under the direction of an officer,
while two more stood guard over a prisoner, holding
him firmly by each arm.

'What are they doing?' she asked, as villagers
appeared from doors and alleys and gathered round
to watch.

'They are going to flog him.'

'Why?'

'He disobeyed the order not to come into the
village. He broke the arrangement the Colonel made,
and he is to be punished in front of the villagers, to
prove an English officer's word is meant to be kept.'

'Poor man,' she murmured.

'Poor man!' he scoffed. 'Even the rawest recruit
knows what to expect if he disobeys an order. The
man knew what he was risking.'

'Why did he do it?'

He laughed lightly, dismissing her concern. 'Some
men just like to test their mettle now and then; it
puts an added spice into their lives . . .'

'I should have thought there was spice enough
without that,' she said. 'You are fighting a war, are
you not?'

'Oh, yes,' he said, as if he enjoyed shocking her.
'But there are some devilish boring bits in between.'

He stopped near the triangle, evidently intent on
witnessing the flogging. Louise had no desire to watch
and kept her eyes averted as the guards removed the
man's shirt and strapped his wrists high on the tripod.
The drum began to roll, but it was almost drowned
by a piercing scream and, in spite of herself, Louise
looked round to see Maria throw herself across the
man as if to protect him. 'No! No!' she shouted. 'No!
I asked him to come to me. I asked him!'

She was lifted bodily and carried away, and the

drummer began to beat the time for the whip as it rose and fell on the man's back—thirty-six times. At the end, he was barely conscious and his back was raw. Someone threw a bucket of water over him and his hands were untied, allowing him to sink slowly to the uneven paving of the square.

'You'll pay for this!' shrieked Maria, addressing the punishment squad and the officer who had ordered it. 'You'll pay with your lives, all of you, see if you don't!' She subsided into Portuguese, while her cousin and his wife held her back from attempting physical retaliation. 'Tommy, Tommy,' she sobbed at last, and they let her go, to follow the two men who dragged her lover between them.

'That was horrible,' Louise said, appalled by the brutality of the punishment and Humphrey's apparent indifference to it. 'The poor man only went to see Maria; they are in love.'

'You know them?' he asked in surprise.

'Maria brought me here. Her brother threw her out for consorting with an English soldier. She followed the march and he must have heard about it. He only came into the village to be with her.'

'That is no excuse, and he knows it. Come now, think no more of it. Such punishment is commonplace and you will become accustomed to it.'

'I never will!' she cried. 'It's barbaric, it makes me feel quite sick . . .'

'Then come to my lodgings and let me offer you a glass of wine to revive you.'

'No, thank you,' she said, sharply. 'I'm going to join the other women. You can tell Captain Fourier where to find me when he returns.'

She ignored his protests and hurried out of the village to the women's camp, where Maria was gently sponging her lover's back as he lay in the shade of an olive tree. The girl was dropping tears on his wounds and murmuring endearments. Passing them without speaking, Louise wandered off among the trees, envying them their love.

She stopped and leaned against a gnarled trunk, feeling desolate. Here she was, miles from home,

unwanted by her husband, ignored by the soldiers
and their wives, unable to understand the language,
unneeded by Paul Fourier . . . But why had he taken
her to Lisbon and left her there? What would he say
when he discovered she had followed him out of the
city? She shut her eyes, trying to hold back the tears
which threatened.

She heard a twig snap very close at hand and her
eyes flew open in alarm. Paul was standing not five
feet away, smiling at her. She had no idea how long
he had been there, and her heart began to beat
uncomfortably fast and warmth flooded her cheeks
because she had dropped her guard and he had seen
the real Louise, unhappy and vulnerable. His
expression, when she had first opened her eyes, had
been tender, almost sad, but now it had hardened
again and her own smile, hiding her hurt, was brittle.
'You startled me!'

He laughed. 'Did you suppose I was a Bluecoat?'

'No, of course not.'

'Why not? I am, after all, French.'

She wondered why he had reminded her of that; it
sent her thoughts whirling towards spies and betrayal
and all the things she had made up her mind not to
think of.

'By birth perhaps, but by adoption, you are
English.'

He moved towards her and reached out to touch
her cheek; his hand was cool and gentle. 'Yes, that's
true. Tell me, why did you not stay in Lisbon as I
instructed.'

'Do I have to follow your instructions?' she
demanded. 'Have you the right . . .'

'I have the right.'

'Because you won me in a game of cards, I
suppose . . .'

'No, I was going to say because of my greater
experience of war.' He was smiling, that half-mocking
smile that made her so annoyed. 'You would have
been entirely safe in Lisbon.'

'I know no one there, no one at all, and I cannot
speak the language. I want to be with my own kind.'

'Your own kind,' he repeated. 'You think you will find them here, among the camp-followers?'

'At least they speak the same language!'

'You could have stayed with Alicia; she would have introduced you to other ladies who had remained behind.'

'Alicia!' she said, before she could stop herself. 'Alicia Barton thinks you are a spy.'

He gave a hoot of laughter. 'Is that so? Well, I don't suppose she is alone in that.'

'Does it not worry you?'

'No, why should it? What can she do?'

Louise, realising she had already said too much, decided not to mention the rest of the conversation she had overheard, and shrugged her shoulders. 'Talk,' she said.

He stepped close to her and put his hand on the tree trunk above her head, so that he was leaning over her. 'And you?' he asked, softly. 'Do you believe I would betray my adopted country?'

'I do not know what to believe.'

'Then there is no point in this conversation,' he said. 'When we reach a convenient town, I shall try to arrange for you to be escorted back to Lisbon.'

Before she could retort that she would not leave unless she chose to, he had gone, striding away between the trees, back to his men.

She had angered him and now she was entirely alone; there was no one to whom she could turn for help or reassurance. So be it; she would stay with the march for no reason other than her own stubbornness.

In the next few days, they followed the north bank of the Tagus, spending a night outside Vila Franca de Xiro, and then on to the ancient town of Santarém, built on a rocky promontory overlooking the river and its surrounding marshy plain, where the white houses of the inhabitants stood on stilts.

Louise was becoming used to the routine, sleeping out of doors or in cattle sheds or deserted cottages, lighting fires, cooking, washing, and every night lying down with aching limbs and blistered feet. And for what? The other women, whether wives or whores, had their reasons—love perhaps, or money—but for Louise there was neither. The money Paul had given her was fast dwindling, and she would not go to him for more. She was not even sure if he was aware that she was still there, still pushing her weary body onwards. She had seen him riding his stallion up and down the lines ahead of them, but he never rode back to where the women followed with the supply wagons and baggage carts, and the small herd of cattle brought along for meat. She told herself she did not care, but if that were true, what was she doing there?

The day after leaving Abrantes, the scene of a battle the year before, according to Hetty, they turned north away from the river and into the mountains. Louise noted an increased tension in everyone, a greater alertness; patrols were sent out more frequently and the women stayed together, trying to keep up with the column and its rumbling wagons. She guessed they were moving into more dangerous territory, and she could not rid herself of the feeling that their progress was being watched, perhaps by those very horsemen she and Maria had seen.

Now they were in rugged country, with huge rough boulders and weird-shaped pinnacles of rock reaching into the heat-filled sky. There was little vegetation on the higher slopes except heather and broom, which covered the barren earth like a golden carpet. Swiftly-flowing streams, starting high in the mountains, cut steep-sided courses down to the lakes and rivers, impeding their progress. Fording-places were difficult to find, and bridges, where they had not been blown up, were so narrow that the column took hours to cross. It was at times like these that she felt her nerves especially on edge. And Hetty didn't help.

'Gives me the creeps,' she said one evening as they approached yet another bridge on the narrow road, beyond which was a tiny walled village. 'That's Spain over them hills, and them Frenchies ain't far away . . . I can feel it in me bones.'

They stopped suddenly as the column ahead halted. Orders were given, and the men broke ranks and made for the wood, leading the guns and supply wagons into its shelter.

'Looks like we're making camp early,' Hetty said, leaving the road to find a spot to make the usual cooking-fire. But before she could do so, Paul rode up and dismounted.

'Don't light any fires,' he ordered. 'Stay low and quiet. We're crossing the bridge after dark.'

'I knew there was something funny goin' on,' Hetty said. 'It's too quiet.'

He smiled, and then turning to Louise, inclined his body in a stiff bow. 'Mrs Oakingham.'

'Captain Fourier.'

'Do you have all you need?'

Now was the time to tell him, since he had asked, to tell him she needed . . . what? Money? She would not ask for it. Protection? Love, even? No, she would not humble herself.

He handed his horse's reins to Pringle, who had followed him up the road to spend some time with his wife, and walked over to her, taking her elbow and leading her further into the trees, away from the crowd.

'I am sorry I have had no opportunity to make better provision for you,' he said stiffly. 'I did not intend that you should have to walk with the women . . .'

'You once said you had nothing but admiration for them,' she said, leaning against a tree and attempting to laugh. It was a brittle sound, forced from her by pride.

'And so I have, but that is not to say that you need to live in their company.'

'They are all you said they were,' she said with conviction. 'And, besides that, they have a great deal to talk about and manage to stay cheerful no matter what. I am proud to be one of their number.'

He stood looking at her with his slightly mocking smile, then said, 'I shall find a room for you when we

reach Castelo Branco; it won't be as comfortable as
Lisbon, but it will be better than this.'

Her answer died on her lips because the quiet of
the grove was suddenly broken by the whine and
thump of an explosion not far away, and the solid
tree against which she had been leaning shook like an
aspen. She flung herself away from it and into his
arms.

He held her tight against his chest, murmuring into
her hair. 'It's all right, my love, you are safe here.'
His lips brushed her hair before he drew away and
lifted her chin with his forefinger. 'Stay here, do you
hear? This time, for your own sake, do as I ask and
stay here. I'll be back.'

Then he ran off between the trees as another
explosion followed the first, and above it she heard
shouts and screams and the neighing of frightened
horses. The ground shook, and she stood a minute
too terrified to move, gazing with unseeing eyes at
the spot where she had last seen him. He had run
straight into the second explosion, she was sure of it.
She moved at last, running through the trees towards
the noise. If he was dead or dying she had to find
him, had to be with him whatever the danger. He
had called her 'love', and shown he could be gentle,
and she became aware of a slow awakening of an
emotion within her she thought had died. Now she
understood how Hetty and Maria and all the other
women felt who followed their men into battle. She,
too, wanted to be in the thick of it.

The camp was a shambles. Dead and dying men
and horses lay among uprooted trees and newly
unearthed rocks. The men had been taken by surprise,
but they were trained soldiers and it was not the first
time they had been caught unawares. They were
grabbing rifles and muskets, and re-grouping. Under
the direction of their officers, they were preparing to
defend an almost indefensible position. The wood
sloped down to the valley, surrounded by bare hills;
the white road ran along one side of the wood and
the river through its centre, emerging at the bridge
that formed the entrance to the village.

Louise looked about, expecting to see blue uniforms, but there was none. Another explosion shook the ground, and more trees and rocks and bodies were flung into the air.

'How in God's name did they get a cannon up in them hills?' asked one soldier, while busily ramming powder and ball down the barrel of his musket. 'There ain't no way we can reach 'em.'

She ducked behind a boulder as another missile screamed down on them. When the dust settled, she peered out and saw half a dozen green-jacketed riflemen leave the small protection of the trees, cross the open road and fling themselves behind the cover of scrub on the other side. She watched in spellbound admiration as they ran, crouching, darting this way and that, climbing up towards the place where the cannon was hidden. Any minute now the gunners would see them and would deflect the gun down on to them; they had to get under its trajectory before that happened. There were other groups going left and right, swarming up the hill.

Another round of canister scattered everyone, and the sound had hardly died away before Pringle dropped down beside her and grinned. 'Captain said I was to take you to Hetty.'

'Where is she?'

'Down the road a spell with the other women; they're safe enough there.'

'How do you know?'

'There are some rules in this war,' he said off-handedly. 'The Bluecoats know where the women are; they aren't interested in them. But they aren't goin' to pick out a single woman what's silly enough to get herself mixed up with the men . . .' He pulled her down and sheltered beside her as another explosion rocked their hiding-place.

'Will they come down here?' she asked, lifting a mud-streaked face and pushing her hair back from over her eyes. She gasped when she found that her hand was smeared with blood.

''Tis only a scratch,' he said, looking at her head.

'Now, when I say "go", you get up and run, d'ye
hear?'

She nodded.

He got to his knees and peered round as rifle-fire
echoed across the road. 'They've seen the skirmishers,
though they can't get the big gun down on 'em now,'
he said. 'It'll give us a breather.' He turned back to
her. 'Now, go!' He pulled her to her feet and,
crouching low, almost dragged her through the trees,
ignoring the dead and wounded.

At the edge of the trees, he stopped. They had to
cross open ground before gaining the shelter of
another group of trees where the women huddled.
He waited for the next explosion, but before the
sound had died away, set off across the space, pulling
Louise after him.

A horseman galloped past them on their left,
heading back down the road the men had marched
along earlier in the day. It was not until they had
gained the safety of the trees and the sound of the
galloping hooves had died that she realised it had
been Paul, leaving the scene of the carnage in what
looked suspiciously like flight.

CHAPTER SIX

HETTY RAN FORWARD with a cry of relief and flung herself into Pringle's arms. He stood for a minute holding her before kissing her fondly and then, telling her to look after Louise, dashed back the way he had come.

The girl bathed Louise's very superficial wound as the bombardment went on; more trees were uprooted, more men killed and maimed, and then the cannon was turned on the bridge, the only way forward to the place where they were to meet the enemy. But the enemy had come to them, forcing them to stop and defend themselves, while reinforcements were still a day's march away. If the French could blow up that bridge, it would delay the British advance and give them time to prepare. Built by the Romans, it was solid, and although pieces of stonework and chunks of masonry flew into the air and landed in the river, it withstood the first few hits. But for how long? The helpless watchers in the women's camp could only guess and pray for deliverance. A cannonball found the village, and they saw roofs disappearing in a cloud of dust.

Maria, who had hitherto remained unmoved by the carnage, cried out in dismay. 'Oh, no, not the homes of my people! Not that!' Then she fell to muttering in Portuguese. Louise was shocked by the expression on the girl's face; it was one of hate and anger, frightening in its intensity.

The men who had tried to climb the hill had nearly all been killed; their bodies lay sprawled among the rocks for everyone to see. More set off on what seemed a suicidal mission, then others, left and right, intending to encircle the offending gun. The women

watched wide-eyed, their fists to their open mouths as
the men scrambled up. The gun's barrel, hidden from
their sight, was deflected downwards and a ball landed
among the climbers, scattering them.

They waited for the next explosion, but instead
they heard musket and rifle-fire high up on the hill,
and then silence. After the ear-shattering noise that
had gone before, it seemed almost quiet enough to
hear a pin drop. No one dared move, hardly dared
draw breath. The cries of the wounded were the
loudest sounds. Still the women waited, scanning the
hill. The surviving skirmishers, almost at the top,
paused in their climbing, unsure of themselves, and
then doubled their pace and disappeared over the
brow of the hill.

Nothing happened, no cannon roared, no rifle fired;
the dust settled, and the wounded continued to call
for help. High in the cloudless sky a pair of vultures
hovered.

'Come on,' said Hetty at last. 'It's over.' She ran
out from the protection of the trees and across the
open ground, followed by Louise and the rest of the
women.

Louise was intent on doing what she could to help.
The destruction was dreadful, and she was almost
physically sick at the sight of the dead and wounded,
but she managed to control her heaving stomach
enough to get to work, binding wounds, fetching
drinking-water, soothing and comforting.

She was horrified to see the living robbing the dead
of their meagre belongings and even tried to prevent
one young soldier from taking the boots of his dead
comrade. He pushed her roughly away and calmly
continued to replace his own badly worn footwear
with some which were only slightly better.

'Leave him be,' Hetty said to her. She had found
Pringle alive and well, and had turned her attention
to the others. 'A dead man don't need boots, do 'e?
And the livin' still 'ave some marchin' to do.'

Louise shut her eyes to what was going on, to
pockets and packs being emptied, even rings being
pulled from stiffening fingers, and knelt on the ground

to bind up the leg of a man whose foot had been blown off. It was a gory mess and she was making a poor job of it, when the rag she had been given to use as a bandage was taken from her and steadier hands than hers completed the task. She scrambled to her feet and turned to thank her helper. It was Paul.

'Oh, you decided to come back, then?' she said, flatly. 'Now the battle seems to be over.'

He ignored her innuendo. 'I told you to stay where you were,' he said. 'Will you never learn to obey? It's just as well I saw you; you might have been killed. As it was, I had to detach Pringle to take you to safety at a time when I needed him.'

'Needed him to cower behind!' she snapped. 'Do you expect me to stay away and do nothing when my countrymen are dying? Englishmen,' she added emphatically. 'Brave British boys. And while there are English women prepared to risk their lives to help the men, I'll not run away and hide.' She looked away from the anger in his face at the horrifying scene about her. Some of the women tended the wounded with a skill born of long experience; some still wandered in and out among the corpses, looking for their loved ones. 'I am needed,' she said.

That simple sentence, spoken with conviction, gave her the courage to face things as they were, to stop yearning for what could not be. She had found a purpose in her life. It enabled her to ignore the uncomfortable beat of her heart because he was looking at her with a mixture of humour and anger. He had no call to be amused, just because she showed a spunk he did not seem to have, and he certainly had no right to be angry.

'Unlike some,' she added firmly, when he did not take his gaze from her face. 'I do not run away.'

His brown eyes hardened. 'Your meaning, ma'am?'

She could not help it, she had to score against him. 'You left your men to die, you took that fine horse of yours and galloped away . . .' She stopped in mid-sentence as his hand came up and hovered above her cheek. They glared at each other for several seconds before he dropped his arm and strode off. She sank to the ground beside the wounded Rifleman, and allowed the tears to fall on her torn and blood-spattered skirt.

'You didna' oughta ha' said that.' He spoke quietly. 'The Cap'n's just about the bravest man you could meet.'

She got up and ran from the scene, trying to find refuge from her turbulent thoughts in solitude. A soldier with his foot blown off had, in the middle of his pain, called his officer a brave man; such loyalty, such generosity had been unexpected, and it made her feel exceedingly humble. She was ashamed, not so much for herself, but for Paul, who did not deserve it. She stopped, leaned against a pine, its resinous smell filling her nostrils, and slowly slid down its trunk to the ground, putting her head in her hands.

''Tis always upsetting the first time,' said a voice. 'You will become used to it.'

Louise opened her eyes to see Maria standing over her. The girl had washed and changed her clothes; she looked spruce and clean, and her dark hair shone. She was carrying her bundle.

'Used to it!' Louise exclaimed. 'How can you say such a thing? How can you be so hard?'

The girl shrugged. 'Tommy is alive—that is all I care about.'

'And the others?'

'There are too many for one person to cry over. We must all weep for our own.'

'You don't like us, do you?' Louise asked suddenly. 'You don't like the English, even though you love one of our soldiers.'

'Should I?' The girl retorted. 'What have you ever done for us except make a poor country even poorer?'

'It would be worse if the French won.'

'What do you know of it?' she demanded. 'You know nothing! Go back to your own country. Go back to England.'

But there was no going back; the battalion crossed the bridge next morning and marched forward again. Even supposing Louise wanted to return to Lisbon,

over sixty miles behind them, no one could be spared
to accompany her. Maria might have been persuaded
to, but then Maria had disappeared. So, too, had
Tommy. They had been marching another two days
when Louise learned from Hetty that he had deserted.

'He's a fool,' Hetty said, as they tramped in the
wake of the men. 'And a dead 'un if he's caught.'

'Then let's hope he isn't caught,' Louise told her.

Hetty let this pass without comment, preferring to
save her breath for walking, especially now the pace
had been stepped up and they were covering fifteen
miles a day over very rough terrain.

Louise was becoming hardened to the life; her feet
were no longer blistered and the heat did not bother
her quite so much, perhaps because the altitude was
higher and there was a cool breeze, perhaps because
her face and arms now had a protective tan which
would have horrified her contemporaries in England
if they could have seen her. But though she was
becoming physically tougher, emotionally she still felt
weak and vulnerable. The other women had come to
accept her; they no longer took account of the fact
that she had been brought up as a lady; she was one
of them.

She had to admit she envied Hetty; her husband
came to her every night when he was not on picket
duty or going on patrol; they enjoyed some sort of
married life together, even if it was exposed and
uncomfortable. The Rifleman, though politely passing
the time of day with Louise, never mentioned Paul,
and Louise knew it was a deliberate omission; he had
probably learned of the accusation she had hurled at
his officer.

The attack on the bridge was still a subject of
conversation and speculation. Many felt they had
been betrayed.

'How did them Frenchies know we was there?'
asked Meg, a big raw-boned woman who carried her
husband's pack because, although injured, he was
considered fit enough to march.

'But anyone could have seen the column from

the ridge,' said Louise, remembering the French horsemen. 'It would be impossible to keep it hidden.'

'Yes, but why were they so far ahead of their own lines?' someone asked. 'And how did they get a cannon up into the mountains without being seen?'

'There are paths all over the hills,' Louise explained. 'I came along one myself to join you.'

'You had a guide.'

'The French could have had a guide, too,' Louise said, and wished she had not spoken.

'Oh, they had a guide, you can be sure,' Meg sneered. 'And he ain't a million miles away.' She looked up to where the men marched ahead, with Paul, head and shoulders above the rest.

'You can't mean Captain Fourier?' Hetty said, shocked to the core. 'He wouldn't do anything like that . . .'

'Why not? He's French, ain't he?'

'Not any more.' Louise felt she had to defend him, though full of doubts herself. 'He was brought up in England.'

'Well, you would speak up for him,' someone else joined in. 'No doubt you're in league with him.'

Louise turned to her. 'Don't be silly! Would I be marching with you if I were in league with the French?'

'What better place to hear and see.' The woman's laughter was hollow as she added, 'It's a funny thing, how he made sure you was safe afore he rode off. He wasn't goin' to stay and be blown to bits by his own kind . . .'

'That's nonsense!' Louise protested, while the doubts grew. 'The firing stopped almost as soon as he left.'

'So it did, but it was the Spanish *guerrilleros* who stopped it. When our men got to the gun, they found the crew all dead at their stations and not a livin' soul in sight. The *guerrilleros* had killed them all and gone back to hiding in the hills.'

'Yes, that's true,' said Hetty. 'That's the way they work. They come out to fight, and then disappear again like ghosts in the night.'

'But Captain Fourier came back,' Louise said feebly, hearing again the bitter words she had spoken and wishing them unsaid. But if all the rumours about him were true, did he not deserve her wrath?

'I'll hear no more agin him,' Hetty stated. 'Another word out o' any on you, and you'll have me to answer to. He's brave and good and clever . . .'

She ignored the chuckle behind her, and the comment, 'He's clever, you can be sure o' that!' Instead, she quickened her pace to catch up with the tail of the column ahead of them. It was nearly time to stop for the day, and she wanted to be on hand when Pringle needed her.

Many of the women who trailed so loyally behind their men had been in the Peninsula two years or more; some had travelled the same ground the previous October on the long retreat to the safety of the Lines of Torres Vedras. They knew the names of the towns and villages, and of the swift rivers whose deep gorges dissected the hills and slowed their progress. It was from one of these that she learned that the name of the walled city with the white castle was Castelo Branco, and although they stayed one night in its environs, Paul did not come to tell her he was leaving her there.

He seemed to have disappeared again; she had missed his tall figure on the big horse, riding up and down the lines, but fearful that the arguments might start again, she could not bring herself to ask his whereabouts. She did not see him until two days later when he rode into the camp they had set up in an orchard, dismounted and hurried to report to his superiors, not even glancing in the direction of the women, and the next morning they set off in a north-easterly direction towards the Spanish frontier.

She did not know whether to be glad or sorry, glad that he was not leaving her behind in a strange town, sorry that they would have no opportunity to talk. But that, in itself, might be a blessing; they seemed always to strike sparks off each other and she found herself saying things which she would not have dreamed of to anyone else, and she could not begin to understand why. She would have to content herself with the company and conversation of the women, who saw the march as the start of Wellington's campaign of revenge for the humiliation of the previous October.

'That was a time, that was,' said Hetty, slightly out of breath, for they were walking steadily uphill. 'You should ha' seen it. There never was so many Frenchies in one place afore, thousands and thousands of 'em. But we was ready; we took to the hills and waited.'

'But it was a retreat,' said Louise. 'I heard about it.'

'Of course,' said Hetty, remembering something Jamie had told her. 'Your husband was there, wasn't he? Lost at Busaco, wasn't he?'

Louise said nothing. She had completely forgotten Paul's tale of her missing husband and now she wished he had told her something of that battle, so that she had no need to appear so ignorant.

'If we go that way, you'll be able to make enquiries for him,' Meg put in, unaware of Louise's discomfiture. 'He might even be there still. Now that would be something to celebrate, wouldn't it?'

'We ain't goin' that way,' Hetty said, always knowledgeable. 'We're going to Almeida. Jamie said so.'

'She can still ask.' Meg rounded on Hetty, then turned to Louise. 'Tell me, what does he look like? Is he handsome? What colour is his hair? Does he wear a moustache?' She laughed suddenly. 'But that don't signify, do it? He could easily grow one or shave it off . . .'

Louise smiled, trying to imagine Dick with a moustache, and wondering if it would make him look more mature, less boyish. 'Yes,' she said. 'He could.'

'Was he wounded?' Hetty asked. 'You could go to the convents; they looked after all the casualties.'

'I don't know,' Louise said, wishing the cross-examination would stop. 'I know nothing at all of what happened.'

'That's queer,' said Meg. 'Didn't his commanding officer write to you?'

'No one missed him until much later.' Oh dear, she thought, she was making things ten times worse.

'That was easy done,' Hetty said, unwittingly coming to her rescue. 'You never saw such a muddle; regiments were all mixed up and the men so weary they dropped out by the roadside and no one waited for 'em. And the rain! Turned everything into mud, it did, even your food tasted of mud, what little there was of it. Down a road just like this one we came, all weary beyond imagining; we knew the Bluecoats were right behind us and we daren't stop for anything. We had to keep ahead of the rearguard, 'cos if we got in their way and slowed 'em down, we was all doomed. There weren't no carriages, and all the carts were needed for the wounded, so even the fine ladies had to walk.'

'How dreadful,' murmured Louise, looking round her at the young vines on the south-facing slopes, the pine woods, the occasional sheep which bolted among the rocks as they approached. It was almost as if the animal knew that an army on the march was always hungry and would not hesitate to kill for food. It was so hot and dry now that she found it difficult to imagine the mud Hetty had described.

'That's how it was,' Meg said. 'We got back behind the Lines and lived to fight another day.

'Why do the 95th wear green uniforms?' Louise asked Hetty.

''Cos they're special.'

'How?'

'Well, for a start, they have rifles and not muskets; that means they can shoot a man down at half a mile.' Hetty knew she was exaggerating, but the story, like myths of old, had grown with the telling and no one was inclined to deny it, if it frightened the French. 'The men are trained marksmen; they shoot on the run and shoot to kill. If the army wants a hard job done, they send for the 95th. They're the best skirmishers in the whole British army.'

Louise smiled; Hetty obviously had as much pride in her husband's regiment as he did himself, and whenever she spoke of it, nearly always said 'we'. In fact all the women were like that; they talked as if they had actually had a hand in all the victories and defeats, and she supposed, in a way, that was so. It was pride in their menfolk.

She wished she had a man she could be proud of, someone she could look up to with respect and love. But there was only Dick, whom she despised, and Paul, whom she doubted. And yet, in spite of those doubts, she was prepared to follow him. Why else was she there?

The following day they came upon Wellington's main army, cantoned about the farmland slopes surrounding the Spanish village of Fuentes d'Onoro, the plateau the General had chosen to halt Masséna's advance and prevent him relieving the besieged fortress of Almeida. Louise was bewildered by the bustle and movement, and though she asked what was happening, the women could not or would not enlighten her. It was enough for them to know a big battle was about to take place, that more men would be killed and injured, animals and crops would be destroyed, that villagers, cowering in terror behind their shutters, might lose their homes. There was no place for the women in this and they retired to a vantage-point in the hills to watch from a safe distance, ready to come forward when it was all over, and do whatever they had to do.

It was a colourful sight. The red jackets of the English infantry, the magnificent rainbow hues of the Spanish contingent with their gold fringes and braid, the sombre brown of the Portuguese, mingled and sorted themselves out in some semblance of order. Among them rode a figure in a plain blue frock-coat and grey trousers, wearing a small bicorne hat without any decoration at all; he passed from one end of the lines to the other, stopping here and there, using his telescope to survey the distant landscape, then galloping to some further point, followed by two or three officers at a respectful distance.

'There's old Hooknose hisself,' someone said. 'Now we shall see something to remember.'

They spent the night huddled together on the

hillside, not daring to light a fire for fear of giving away their positions to an enemy who could not be far away. They could hear the sound of horses, the rattle of harness, a sort of scuffling, whispering sound like wind through tall grass, and here and there they could see a pinpoint of light but had no way of knowing if it were friend or foe. They were awoken in the half-light between night and day by the sound of firing.

'It's started,' said Hetty, getting out from under the cape she carried as a blanket and folding it up, to stow in her pack. Louise followed suit and went with her to stand on a promontory above the valley which afforded a good view.

The French had crossed the bridge behind the village and were driving the British rearguard in front of them. Louise, standing high above, saw the French storm it, firing as they went, forcing the allies back street by street. She gazed in dismay at what she thought was a humiliating retreat, but none of the women seemed concerned, and their placid acceptance irritated her.

'Tain't over yet,' Hetty said, as the 71st, behind whom she had marched, were ordered to counter-attack from their position on the flank. The Highlanders, raring to go, gave a blood-curdling yell which could be heard clearly by the women, and charged down with fixed bayonets. The village changed hands again. The French, temporarily displaced, remained on the outskirts, letting off shots whenever a Scotsman was foolish enough to raise his head above the cover of the surrounding walls. Darkness fell and at last the battle died, while the opposing sides re-grouped and moved their positions, each trying to outmanoeuvre the other. The women dared not move for fear of becoming entangled in the deployment, and in any case they were not sure how near the enemy was.

'The night before is the worst,' Hetty said. 'You imagine all sorts of things, and you're afraid to fall asleep in case you're taken by surprise, so you just wait and wait and wish it was all over . . .'

When the sun rose over the mountains, they realised that the main core of the fighting had moved round behind them. They could hear, but they could not see.

'Great God, we're cut off!' Meg exclaimed.

They were surrounded by the enemy, their way down to the road cut off by blue-coated French cavalry who ranged over the plain, intent on severing Wellington's communications with the forces in the village. It soon became all too obvious to the watchers on the hillside, who could do nothing but look on helplessly.

'He's seen the danger,' Meg said. 'Look, the 95th are moving round; they'll meet head on.'

The French were in great spirits as they charged again and again at the green-jacketed rifleman, who coolly formed square and fell back, almost as if executing the drill on a parade-ground in England. Then some English cavalry came to the rescue, and they were safely gathered in. But, a moment later, the fighting was coming uncomfortably close, and the women began to murmur among themselves.

'We can't stay here. We should go.'

'Where to?' demanded Meg, without taking her eyes off the battle; she was doing what she always did in such a situation, trying to pick out her own man, so that she would know where to look for him when the fighting stopped. 'We'd best sit tight, or we'll get in the way.'

'I'm going up there.' The first speaker pointed to a craggy peak, and started to climb.

'You'll fall,' said Louise, but the woman continued up, dislodging loose rocks so that they rattled down on the men taking cover below.

'God in heaven!' Hetty shouted. 'Haven't they got enough to worry about without having you bombard them from behind?'

A single shot echoed round them as a ball spat into the rock only yards ahead of the panic-stricken woman. Instinctively they dived for cover, and the woman, doubled up, ran to rejoin them.

'Now see what you've done!' said Meg. 'If you ain't careful, you'll go in a Bluecoat's stewpot tonight.'

'Or his bed!' someone said, and forced a laugh from them all.

The village changed hands for the third time as the French were driven out street by street, church by church, followed, it seemed, by almost the whole army. By early afternoon the enemy had retreated beyond the river.

The band of women gave a concerted cry of relief and began to pick their way down, anxious as always to find their men. For some, Louise knew, there could be only heartache, for others, months, perhaps years, of devoted nursing. Some might be lucky. Her own gaze was directed at searching out a figure on a big black horse, but he was nowhere to be seen and she found herself praying that he had not been hurt. She and Hetty separated from their companions, and made for the road which led south.

The atmosphere between the women was tense, almost hostile; Louise knew it had something to do with the way she had behaved towards the Captain— her heated accusation of cowardice was common knowledge—but she knew it would do no good to try and explain how she felt about him; since she could not understand it herself, how could she expect to convince anyone that, even suspecting he was a spy, she could not help being drawn to him?

It was not love; love was something good and fine. This was a physical awareness of his power, his strength, his supreme self-confidence. He might make a great lover, but as a husband . . . Her experience of husbands did not lead her to hold out much hope in that direction.

'What's so funny?' Hetty asked, and Louise realised with a start that she had chuckled aloud at her own ridiculous thoughts.

'Oh, nothing,' she said. 'It's just relief that the fighting is over, I expect. I feel suddenly carefree.'

'It won't last,' Hetty said gloomily. 'When we find the men . . .'

'Oh, we shall find them safe and well,' Louise assured her. 'Paul will see to that.'

'I don't know how you can speak of him in that way!' Hetty exclaimed. 'He has done so much for you.'

Louise stopped in her tracks and confronted the girl. 'What has he done for me? Brought me to this barren land, left me among strangers, turned his back on me . . .'

'And do you wonder?' Hetty cried. 'After what you said to him? And you brought yourself here; he told you to stay in Lisbon.'

'Would you have obeyed if he had ordered you to stay?'

Hetty chuckled. 'No, but I know where my husband is. You may not know where to find your husband; but, then, neither do you care. That's plain to see. I have no sympathy for someone so selfish.'

'You have no right to say that! You know nothing of my affairs.'

'Nor want to,' said Hetty, quickening her pace and leaving Louise behind.

It was not until the girl had disappeared into a belt of pines that Louise, suddenly finding herself alone, hurried to catch her up. The trees, though sparse, offered some shade from the merciless sun, and she slowed to a dawdle. She would not allow herself to become dependent on Hetty; she could find her own way, in her own time. She stopped at a pool and bathed her aching feet, splashed her face and arms, and felt refreshed. As she was rooting in her pack for a crust of bread, she heard a sound immediately behind her. Her hands froze, her body became rigid with fear.

'*Une femme; une belle femme*,' said a man's voice.

Slowly she turned her head, and gasped. Before her stood a man, a magnificently uniformed man, with high plumed hat and dark curly moustache. His legs were encased in tight white breeches and shiny black boots; his blue jacket was covered in gold braid and rows of silver buttons. He snapped to attention and bowed. '*Bonjour, mam'selle*.' He held out his hand and took hers, drawing her to her feet. It seemed to her that she had seen him before, and a picture flashed into her mind of the horsemen she and Maria had noticed near Casavienti, miles behind the British lines. Could it be the same man who had led those? Or was it just the uniform?

She managed to control the tremor in her voice as she asked, 'Who are you?'

'*Ahh, Anglaise*,' he said thoughtfully. '*Capitaine Henri Fourier, à votre service.*'

'Fourier,' she gasped. 'Did you say Fourier?'

'*Oui.*'

She could not believe it; the same surname, even a faint resemblance! But it had to be a coincidence. Perhaps Fourier was quite a common name in France.

'What are you going to do with me?' she asked, assuming she was his prisoner.

He took her hand and put it to his lips, then, noticing her wedding ring, said, '*Madame?*'

'Yes.'

'Your husband is perhaps with the English forces?' She did not answer, and he went on, 'Which regiment is he with? Where is he to be found?'

'That I cannot tell you.'

'*Elle a du courage*,' he said, and laughed. 'I will not 'arm you, *madame*, just so long as you 'elp me. I will find your 'usband and he will pay to 'old you in 'is arms again, *n'est-ce pas?*' His smile made him look more than ever like Paul, and it unnerved her.

'I shall scream!'

'If it relieves your feelings, please do,' he said, suddenly dropping the accent and speaking in faultless English. 'But no one will hear you except my men.'

'Your men?'

'Yes, they are all around us. You must have been in a very deep reverie to walk right into our midst without hearing or seeing us.'

'Please let me go.'

'Oh, no, my dear lady, we cannot have you giving away our secrets, can we? I fear you might have to die.' He paused, fingering his moustache and appraising her with his head on one side. ''Tis a great pity.' He sighed heavily and spread his hands. 'But there you are. This is war, and war is pitiless.'

She tried to make a dash for freedom, but her way was barred by another Frenchman and then several more came out of hiding and surrounded her.

'Sit down, my dear,' said the Captain, indicating a fallen log. 'We intend to spend some time here, and we may as well pass it in pleasant conversation.'

Mutely she obeyed, while the men set about building a small fire and cooking a hare which one of them had caught earlier. The smell of it was mouth-watering, and she was hungry enough to accept their food with gratitude when it was offered. Only the officer spoke English and then only when addressing her, and she concentrated all her mind on trying to remember her childhood French lessons enough to understand what they were saying to each other, hoping to learn something of value to tell when she returned to her own lines.

It grew dark, and the men made no move to leave; it was as though they were waiting for something or somebody. Their chatter grew desultory and, apart from a sentry posted on the path, they settled down to sleep. But their leader did not sleep; he remained watchful, and she began to despair of escape.

'What are you doing behind our lines?' she asked, trying to tempt him into giving something away. 'Why are you waiting here?'

'On the contrary, we are not behind the English lines,' he said, then parried with a question of his own. 'You are no ordinary camp-follower, are you? Under that muddy skirt and torn blouse, you are a gentlewoman. You belong to an officer.'

'I belong to no one!' she snapped, pulling the torn edges of her blouse together.

He laughed and put out a hand to touch her, but stopped suddenly as the sound of a walking horse came to them and then the voice of a challenging sentry. The next minute Paul led his horse into the clearing.

He did not immediately see her, and she stifled her cry of pleasure and surprise as he strode towards the

French Captain and embraced him, greeting him in French. The two men turned their backs on the company and strolled away, speaking in undertones for some minutes, and though Louise strained her ears, she could not hear what they were saying, except to catch the words 'Badajoz' and 'Albuera'. She was trying to move closer when the Frenchman turned and pointed to her, addressing Paul again, apparently explaining with a great deal of gesticulation how she came to be there. Paul turned and came towards her then, holding out his arms.

'Louise, you little fool,' he said, enfolding her. 'I've been worried sick and Hetty is quite distraught; she is blaming herself for your disappearance. I've been searching everywhere!'

Louise listened and marvelled; she wanted him to go on, she wanted to stay in the comforting warmth of his arms and feel safe, but the reality of the situation intruded; it was a fool's paradise. She pulled herself away. 'Have you?' she said. 'Have you? And how did you know where to find me?'

'I didn't know, but thank goodness I have. We must get you back to safety.'

'But are we not prisoners of the French Captain?' she asked, pretending naivety. 'He will surely not let us go.'

'He will not prevent us. I have made arrangements with him.'

'Arrangements?' she repeated. 'Pray, sir, do not compromise yourself on my account! I would rather stay a prisoner.'

Both men laughed, shook hands, clapped each other on the shoulder and then parted. Paul lifted her, still protesting, on to the black stallion, while the French Captain woke his men and ordered them to stir themselves. Paul did not look back as he led the horse along the path and down towards the road.

He was a spy; she had no doubts now. He was in league with the French forces, probably giving away the British positions, passing on secret information about their strength and supply situation. It had been a pre-arranged rendezvous tonight; he had not been looking for her and had not expected to find her there. Now he knew his secret was out, what would he do?

She looked down from her perch at the back of his bare head, trying not to be moved by the way his dark hair curled on the nape of his neck. Unlike most officers, he always carried a rifle, proud of the fact that he could handle it as well as any of his men, and when on horseback, he kept it in a sling on his saddle. If she could pull it out, gently and silently, she could fell him with one blow and gallop off to raise the alarm. The path was dark and he was watching the ground.

She managed to ease the weapon out, and was about to lift it high enough to crash the butt down on his head when the stallion snorted, pulling on the reins. It was enough to make him turn. He caught her arm, knocked the rifle from her hand and pulled her to the ground. She struggled fiercely, and they were locked in silent combat for some time, because he was loath to hurt her, and making a noise would bring half the French army down on them. But he overcame her at last and held her against him with her back to his broad chest and one hand over her mouth.

'No, you don't, my fiery one!' he said. 'If you make a sound, I shall be obliged to silence you in a very ungentlemanly way. I shall knock you cold, do you understand?'

She nodded and he took his hand from her mouth. 'I won't harm you, but I mean to take you back to our lines, come what may.'

'Whose lines are "our" lines?' she asked. ''Tis hard to tell from the way you behave.'

Without answering, he mounted the horse and lifted her up behind him. She was reminded of the last time they had ridden like that, through the streets of London. It seemed years and years ago, another age, a different world. And she had trusted him then.

Her arms crept round his waist and gripped the buckle of his belt as they rode silently along the white road.

Lady Oakingham looked up from the paper in her hand as her husband came into the small drawing-room where she sat with a warm shawl round her shoulders and a rug tucked about her knees.

She had been extremely ill since that terrible morning after the betrothal ball when that man's body had been found by an early-rising servant, and she was only now, two months after the event, feeling well enough to leave her bed for a little time each day.

'My dear, you are not reading that again?' he said, sitting on a stool at her side. 'Please put it away, or, better still, let's burn it.'

'But it puzzles me,' she said plaintively. 'What does it mean? What are bigamy stakes? Is it some new card game, or a horse race?'

'I don't know,' he said, for the thousandth time. 'I really don't know.'

'I'm sure it has something to do with Dick's disappearance.'

'Nonsense!' He took it from her, screwing it up and aiming it at the fire that blazed in the grate although it was the height of summer. It missed, and fell into the hearth.

'But how did it get on the library floor?'

'I've no doubt it slipped from the man's pocket when he fell.'

She shuddered, remembering the shock she had felt on seeing the body sprawled across Richard's favourite chair, and blood everywhere. It would not have been so bad had Dick not disappeared at the same time. Everyone, even her own husband, had jumped to the conclusion that Dick had something to do with the man's death, but she did not believe it, not for a minute, and neither did Angela. They were both convinced the man had had an accomplice who had carried Dick off, who might even have murdered him. It was this thought which had made her ill, and kept her awake at nights.

'No,' she said thoughtfully. 'The man was a criminal—you could see that—he was dirty and ragged and smelled vilely of drink, not the sort Dick would consort with, nor who would know how to write, and you must admit it is in a fair hand.'

'Just because he had it on him, it doesn't mean he wrote it, or that he intended it for anyone in this house,' he said, somewhat impatiently. 'Put it from your mind.'

'Oh, if only Dick would come home, I am sure he could explain everything!'

'My dear,' Sir Richard said, soothingly. 'Please don't distress yourself. Dick will come home in his own good time.' He paused, and added under his breath, 'If he dare.'

'What did you say?'

He did not have to answer because a footman came to announce a visitor. 'A Mr Reuben Black,' he said. 'He asked most particularly to speak to you both.'

CHAPTER SEVEN

A SENTRY CHALLENGED them. 'Who goes there?'

'Captain Fourier. And I've found Mrs Oakingham.'

The soldier came forward and peered at them both. ''Tis good to see you safe, ma'am,' he said, addressing Louise, then turning to Paul, saluted and added, 'The Commander in Chief wants to see you, sir. Message came to tell you the minute you got back.'

Paul acknowledged the order and they rode on into the town. It was packed with soldiers intent on celebration; they were singing and dancing and doing their best to drink the local cellars dry. Broken casks and smashed bottles littered the streets, light spilled from open doorways as men, and women too, came and went. The smell of cooking food and overflowing wine was everywhere. It seemed as if the small place could not contain a single soul more, and Louise began to think she would rather spend the night outside in the fields, where it was quiet.

They went on up the hill, where Paul stopped near one of the churches and lifted her down. Then he dismounted and turned to face her, taking her shoulders in his big hands, and the grip was tight enough to hurt. 'You have seen things tonight that you should not have seen,' he said quietly. 'I must ask you to keep them to yourself.'

'No!' she hissed. 'You are a spy. Deny it if you can!'

'I cannot deny it,' he said. 'But you must accept there are good reasons . . .'

'Good reasons!' Her voice rose shrilly and then dropped again. 'What good reason can there be for betraying your comrades, men who have fought and died for you? I mean to expose you.'

'To whom?' His voice was level and cool.

'To anyone who will listen. To the Duke of Wellington himself.'

'And you expect to be believed?'

'Why not? There are already rumours.'

'They amount to nothing, just the talk of ignorant people who always have to find a scapegoat. They will be disregarded when set against my record. I have proved myself to be a loyal soldier and a good officer; I am trusted by my superiors, and ask only that you trust me too.'

'I can't,' she whispered helplessly. 'There are too many suspicious circumstances, they all add up.

'Your behaviour has been suspicious, too,' he said. 'You came searching for a non-existent husband—or at least one who is certainly not to be found here— and you follow the battalion with no good reason and against my express wishes . . .'

'I had a reason.'

'What was that?'

She could not answer, because he was himself the reason, because she could not bear the thought of losing him, because she had been lonely and afraid and locked in a marriage from which she could not escape. He had offered her the means of escape and now she was more embroiled than ever, imprisoned in her own hopeless longing.

'I am waiting for an answer,' he said quietly.

'And I refuse to give it. You have no right . . .'

'But I have the right,' he explained. 'This gives me the right.' And, pulling her down an alley, he took her in his arms and pressed his mouth to hers in a kiss which took her breath away. She squirmed at first, her anger with him still hot, but he held her firmly, and gradually the will to resist left her and her wrath cooled. She clung to him, allowing her muddled thoughts to become submerged in a sea of sensuous desire. She loved him, she could deceive herself no longer, and now he knew it too and that gave him the upper hand. But at that moment she did not care, she cared for nothing except that he should go on kissing her.

He moved away from her at last, as some drunken revellers almost fell over them in the dark. 'Shorry, shirr,' one said, and they reeled away.

The spell had been broken, but she remained in a daze as he led her by the hand and pushed open the door of a small cottage tucked out of sight behind the church.

'Hetty!' he called. 'Hetty!'

The girl appeared from a back room, carrying a candle. 'You found her—God be praised!' She hurried forward. 'Come into the back room; there's food and wine and a good bed . . .'

Louise glanced back at Paul, wondering if he was included in the invitation, but he took no more than a couple of steps into the room.

'What happened to you?' Hetty asked. 'I thought you were right behind me. When I found you weren't there, I was worried, but I daren't go back because we heard the Bluecoats were on the move again and we were ordered to come here. What happened to you?'

Louise opened her mouth to tell the truth, but could not utter a sound, she could not say the words that would condemn the man who stood behind her. Instead she dropped her head into her hands and burst into tears.

'She became lost among the trees,' Paul told her quietly, putting his arm round Louise's shaking shoulders. 'It's been a very trying day for her, one way and another . . .'

'Of course, you poor thing,' said Hetty, moving forward to take Louise's arm. 'I'm sorry I said all those unkind things to you.' She led her away from Paul. 'Come and sit down and eat something, you must be famished.'

'I'm not hungry,' Louise murmured, remembering the meal she had eaten with the Frenchmen; she still could not carry out her threat to denounce the Captain, and allowed herself to be taken into the back room.

Behind her she heard Paul say, 'Look after her,

Hetty. Keep watch over her and, whatever you do, don't let her out of your sight again.'

'I won't,' Hetty said, cheerfully.

'And don't leave the house until the sun is well up,' he continued. 'Now, that's an order, Mrs Pringle, and I mean it to be obeyed.'

'Yes, sir.'

Louise suddenly became aware of the implications behind his instructions and turned towards him. 'No, I won't be held a prisoner!'

But he had gone, and she saw only the back of the door as it closed.

'You're not a prisoner,' Hetty soothed. 'The Captain is only thinking of your safety.' When Louise did not answer, she added, 'You know, if the women make too much of a nuisance of themselves, they get sent back to England. You wouldn't want that, would you? You wouldn't be able to look for your husband.'

Louise's thoughts flew to Dick and Reuben Black and Will Fletcher and the threats to her life; she could not decide where she was in the greatest danger: in London because she blocked her husband's wish to marry a second time, or here, where she had information it was dangerous to know.

She tried to eat the food Hetty offered her, but she had no appetite. Her energy was spent, both physically and emotionally and she dropped on to the bed—the first she had seen in weeks—and slept almost immediately.

It was Hetty, opening the shutters, who woke her. She did not want to wake up, did not want to face the day. She was torn by indecision, whether to denounce Paul and kill forever any chance of happiness, or say nothing, knowing her silence might lead to thousands of casualties which could be prevented. She prayed for guidance, a clear sign to tell her what to do. But nothing came to her, as she lingered over her toilette, then found needle and cotton from her pack and sat down to mend her torn blouse. It was a delaying tactic and she knew it, and it frustrated Hetty.

'Do that later,' she said. 'I must go to the hospital; Jamie's wounded.'

'Oh, I am sorry,' Louise said penitently. 'Is he very bad?'

'No, took a ball in his arm, but it went right through. He's lost a lot of blood, that's all. But he needs me.'

'Of course he does. You go to him; I'll stay here.'

The girl hesitated, remembering her orders, then pulled herself up sharply. 'You know I can't leave you. The Captain said . . .'

'It doesn't matter what he said; I can look after myself,' Louise interrupted her. 'Besides, I've got something important to do.'

'Come to the hospital with me first, then, it's only in the church. We'll do what you have to do afterwards.'

Louise sighed, put away her sewing, and stood up. 'Very well.' If Hetty was going to behave like a gaoler, so be it, she would just have to take her with her to find a senior officer to talk to, someone who would believe her story. The delay did not mean she would change her mind, did it?

The scenes in the hospital were sickening. Men lay on litters with their shattered limbs bound in dirty bandages waiting their turn for amputation; others with bandaged heads and bodies sat or wandered about in a daze. Hetty picked her way between the mattresses laid side by side on the floor, passing through the nave and entering a small side-chapel. Here the men were not so badly injured; they were smoking pipes and playing cards, joking with each other. Rifleman Pringle sat propped against a wall with his arm in a sling. Hetty stooped to kiss him, then produced food from the bundle she carried. It was not much—bread and cold pork—but he fell upon it hungrily, then offered the remains to his comrades.

'How goes it?' he asked her.

She shrugged. 'Quiet. The burial-parties are out, but it seems there's more o' them than us, thank God.'

'Any sign of moving on?'

'Not that I can tell. Seems both sides are watchin' and waitin'; no one is inclined to start it all up again.'

'We are goin' after 'em aren't we?' he queried. 'We ain't come all this way, jus' to stop when we've got 'em on the run.'

'I dunno,' she said. 'I didn't see patrols goin' out, and the officers, most on 'em, are still asleep.

'Perhaps we're just goin' to have a couple of days' rest. We could do with it. It'll give me arm time to heal.'

'You aren't going back on the march,' she said sharply.

'Why not? This ain't bad.' And he lifted his arm in its sling.

'It's bad enough.'

He did not argue with her; they both knew he would do whatever he was ordered to. He looked up and saw Louise standing in the doorway. 'Mornin', Mrs Oakingham.'

'Good morning, Pringle,' she said cheerfully. 'I'm glad to see you are recovering.'

'Mrs Oakingham got lost yesterday,' Hetty told him. 'She was up in the hills alone in the dark, with all those Frenchies prowling about. Cap'n had to go and find her.'

'It's best to keep with the other women,' he said, addressing Louise. 'It don't do to wander off. And if the Cap'n was to go missing while he was lookin' for you, why, that would be one good officer less to fight old Boney, and that won't do at all . . .'

Louise realised that no one in the 95th would listen to her accusations however convincing they sounded, and even to her, in the light of a new day, they seemed feeble and imagined.

She left them and went back into the main body of the church. A surgeon in a mud-spattered apron followed two stretcher-bearers carrying a wounded man, who cried out in agony with every step they took.

'Put him on the table,' the doctor said. 'I'll be there directly.'

Discover a world of romance and intrigue in days gone by with 2 Masquerade historical romances FREE.

Every Masquerade historical romance brings the past alive with characters more real and fascinating than you'll find in any history book.

Now these wonderful love stories are combined with more real historical detail than ever before with 256 pages of splendour, excitement and romance. You'll find the heroes and heroines of these spellbinding stories are unmistakeably real men and women with desires and yearnings you will recognise. Find out why thousands of historical romance lovers rely on Masquerade to bring them the very best novels by the leading authors of historical romance.

And, as a special introduction we will send you 2 exciting Masquerade romances together with a dazzling diamond zirconia necklace FREE when you complete and return this card.

As a regular reader of Masquerade historical romances you could enjoy a whole range of special benefits — a free monthly newsletter packed with recipes, competitions, exclusive book offers and a monthly guide to the stars, plus extra bargain offers and big cash savings.

When you return this card we will reserve a Reader Service subscription for you. Every 2 months you will receive four brand new Masquerade romances, delivered to your door postage and packing free. There is no obligation or commitment — you can cancel or suspend your subscription at any time.

It's so easy, send no money now — you don't even need a stamp. Just fill in and detach this card and send it off today.

Plus this beautiful diamond zirconia NECKLACE – FREE

FREE BOOKS CERTIFICATE

Dear Susan,

Your special introductory offer of 2 free books is too good to miss. I understand they are mine to keep with the free necklace.

Please also reserve a Reader Service subscription for me. If I decide to subscribe, I shall receive four brand new Masquerade romances every other month, for just £6.00, post and packing free. If I decide not to subscribe, I shall write to you within 10 days. The free books are mine to keep in any case.

I understand that I may cancel or suspend my subscription at any time by writing to you. I am over 18 years of age.   2A7M

Name _____
(BLOCK CAPITALS PLEASE)
Address _____

Signature _____

_____
Postcode _____

The right is reserved to refuse an application or change the terms of this offer. You may be mailed with other offers as a result of this application. Offer expires 31st August 1987. Independent Book Services P.T.Y. Postbag X3010, Randburg, 2125 South Africa please write to: Readers in Southern Africa please send for details. Overseas please send for details.

To Susan Welland
Reader Service
FREEPOST
P.O. Box 236
CROYDON
Surrey CR9 9EL

NO STAMP NEEDED

SEND NO MONEY NOW

He looked at the sea of patients round him, some of whom he had already attended to, others queueing for his ministrations, still more waiting only to hear prayers for the dying, murmured in Latin by the Spanish priests. His eyes were red-rimmed and dark-circled, his cheeks hollow, his bare arms caked in blood. He looked like a man haunted by failure.

'You,' he said, addressing Louise. 'Come with me. I need your help.'

She hesitated only a moment, then followed him into another of the side-chapels, where he turned to her, pointing to a man on the table. 'I want you to hold that leg.'

The patient had already been strapped down by the stretcher-bearers, filled with as much rum as he could swallow and his mouth gagged with what looked like part of a leather harness. She moved forward slowly, dragging her feet.

'Come on,' he said sharply, picking up a knife. 'I haven't time to waste. You are up to it, aren't you?'

She pulled herself together and did as he asked.

'Good,' he said at last, standing back from his handiwork to allow the men to carry the now-unconscious patient away. He looked even more gaunt than before and he was covered with blood. 'Good girl,' he said, smiling at Louise. 'Go and have a rest and come back again this afternoon. I need people like you.'

His praise was like music to her; she was needed—the surgeon needed her, she could do some good in this terrible war after all. 'I don't need rest,' she said. 'But there is something I must do; then I'll come back.'

She moved off through the church with its cries of pain, its stench, its misery, and out into the sunshine of the streets, where the heat beat down and drove everyone indoors.

If one thing above all others had convinced her where her duty lay, it was to see and hear all those wounded men in that church, wounded fighting for freedom, men who trusted the officers who led them. She told herself that she could not love a man who

betrayed them, who shut his eyes to their suffering,
that it was not love she felt for Paul Fourier, but a
physical attraction that would fade with the passing of
time. If she kept her mind firmly centred on that, she
could steel herself to do what she had to do. And she
knew only one man who would even begin to listen
to her. She went in search of Humphrey Barton.

She found him in one of the bigger houses in the
village which the officers of the 71st had taken over.
He was sitting at a table enjoying a meal of bread
and sausage and the red wine of the district, while his
servant, whistling in an adjoining room, polished his
boots and cleaned the mud from his jacket. The night
before had been a long one, the revelry sustained
almost until dawn, and Humphrey had a headache
not improved by the tuneless whistling. None the less
he sprang to his feet when she entered and then,
noticing the blood spattered all over her, came
forward in alarm.

'Why, Mrs Oakingham, are you hurt? Here, sit
down.' He pulled out a chair for her.

'No, I'm not hurt,' she said, sinking gratefully into
the chair. 'I've been helping at the church.'

'Very praiseworthy,' he said. 'But hardly fitting for
a lady such as yourself. There are others more suited
to the task.'

'I am very well suited to the task,' she said, and
smiled with weariness. 'I did not faint; I did not
flinch. I stood and held a man's leg while it was
severed from his body and I helped to bind the stump
afterwards. I felt some satisfaction in a job well done,
a life saved.'

'Who would believe it?' he murmured, sitting down
again and eyeing her appreciatively. 'A woman with
the stomach of a man!' He laughed at her discomfiture.
'Don't look so shocked; I meant it as a compliment.'

'I didn't come to listen to compliments,' she said,
with some asperity. 'Do you know where Captain
Fourier is?'

'I'm afraid, dear lady, you have missed him,' he
said, and there was a note of satisfaction in his voice.
'You will have to make do with me. I'll prove a good

substitute, I promise you. In fact, you may never wish to return to the gallant Captain.'

'What do you mean, "missed him"?' she asked, ignoring his hints.

'Simply that the Captain, like the General, is an early riser; they were gone before dawn.'

'They?' she repeated.

'Fourier and the Duke,' he said. 'Along with one or two others.'

She gasped. 'You mean the Duke of Wellington himself?'

'There is no other duke, unless you count that peacock of a Spaniard who struts about full of his own importance.' He paused. 'Though I did hear the new French commander is a duke—Duke of Ragusa, if our intelligence is correct.'

'Intelligence?'

'There are spies on both sides, Mrs Oakingham.'

'Where have they gone, Paul and the Duke?'

'He shrugged. 'I can't be sure, though I did hear Albuera mentioned, and that's 150 miles away.'

'Albuera.' She repeated the name, hearing again the low voices of the two Captains, one French, one English, or at least pretending to be English. It was a name she had heard them say more than once.

Humphrey was looking at her intently, watching the different expressions cross her face. 'Mrs Oakingham,' he said, leaning forward to try and take her hand. She pulled it away. 'I think your session with the sawbones has had a more profound effect than you thought, you look decidedly faint.

'Where is this place?' she asked. 'Where is Albuera?'

'Almost due south,' he said. 'It's the nearest place in our hands to Badajoz. The French are under siege there—or they were,' he added. 'It is conceivable that they may have broken out, but I doubt it.'

'He is in great danger,' she said, her remaining doubts squashed beneath the weight of circumstantial evidence. 'He must be warned.'

He laughed. 'Paul can look after himself. Have no fear for him, it is I who need you! Can't you see how much I want to look after you? There is no need for you to wear yourself out nursing casualties; others can do that. You needn't walk with the women either. I can find a carriage for you to ride in, and you needn't sleep on the rough ground, getting wet and cold. I will find you a soft bed and warm blankets and . . .'

She jumped up suddenly. 'I didn't mean Paul. It's not Paul who is in danger, it's the Duke of Wellington. Paul is leading him into a trap. He'll be killed.'

He sprang to his feet, moved over and took hold of her shoulders, almost shaking her. 'What did you say? Say it again.'

She repeated her accusation, almost choking over the words.

'Do you know what you are saying?' he asked. 'If it's true . . .' He paused. 'God in heaven, without the Peer we're done for, the war is lost.' He took her chin in his hand, forcing her to look up at him. 'How do you know this?'

As she told him, she became aware of a gleam of triumph in his eyes, but it was too late to change her mind; she had to go on.

He yelled to his servant to bring his jacket and boots and fetch his horse. 'I'll have to go after them,' he said. 'And if I get my hands on that traitorous Frenchman, I'll cut him to pieces.' He paused and turned to Louise, who sat staring at him, frightened by the intensity of his anger. 'No one can save him now, not you, not Alicia, the faithless bitch, nor his loyal men. He is as good as dead.'

The servant hurried in with his uniform and accoutrements and went to help him to dress, but Humphrey pushed him away, impatient to be gone. Shrugging his shoulders into his jacket, he pulled on his boots, clapped his shako on his head and ran out, clutching his belt, sash and sword in his hand.

Louise and the servant faced each other, saying nothing, listening to the sound of the horse's hooves galloping away, then the man went back to the kitchen and slowly, very slowly, Louise dragged herself back to the church.

There was work to do there, good work, and she

was needed, the surgeon had told her so, and however much the sight of those appalling injuries sickened her, she would steel herself to be useful.

She worked at the hospital without stint for over a week, expecting, almost daily, for news to filter through that the Duke of Wellington had been captured, or, what was worse, assassinated. But nothing happened; the normal routine of amputation, of digging spent balls out of men's bodies, of nursing, went on uninterrupted. She told herself it would take more than a week for the double journey, even on horseback, and in any case the news might be suppressed for reasons of morale.

The French kept a watchful eye on the village from the other side of the river and indulged in periodic displays of strength by parading and drilling in full view of anyone watching from the upstairs windows of the houses. Neither side seemed disposed to make war unnecessarily, and so long as each respected the other's terrain, they could get on with the daily business of living, eating and sleeping unmolested.

But Louise knew it would take only a small spark to ignite an explosion, a spark like the killing, wounding or capturing of the Great Duke. To the men under his command, he seemed invulnerable; while he remained at their head, they would win, whatever the odds. She dared not think what would happen to their spirits if they heard he had been harmed. She prayed that Humphrey had been in time to prevent it, but her prayers for the Duke were laced with others. 'Let Paul escape, let him go back to the French lines and stay there where he belongs; don't let him be killed . . .'

On the day the French decided to retire to Salamanca, Hetty came to her at the church. 'We're moving,' she said. 'Are you coming or no?'

'Where are you going?' Louise dried her hands on the sacking apron she had been provided with and rolled down her sleeves. Most of the men had either died or were recovering, and she had little to do.

'Dunno. Pringle says we're goin' to join the Cap'n.'

'Paul?' queried Louise. 'Does Pringle know where he is?'

'Not exac'ly, but it's south, and that suits me. We might get a bit o' leave behind the Lines.' She paused. 'Well, are you coming? You can stay here with the other women if you like.'

'No,' said Louise, quickly, throwing off her apron. 'I'm coming with you. I'll go and fetch my pack and meet you on the road.'

It took only a few minutes to wash and collect her few belongings before hurrying to join the muster. Then they started off down the white road again, retracing the steps which had brought them there a little over a week before.

It was unbearably hot and the march was forced to light infantry pace, accompanied by the beat of a drum, and it was all they could do to keep up with the column. The women dropped behind during the day and caught up with the column only when it stopped to bivouac for the night, trailing into the camp in twos and threes after dark. There was no chatter as there had been on the northward march; they were too exhausted. It seemed they had hardly stretched on the hard earth and pulled cape or blanket about them, when the bugle woke them and the torture began again.

Louise did not know why she stayed with them; unlike the other women, she had no man to look after, nothing to look forward to at journey's end. She had signed Paul's death warrant, and the deed lay heavy on her heart; she would never get over it, not if she lived to be a hundred. But given the same circumstances, she would repeat it, she told herself over and over again, as she put one aching foot in front of the other; she had had no choice. Her ability to choose, to order her own life, had stopped the day she married Dick Oakingham. That was her last free decision; ever since then she had allowed herself to be carried along on the tide of events, swept along like a piece of flotsam.

And she was still married to Dick Oakingham, she

reminded herself; he was still her husband, and she would do well to remember it.

The news of the war came late to Edgware: it was often weeks after the event when Monsieur Fourier heard news of victory or defeat. It came to him through letters from his son, from published news-sheets, specially ordered from London, and from reports of the daily happenings in the House, where Wellington had his critics, many of them vociferous in their demands that he should be recalled and someone else sent who was not forever retreating. Sometimes he received a visit from one of Paul's men, repatriated because of wounds or sickness, and their graphic accounts filled in the details omitted by the published reports. He spent some time each day piecing together the information that came his way, building up a picture of events.

He could no longer fight, but that did not mean he had no interest in the defeat of the dictator who had over-run all Europe except that small corner of the Iberian peninsula; he had to be stopped. Paul was involved in that and he was proud of his son, even though he did not always understand him.

Neither did he understand Paul's interest in Mrs Oakingham; no, he corrected himself, that was not quite right, he did understand it. Anyone with an ounce of manhood would be attracted to the girl; she was beautiful and spirited and she had courage, a great deal of it. What he could not fathom was why he had chosen to take her to Lisbon with him. He would be unable to stay there with her; he had to go off and fight, and she must be very lonely. Besides, she was a married woman, she had told him so herself, and he could not believe Paul was an adulterer. What possible outcome could there be? Divorce? She did not seem to be the kind who would countenance that, and neither would Paul.

He sighed and reached for the latest copy of *The Thunderer*, received that morning from London, and spread it out on the table to read it, as was his custom, from beginning to end.

Ten minutes later he looked up with a start and gazed into the middle distance, then re-read the piece which had so surprised him. 'The betrothal is announced between Mr Richard Oakingham, son of Sir Richard and Lady Oakingham, and Miss Angela Trent, only daughter of Mr and Mrs Frederick Trent. The wedding ceremony, which had been postponed because of the illness of Mr Oakingham, will now take place in August . . .'

There was more, but he did not bother to read it; instead he shouted for his wife and began wheeling himself about the room in an agitated manner until she answered his summons.

'Pierre! Pierre, whatever is wrong? Could you not ring for a servant?'

'I must go to London,' he said. 'Get the coach to the door.'

''Ow can you go to London? 'Ow will you get about?'

'The wheelchair can go on the roof of the coach. Benton can lift me in and out of it, as he is used to doing here . . .'

'But . . .'

'I mean to go,' he said, interrupting her. 'And I mean to go today.'

'Why? Why such 'aste?'

'Mrs Oakingham's husband is going to commit bigamy, and I must put a stop to it.'

'Mrs Oakingham?'

'Yes, you know, the young lady Paul brought here just before he left for Lisbon. The one who lost her baggage and left in a hurry . . .'

'Oh, that young lady! I thought she was a widow.'

'She is not, and neither is her husband a widower, though whether he realises it or not is another matter . . .'

''Ow do you know this?'

He was in no mood to pander to her sensibilities, and almost snapped, 'Because Mrs Oakingham is in Portugal with Paul.'

'With Paul!' she exclaimed. ''E would never do anything so ungallant.'

'He has told me so in his letters,' he said. 'Now please stop arguing, Marguerite, and make the arrangements for me.'

'If you insist on going, I shall come too,' she said firmly. 'You may need me . . .'

'Poppycock!' he said, but was all the same relieved, because that was what he wanted. He had not been to the capital for years, and then he had had two good legs. Besides, he needed her moral support.

It would not be an easy interview, even supposing Sir Richard did not know of his son's previous marriage, but if he were aware of it and was condoning the bigamy, it could be more difficult, even dangerous. A strange killing had already taken place in the house—it had been widely reported—and a man in a chair without the use of his legs would present an easy target.

Marguerite seemed not to have thought of the danger and he did not bring it to her attention as they journeyed in the comfortable family coach, stopping first at St James's and luckily finding David Marriott at home. For safety's sake, Pierre needed witnesses to the disclosure, and David Marriott was the obvious choice. The young man's name had been mentioned by Louise when she unburdened herself, and he was a lawyer.

On learning from his servant that his caller was disabled, David hurried out to the coach to speak to him.

'I have some important information to convey to Sir Richard and Lady Oakingham,' Pierre said, when the formalities of introduction had been completed. 'I would be most grateful if you would accompany us . . . In your capacity as a lawyer, I mean.'

David looked doubtful. 'I don't know if I am the right person to ask,' he said. 'I am related to the family; Lady Oakingham is my aunt.'

'I am aware of that, and you are exactly the right person.'

'Very well. Will you come in? May I offer you some refreshment?'

'My 'usband is in some pain,' Marguerite put in

quickly. 'The journey 'as been exhausting for him, what with the jolting. The roads, you know, are disgraceful . . .'

Pierre smiled. 'My wife exaggerates, but in truth it would be better if I had to climb in and out of the coach only once. If you would be kind enough to come now, I'll explain as we go.'

David returned indoors to fetch his coat and hat and give instructions to his servants, and then joined the Fouriers in the coach.

'Now,' he said, settling himself in his seat. 'How can I help you?'

'It is not we who need your help, but your cousin Richard.'

'Dick?'

'I believe he has recently announced his betrothal to Miss Angela Trent.'

'Yes,' the young man said warily, wondering what Dick had been up to; ruined the Fouriers' daughter, he shouldn't wonder, and they were bent on restitution—marriage, perhaps, or money. If such a disclosure upset Angela in the slightest degree, he would personally throttle his cousin. In the meantime, he would do well to tread carefully. 'The announce-ment was to have been made some months ago,' he said. 'It was postponed for family reasons.'

'I believe your cousin is planning to commit bigamy,' Pierre Fourier said quietly. 'He has a wife alive and well.'

'Bigamy!' This was worse than he had feared. 'Are you sure? I know Dick is something of a rake . . .'

'I am sure. And for Miss Trent's sake, if not for his wife's, he must be stopped.'

'Yes, yes,' David said, his thoughts with Angela. The poor girl would be heartbroken and mortified by the shame of it—if it were true. 'He is sure to deny it,' he added. 'And you realise my uncle, Sir Richard, will require proof? Rumour and supposition will not do, nor the accusations of a rejected lover.'

'Proof can be obtained, but it might take more time than we have before the proposed wedding day.'

'Why? Is your daughter not the young lady in question?'

'We have no daughter.'

David leaned forward and studied the older man's face; it seemed honest, and the dark eyes did not flinch from his. 'Then who is this woman whom Dick has married? Why has she not come forward herself?'

'Because she does not yet know of the announcement. She is in Portugal, and will have to be fetched back . . .'

'Tell me her name and how Dick came to meet her.'

'I think, Mr Marriott, you will know how he met her when I tell you that her name, until she married your cousin, was Louise Topham.'

''Ow did you know that?' Marguerite asked her husband in the silence that followed.

'She told me so herself.'

David was stunned. He could find nothing to say, nothing at all. He leaned back on the squabs and shut his eyes, picturing Louise as they had first seen her, galloping her pony across the fields of Haleham, with auburn hair loose, angry with them for daring to interrupt her ride. She had grown up to be beautiful, and Dick had seen a lot of her—that was, until she disappeared. Had they been married? When everyone was speculating on her whereabouts, had Dick known all along where she was? But why the deception? And why this second attempt at marriage? His head was whirling and he did not know whether to believe the Frenchman or not.

'I think we have arrived.' Pierre Fourier leaned forward and touched the young man's arm, breaking into his reverie.

He pulled himself together. He had to appear calm and in command of himself; he would be asked for his advice, and in spite of his own inclination to expose Dick for what he was and bring down all the retribution he could think of on his head, he had to think of others, his uncle and aunt, Louise, Angela. It was Angela he pitied most at that moment.

Jumping down, he went to the door, while the

coachman and valet climbed up and unstrapped the cumbersome wheelchair. By the time a footman had been despatched to announce their arrival, Pierre Fourier was seated in the chair and being carried up the steps to join him at the door.

They were shown into the library, which was on the ground floor, and Sir Richard and Lady Oakingham joined them there.

'Monsieur and Madame Fourier have something very important to say to you,' David said, after making the introductions. 'And it would be as well for Dick to be present.'

'He is getting ready to take Angela and her parents to supper and the theatre,' Lady Oakingham said. 'Is it important?'

'Very important,' David said, reaching for the bell-rope to summon a servant. 'We must hear what he has to say.'

'This is all very mysterious,' commented Sir Richard, trying to appear at ease, but the grim expression of his nephew and the presence of strangers filled him with foreboding. Dick's explanation for his sudden disappearance and just as sudden reappearance had been less than convincing, although Felicity and Angela had been entirely won over. He had a horrible feeling that his son's misdemeanours were about to catch up with him. Not that he cared tuppence about that, except for his concern for his wife; he wished she could be spared the interview. He sent the footman to fetch Dick, and then turned back to David. 'Do we really need the ladies to be present?'

'It would be best.' David was determined that everyone should learn the truth. 'You will only have to repeat it afterwards.'

'Repeat what?' demanded Lady Oakingham. 'I beg of you, David, don't keep us in suspense. Say what you have to say.'

Dick strolled into the room in his shirt-sleeves, still tying his cravat. 'I'm sorry to appear half dressed,' he said smoothly. 'But I was told the matter was urgent.'

'It is,' said David. 'And I don't think you will be taking Miss Trent to the theatre tonight.'

'Oh?' Dick smiled, still unaware of his danger. 'If you make haste and get this over with, I shall still have time . . .'

David turned to the Fouriers. 'This is Monsieur and Madame Fourier.' He paused, while Dick bowed, still smiling. 'They are proposing to bring Louise back from Portugal to confront you.'

The smile faded from Dick's face and he suddenly went very white, clutching at the back of a chair for support. Then, pulling himself together, he said, 'Louise is dead.'

'She is not dead,' Pierre said. 'She is alive and well.'

'Louise?' queried Lady Oakingham. 'Who is Louise?'

'Her name was Louise Topham, Aunt,' David said, standing with his back to the fireplace so that he could command the attention of everyone. 'You remember the rector's daughter at Haleham, who disappeared? She became Louise Oakingham, your daughter-in-law, just over a year ago.'

'This is pure invention,' Dick said, trying to bluff it out. 'And who are these people to interfere in our lives?'

'The bigamy stakes,' murmured Lady Oakingham. '*L. is alive and well*. That's what it said. "L" is Louise, isn't it?'

Dick did not answer her but continued to bluster at David. 'Louise was drowned in the Thames, drowned after she had been carried off by . . .' He stopped, and looked accusingly at Pierre.

'By our son,' Pierre finished for him.

'Then ask your son how she died!'

'She did not die. She is with him now, in Portugal.'

'And I must ruin my life for a harlot!' he shouted. 'She doesn't care for me nor I for her. Reuben said she was drowned, and I believed him.'

'I never did like that one,' Sir Richard stated. 'He is ill mannered, uncouth and shifty; not the sort I would like my son to make a friend of.'

'Who is Reuben?' David asked.

'He came to see us a week or two ago,' Sir Richard said, speaking in flat tones; it was no good becoming hysterical, and unless he remained calm, that was just what his wife would do, and also his son. Dick was dangerous when cornered, he knew that. 'He had a rather involved story, which your aunt chose to believe . . .'

'You believed it, too,' she put in.

He ignored the interruption and paced the room, while David moved across and placed himself between his cousin and the door.

'I chose to believe it because I didn't want to believe the alternative,' he said. 'Now I am not so sure . . .'

'Dick disturbed two intruders on the night of the ball,' Felicity said, deciding that explanations would be more convincing coming from her. 'I suppose they thought there would be rich pickings with us having so many guests, and perhaps not as watchful as we might have been.' She paused, but no one interrupted, and she went on, 'They attacked Dick and he put up a fight, of course.' There was no 'of course' about it, but again no one interrupted her. 'Unfortunately, one was killed and the other ran off. Dick went after him, and chased him half across London before he lost him. Then when he stopped, he realised how suspicious the circumstances would look and he dared not return. He spent weeks searching for the fellow to bring him to book, so that he could prove his innocence . . .'

'And?' queried David, although he had heard the story before.

'I couldn't find him,' Dick said. 'Reuben persuaded me to come back anyway. The dead man was a known criminal, no one would doubt my story . . . I was worrying needlessly.'

'And what about that scrap of paper?' Sir Richard demanded. 'You were being blackmailed, is that not the truth? Whoever wrote it knew you were married to Louise, and he had to be silenced . . .'

'You killed him, didn't you?' David said. 'You killed him so that you could commit bigamy.'

Dick made a dash for the door, but David stopped him, and held him. 'Not so fast, my fine friend! If you go out of that door, I, as a man of law, will be obliged to set the wheels of justice turning. I do not want to do that because it will hurt too many people I love, my uncle and aunt, Louise, Angela—Angela most of all.'

'Angela!' Dick laughed harshly. 'So that's the way the wind lies! Well, well, well, and I thought it was little Louise who tickled your fancy.'

'I am very fond of Louise,' David said sombrely.

'More than fond at one time,' said Dick. 'It seems to me you can't find someone for yourself, but have always to hunger for my leftovers. Well, you may have joy of her, as it seems I have to forgo the pleasure.'

'I'm glad to hear it. And what of Louise? Shall we fetch her back? Will you make her a good husband?'

'What! After she's run off with the Captain?'

'My son will not have taken advantage of her,' Pierre said firmly. 'He believed she was in danger from your accomplices, and he took her for her own safety.'

'You expect me to believe that?'

'Why not?' demanded David. 'You have expected us to believe even wilder tales than that.'

'Yes, but Louise is beautiful and young, and . . .'

'And you 'ave not forgotten 'er altogether,' said Madame Fourier. 'You still love 'er just a leetle.'

Dick turned to her as the only person in the room who appeared to show him any pity, opened his mouth to speak, then shut it again, because he had no easy answer and he had never been very good at expressing himself.

'Well?' demanded David. 'Is Madame Fourier right?'

'Louise is my wife,' Dick said, deciding there was no point in denying it. 'But I truly believed she had drowned.'

'And now you know she did not?'

Dick slumped into a chair. 'What can I do?'

'Angela must be told.'

'Yes, I suppose so.'

'There is no "suppose" about it,' David snapped. 'I shall personally go and call on her in your place this evening, though I hardly think the poor girl will want to go to the theatre now.'

'No.'

'And Louise must be brought back.'

'Yes.' Dick's replies were delivered in a flat monotone of hopelessness.

'And you should be handed over to the law to face a charge of murder.'

'Oh, no!' cried Lady Oakingham. 'It was an accident. The man was an intruder, everyone knows that . . .'

'Can we not avoid the scandal?' Sir Richard asked. 'I am prepared to believe Dick had no intention of killing the fellow. Why not let sleeping dogs lie? We can devise some punishment of our own without disgracing the family name . . .'

It was at this point that Pierre Fourier intervened. 'I think it's time *Madame* and I left for Edgware,' he said, signalling to his wife to take her station behind his chair. 'This is now a family matter, and we shall leave you to settle it as best you may.'

'Indeed yes,' said Sir Richard. 'But we would appreciate your discretion.'

'Of course, of course,' Pierre said, inclining his head at everyone as Marguerite turned his chair to push him into the hall where Benton waited. Passing Dick, he added, 'I hope today, sir, you have learned a lesson and will, in time, come to realise what a treasure you have in that young wife of yours.'

'*Oui*,' said Marguerite. 'I do believe you know it already, in your 'eart, *n'est-ce pas?*'

'You are an old romantic,' Pierre commented, as he and his wife began the journey home. 'You know a man like that does not know the meaning of the word 'love', or if he ever did, he has forgotten it.'

She smiled. 'Perhaps 'e will discover it again when 'e is reunited with 'is wife.'

'Perhaps,' he said. 'But I don't know what Paul will say. I rather fear we have put the cat among the pigeons.'

CHAPTER EIGHT

'YOU KNOW,' said Louise, one day as they walked. 'I don't think our destination is Lisbon, we're too far east.'

'I was thinkin' the same,' Hetty replied 'We'd not be forced at this pace if we was goin' on leave. At the end of the march, the men will have to fight again.'

The column, with its guns, limbers and supply wagons, was half a mile ahead and the rest of the women, including some children, were at least two miles behind. It would be very late when the last stragglers found their way into camp that night.

'Have you had any news? ' Louise asked, trying not to sound too eager.

'Only rumours.'

'Rumours?' Louise's heart began to beat painfully quickly. 'What rumours? When did you hear them?'

'A despatch rider stopped on his way back to Fuentes d'Onoro yesterday,' the girl said. 'Pringle heard him tell one of the officers there'd been a battle at a place called Albuera; thousands of casualties, he said . . .'

'Albuera?' Louise found herself repeating the name and wondering for the thousandth time what Paul and the French officer had been talking about; the name had figured in their conversation more than once.

'Yes, do you know it?'

'No, no, I just thought I'd heard it before.'

'You probably have. This ain't a very big country, and we have been tramping up and down it for two years now; first we go north, then we go south, then we turn and go north again. It's little wonder we keep hearing the same names.'

'Who won this battle?'

'Don't know. Does anyone ever win? In my book we're all losers, though I shouldn't like you to tell Jamie I said that.'

'And the Duke, what of him?'

'What of him? According to the rider, he got there too late to do anything about it, but he's hoppin' mad about something one of his commanders has done . . .'

'He hasn't been killed or captured, then?'

Hetty looked at her with raised eyebrows, and Louise realised her own agitated manner was betraying her concern.

'Not that I know of, and we'd have heard if he had.' She laughed. 'Generals don't usually go near enough to the front to get hurt, not nowadays, not often.' She paused. 'Though he did nearly get caught last year, when he was out reconnoitring near Badajoz and had to be rescued by the Captain.' She paused and added, 'What's your interest in old Hooknose? You don't know him, do you?'

'No, I've never met him. I just wondered, that's all . . .'

'You'd do better to worry about someone nearer home,' Hetty said, darkly.

'Who?'

'You know who. You haven't once mentioned him, all the way, not one word.'

'Haven't I?'

'No. Have you quarrelled with him?'

'That's none of your business.'

'Nor it is,' said Hetty, philosophically. 'But whatever it is eatin' you, it's made you mighty poor company.'

They went on in silence for some minutes and then Hetty, almost as if she wanted to hurt, said, 'Did you find any news of your husband in Fuentes d'Onoro?'

'No.'

'Didn't think you would. You'll have to go to Busaco, if thats where he was last seen.'

'I don't know that it was.'

'But the Cap'n said . . .'

'He said that was the name of the battle; he didn't
say that was the last place he was seen.'

'Where was it, then?'

'I don't know. I've forgotten.'

'Don't know! Forgotten!' exclaimed Hetty. 'I'm
damned if I'd forget if someone said they'd seen my
old man and he'd been missin' a year.'

'These Portuguese names confuse me,'

'That's a rum do,' Hetty said. 'It makes me
wonder . . .'

'Well, don't,' Louise said sharply. 'I would much
rather not talk about it.'

So they did not talk at all and on 24th May, ten
days and one hundred and fifty miles after they had
set out, they walked into the fortress of Elvas, to find
Wellington fit and well, although, according to
rumour, depressed by the enormous casualties on
both sides and fuming at the incompetence of the
officers he had left in command. Rumour said nothing
of an attempt on his life, or of the arrest of a certain
Captain Fourier.

The relief column did not stay long in Elvas but
pressed on southward, driving the French army before
them. Hetty, determined to follow Rifleman Pringle
wherever he was sent, rejoined the march, leaving
Louise in the town.

She could see no point in going on; she had no
idea where Paul was and, in any case, she told herself
a hundred times a day, they had no future together
and she should be doing her best to forget him. The
only way she could think of to do that was to work,
and she knew where she was needed.

The heavily fortified town was bristling with soldiers
of all nations; there were horses and wagons, carts
and limbers, guns and all the impedimenta of an
army. Somewhere, not far away, a company was
doing rifle practice; she could hear the familiar
commands, followed by the shots, though she could
not see them, and her thoughts, in spite of her good
intentions, turned to Paul. He always insisted on
frequent practice to speed up the rate of fire,
maintaining that seconds could mean the difference

between life and death. Where was he? Had he
rejoined his men?

She wondered where the civilian population was;
hiding she supposed, in their cellars or in the many
beautiful churches or perhaps scattered in the hills
about the town; there were few to be seen in the
streets.

She made her way to the convent, which had been
turned into a hospital, and found the surgeon with
whom she had worked before, and offered her
services.

'Thought you'd had enough of blood and bones,'
he said, cheerfully. 'But I won't pretend I'm not
pleased to see you. There's more than enough to do.
Come, I'll show you where to make a start.' And he
led her into the largest of the cloisters.

Here the scenes were very like those at Fuentes
d'Onoro, but many times worse. The men's injuries
were appalling and she marvelled that the human
body could withstand so much. And there were so
many, tended by fellows less badly hurt, by wives, by
Portuguese and Spanish women, by nuns, by anyone
with the will and stomach to help.

She was kept too busy to think of her own situation
or to wonder what had happened to Paul, but both
were thrust forcefully to her attention two days later,
when he was carried in on a litter with a flesh wound
to the head.

She did not immediately realise who it was; his
face was caked with dried blood and his once
immaculate uniform was torn and mud-splattered,
and he wore no boots. As soon as the stretcher was
placed on the blue-tiled floor and neatly squared up
with the hundreds of others there, she bent to remove
the blood-stained bandage which bound his head.

It was then that she recognised him and she was
glad, in a way, that he was only half conscious and
delirious; he could not see the expression of anguish
on her face.

'Had the devil's job to get him here,' one of the
bearers said. 'Didn't want to come at all, but then he
passed out and there weren't no more arguments.'

'Hey, miss,' said the other. 'You ain't goin' to faint, are you? He's no worse than all the rest. Fact is, he's not bad hurt like some o' the others. Go outside 'til you feel better.'

She pulled herself together. 'No, no, I'm fine. It's just that I know him.'

'Oh, then he's in good hands.'

'Yes,' she said, dimly aware of their leaving. 'I'll look after him.'

He remained unaware of her ministrations for two days, and in that time she hardly left his side. She cajoled the Mother Superior into letting him have a small cell-like room to himself, where there was a truckle bed and a mattress and here she nursed him, kneeling on the hard floor at his side for hours on end, changing his bandages, washing his hot body with cool water, holding his hand, listening to his ramblings, partly in English, partly in French, and praying for him. She had not prayed for a long time but now, while he slept, she went to the chapel and knelt before the altar in supplication, then returned to her vigil. Although she had prayed for his recovery, she had no idea what she would do when he regained consciousness and saw her; he would surely know she had betrayed him, and he would not forgive her.

She wondered why Humphrey had not insisted on his arrest and punishment. Where was Major Barton? How had Paul come to be injured? Could he have been shot by an Englishman?

Once his eyelids flicked open and she thought he murmured 'Louise', but when she leaned forward and spoke to him, he drifted off again. But he was easier now, less restless, and his features were relaxed. Sometimes she even thought he smiled. She cried a lot, silent salt tears which ran down her face unhindered and dropped on the rough blanket which covered him.

At such times, she pulled herself together with an effort, wiped her eyes and busied herself making bandages from one of her petticoats. There was no place for luxuries like petticoats here, it was enough that she had a good serviceable peasant skirt and a

new blouse one of the nuns had found her, from
heaven knew where. The nun, who could speak no
English, had pointed to Louise and then the garment,
indicating that the girl was hardly decent, and with so
many sick and recuperating men . . .

On the third day, the fever which had accompanied
the wound abated, and she glanced up from rolling a
bandage to find him looking at her, seeing her
properly for the first time since being brought in.

'Louise?' He looked tense again, strained, as if
trying to hold on to something, a thought, an idea,
which kept eluding him.

'Yes,' she said, moving closer to him.

He reached for her hand. 'How long have you
been here?'

'All the time.'

'How long is all the time?'

'Three days.'

'Three days!' he exclaimed, trying to sit up. 'I must
go.'

'You can't,' she said flatly. 'You're ill.'

Dizzily he leaned back against the pillow she had
made of his pack. 'I can't leave my post.'

'You didn't leave it; you were carried here, and by
all accounts, very reluctantly. You can't go back until
the surgeon gives you leave.'

He smiled. 'If I'd known you were here, perhaps I
wouldn't have been so reluctant . . .'

Her heart was beating in her throat, and she
swallowed hard. 'No?'

'No. How did you get here?'

'I came with the reinforcements, with Hetty and
the others, but they went on, I stayed to help with
the wounded . . .'

'And me in particular?' His smile showed no
resentment, but she could not believe he was not
playing some cat and mouse game with her; he would
have his revenge.

'You in particular,' she admitted.

'And a very good job you've done,' he said. 'But
now I must go.' He pushed the blanket away and
looked down at himself, and the expression on his

face as he realised he was naked made her want to laugh. For the first time since she had known him he was acutely embarrassed. 'Did you say you had been here all the time?'

'Yes.'

'No one else?'

'No one at all.'

He chuckled suddenly. 'I have no secrets from you now, have I?'

'Haven't you?'

He caught the innuendo in her voice and the playful mood was immediately gone. His eyes, so soft and velvety a moment before, hardened. 'I must go. There is work to do. What have you done with my clothes?'

She pointed to his neatly folded uniform lying on a small stool. 'They're there. I cleaned them as well as I could.'

'Thank you.' They were out of his reach. 'Please give them to me.'

'No. You are not well enough to leave.'

'I'll be the judge of that. Now, are you going to hand me my clothes or shall I get out and fetch them myself?'

She stood up and took a step towards the stool, then changed her mind; if he were kept in hospital, he could not spy, could he? Not if she watched over him? For his sake and her own peace of mind, she had to make him stay.

'No,' she said, turning back to him. 'You are not well enough to walk, let alone sit a horse, and you are certainly not fit enough to resume your command. No one would expect you to. You've had a very nasty blow on the head.'

'Which I mean to avenge at the earliest opportunity. Louise, I am not playing games with you. Hand me my clothes!'

'They're not all there,' she said. 'You lost your boots.'

'I can find some more.'

He made a move to get out of bed, but he really was still suffering from dizziness and fell back,

knocking his head on the wall behind him. She ran to
him at once. 'Oh, Paul, see what you've done. Now
you've made things worse.' She pushed him back
against the pillow and straightened his legs. 'There
now, lie still and . . .'

She stopped as he gripped her round the waist,
pulling her down on top of him. 'Louise! Louise, my
love, what am I going to do with you?' he asked,
stroking her hair and letting his lips roam over her
face. 'And what good am I without you?' He kissed
her mouth gently at first, but then with more pressure
until her lips parted. She knew she was lost, lost to
all reason. Her feeble attempt to denounce him had
failed and she knew she could never repeat it.
Whatever happened, she belonged to him, it was no
good pretending anything else. She wanted him, her
body was responding to his caresses, and he knew
it . . .

Suddenly they became aware of voices down the
corridor and the sound of footsteps outside. She
hardly had time to scramble away from him before
there was a knock, and Pringle put his head round
the door, grinning from ear to ear.

'Beggin' your pardon, sir,' he said, noting Louise's
embarrassment and the smile on the Captain's face—
'Like a cat what's got the cream,' he told Hetty later.

'Blast you, man,' Paul complained. 'D'you have to
come bursting into a man's room like that?'

'I did make plenty o' noise,' the Rifleman said.
'And if you don' mind my saying so, you don't look
very sick to me. In fact, I'd say you was in the pink
of condition . . .'

'Rifleman Pringle,' said Paul sternly, though there
was a twinkle in his eye. 'You are being insubordinate,
and for that I could have you flogged.'

'Yes, sir.' Pringle continued to smile.

'And if I had my boots to hand, one would certainly
come your way right now.'

'Talking of boots, sir'—Pringle pushed the door
open wider and came into the room—'see if these fit.'
He held out a pair of black polished boots which
seemed almost new. 'Couldn't find yours, sir and in

any case, they were past their best, weren't they? Took these off a Hussar, new out from home by the look of him, not a spot of dust on his jacket and his sword shinin' like it had never drawn blood.'

Paul, encumbered by the blanket he was obliged to hold round himself, could not reach the proffered footwear and was chagrined when Louise got to them first.

'Thank you, Pringle,' she said firmly. 'When the Captain is well enough to leave his bed and walk, I will give them to him.' She stood them down beside the folded uniform, out of his reach.

'Heaven preserve us from petticoat rule!' said Pringle, risking the flogging again.

'Amen to that,' Paul said, winking at the Rifleman. 'Now, off you go, back to the battalion. I'll join you shortly.'

'You will not,' said Louise promptly.

'If I'm not back by tomorrow evening,' Paul said to the departing soldier, 'come back with reinforcements. I may need rescuing.'

As soon as he had gone, they fell together, laughing like a couple of schoolchildren caught in some mischief, but the interruption had cooled their passion and in a way Louise was relieved; it was not the time and place. When, and if, she gave herself to Paul Fourier, it would be in different circumstances, happy circumstances, away from the stench of war, away from passions roused by deprivation and loneliness. She wanted it to be clean and good and right. And this was not right; it could never be right because she had made marriage vows to someone else.

His recovery was swift once he had begun to mend, and in another two days not even she could think of reasons to detain him. By that time, a fresh wave of casualties was being carried in, bringing with them the news that Wellington's second shot at taking Badajoz, just over the border in Spain, was having no more success than the first. Two attempts at storming the ramparts had failed with heavy losses, and the men in the soggy trenches surrounding the

town were falling victim to sickness as often as they fell
to the mortars which rained on them from the walls.

'We lack big guns,' Paul told her. 'Those pennypinch-
ers in the House of Commons never send enough of
anything. If they'd only provide what the Peer asked
for, he'd have this war over in weeks instead of years,
and a lot of lives on both sides would be saved. As it
is, he has to rely on a few ancient cannon hauled from
one battlefield to the next.'

'And the French know this?' she asked, probing.

'Of course they know it! They know they're safe
behind the walls of that fortress and can't be shifted
except by starvation. If the Duke had a few really big
guns and more trained artificers . . .'

'You don't think we can win, do you?'

He shrugged. 'No one wins in a war. Men are killed
or crippled, women made widows, children, orphans.
The countryside is denuded, livestock slaughtered, food
and growing crops trampled, churches desecrated. Look
at this place.' He spread his hands to encompass the
convent. 'Do you suppose it will ever be the same
again? Will the nuns ever be able to get the stench of
blood from their nostrils?'

'What would you have us do?'

He had been pacing the floor, but now slumped back
on the bed. 'I don't know. There is no easy answer.
Nothing is easy, nothing . . .'

She knew the time was near when he must leave; he
was growing more and more restless, and trying to
detain him would only make him worse. Her only hope
was that he would refrain from contacting his opposite
number in the French forces, the man with the same
surname who looked so much like him.

She supposed it was the same throughout the army,
each man had his equivalent on the opposite side, from
the generals down, all men of flesh and blood, with
hopes and fears and loved ones, most of the time
obeying orders without question, because they had been
drilled not to question. The more she thought about it,
the more horrifying and unnecessary it all seemed. And
yet the men, with their shattered limbs and bloodied
heads, brought into the convent by the overworked

stretcher-bearers, remained cheerfully confident. Old
Hooknose would beat old Boney and they would all go
home, to London, to Cardiff, to Manchester and
Leicester, to the Highlands and the Lowlands, home to
a jubilant welcome of victory.

Would she ever go home? she wondered. Would she
ever see the green fields of England again? Would
Paul? Or would he return to France, his birthplace?
But his parents lived in England, had done so for many
years, surely he would want to go back to them?
Thinking of England made her think of Dick, and
because she did not want to do that, she tried not to
think at all. Suffice to live each day as it came, to enjoy
Paul's company, his laughter, his teasing, to try to raise
his spirits when he was suddenly hit by bouts of
depression, depression she felt was almost certainly
brought on by an inner conflict he could not resolve.

He dressed every day now and walked with her
through the cool corridors of the convent, along the
cloisters or among the plum trees. He was almost back
to full strength, and she knew he would soon be
leaving.

He was visited by his commanding officer one day
and she watched them walking together in the precincts
of the convent and knew the time had come.

'You've done a rare job on the Cap'n,' said a voice
at her elbow, and she turned to face the grinning
Pringle.

'He's a very strong man.'

He laughed. 'Strong enough to get his boots back, I
see.'

'Yes.' She paused. 'Pringle, what's the news outside?
Is there any sign of an end to the fighting? I couldn't
bear it if he . . .' She stopped in confusion.

'It'll not be long now,' he said confidently. 'I reckon
the end is in sight. There's reinforcements and supplies
coming from England every day, we're well victualled
and ready to go . . .'

'Go where?'

'Only old Hooknose and God hisself know that.'

'But you have a very good idea?'

He laughed. 'The Duke knows the enemy movements

almost as soon as they know theirselves; we heard they were coming down from the north, and crossing the Tagus . . .'

'They're heading this way?' she queried in alarm.

'Don't worry, Mrs Oakingham. We'll be ready; and you're safe here . . .'

'Another battle, more casualties,' she said dully. Would the slaughter never end?

''Fraid so, that's why we need every man we can muster. Half this lot will be gone tomorrow.' And he indicated, with a sweep of his hand, the hundreds of patients who crowded the hospital.

'And Captain Fourier?'

'Especially Cap'n Fourier.'

And so it proved. Everyone able to walk and fire a gun volunteered to return to duty, and those left behind were moved to a large upstairs dormitory to make way for new casualties. Stretchers were stacked against the entrance, old bandages were washed and rolled, blankets were de-loused, surgical instruments were cleaned and sharpened; somehow or other the medicinal rum-bottle was refilled.

Louise, her parting from Paul still bitter-sweet in her memory, decided to stay and help. He had told her not to follow him and, for once, she did not feel inclined to disobey. She was weary beyond imagining, having had only a few hours' snatched sleep each night since he had arrived. But the days, so few of them, had been ones of great joy, when her love for him had grown until there was no denying it. It had filled her mind and heart and drove out all thought of the future; time enough for that when it was forced on her.

'Mrs Oakingham, I insist you rest,' said the Mother Superior, after watching the girl for some time. 'You have done your duty and more. God could not have wished for a better servant, but even God's servants need to sleep sometimes.'

Thankfully Louise obeyed, and going to the little room so lately occupied by the man she loved, she dropped on the bed and shut her eyes. She did not want to sleep, she felt so near to him there. She could almost feel the warmth of his body beside her, his soft breathing on her cheek, could hear the murmur of his voice. 'I will come back, my darling. I will come back. I love you, now and always.'

His words set her pulse racing, and she had tilted up her head to look into his face and had seen the truth of what he said in the tender expression of his brown eyes. 'And I you,' she had whispered.

She had ignored the little voice in her head, so weak it was easily pushed aside, which reminded her she was playing with fire, that she was not free to love, that he had declared his love for her not knowing she had denounced him. She listened only to her heart and gave herself up to his embrace, nestling in his arms, feeling utterly at home there.

He had kissed her tear-wet cheek and pressed some money into her hand. 'This will be enough until I return. Stay here, do you hear me? Or, better still, go back to Lisbon and wait for me there.' He had held her for a minute longer, then pulling himself reluctantly away, had left, closing the door softly behind him. She had wanted to cry out, to call him back, but she could make no sound. The room had become silent with his going, silent as the tomb, just as it was now. Empty. Even as she decided she would never be able to sleep, she drifted into oblivion.

But it was not a restful sleep and she woke with her troubles more oppressive than ever; the small voice had made itself heard at last and would not be denied. Forcing herself to get up, she went in search of the Mother Superior, noticing, as she went, that there had been no new intake during the night. The threatened battle had not yet materialised.

She found the nun in one of the small chapels on her knees in prayer, and waited patiently until she rose, crossed herself and turned to leave, before moving forward.

'What is it, my child? You look troubled.'

'May I talk to you?'

'But of course! Come and sit down here, beside me.' She led the girl to a stone bench against the wall. It was hard and uncomfortable, but Louise hardly noticed, she was intent on putting her words together, unburdening herself and asking for reassurance and advice.

It was difficult to begin, but once she had made the start, the words poured from her: all her doubts, all her guilt. Afterwards she wondered if the poor nun had been able to understand half of what she said, but it did not really matter, just talking had been good for her. In trying to put her thoughts into words, she had clarified them in her own mind, and the nun's sweet smile, and cool hand on hers, soothed and comforted her.

'You know what you must do, child; your duty is clear. Did you think I would tell you any different?'

'No, I suppose not.'

'Are you a Catholic?'

'No, Reverend Mother.'

'But you are a good Christian, you know right from wrong, you will find your own penance.'

'Yes.'

'God bless you, child.'

Louise bent her head to receive a blessing, then rose and thanked her before fetching her bundle from the little room leaving the convent by its great doors.

She knew what she had to do, but she delayed doing it, preferring to leave the town and wander aimlessly in the orchards and olive groves which surrounded it. Here it was cool and, in spite of everything, peaceful. The sounds of the town, the noise of war, were replaced by the chirping of crickets, and the soft whisper of the breeze; the smell of cooking and horses became the scent of blossom.

She sat on a rock on the hillside and looked across the valley at the huge Roman aqueduct outlined against the deep blue of the sky, marvelling at the engineering skill which had gone into the building of it, and what was even more surprising was that it still stood, untouched by the war. Things did survive such upheaval, what was built on solid foundations outlasted the tumult; the tumult inside her would subside and she would go on living. She did not want to move, but the memory of the nun's words, like an echo of her conscience, drove her to get up at least and shake out her skirt.

Then she suddenly became aware that she was being watched and, startled, twisted round to see Captain Henri Fourier, magnificent as ever, sitting astride his horse, which had its head down to drink at an irrigation channel.

He inclined his head towards her in acknowledgment. *'Madame.'*

Before she could recover from the shock of seeing him so close to the British stronghold, he had cantered away.

The encounter was a kind of confirmation of her decision to return to England; she did not belong in this place of bloodshed and intrigue, of inhumanity and treachery, where you could never be sure who was friend and who foe. It was a place where all the standards she had been brought up to respect were thrown away, where love and marriage had no meaning, where death was forever at your elbow. She loved Paul, she no longer tried to deceive herself on that score, but to remain here with him would be to deny her upbringing, the teaching her father had instilled in her, the advice of the kindly nun. Suddenly she longed for home.

She made her way back to the town and across the square to the town hall which seemed, from the bustling activity around it, to be the military as well as the civic headquarters, and went inside, intent on finding someone in authority who could arrange her passage to England. The incurably sick and wounded were being repatriated every day in the ships which brought the reinforcements and supplies; she might be allowed to travel if she offered to nurse some of them.

The first person she saw, in the vestibule, where a regimental clerk sat, quill in hand, totting up a list of figures, was Major Humphrey Barton.

She stopped in the doorway, undecided whether to go on, while he looked her up and down, as if he were enjoying her discomfiture, then bowed towards her. 'Mrs Oakingham! What a pleasure! I hardly expected to see you again so soon.'

'Why not?'

He turned to look down at the clerk, whose head was bent to his task. He appeared not to be listening, but appearances could be deceptive, as Humphrey knew to his cost. He came forward and put his hand under her elbow to lead her down the corridor.

'Let's look at the garden. It is something of a shambles, I admit, but pleasant and cool,' he said, walking her away out of earshot of anyone in the hall. 'The heat is oppressive, don't you think? How a man can be expected to stand about in it, much less march, I cannot think.' He was unbuttoning his jacket as he spoke.

'You don't march,' she said quickly. 'You always ride.'

'True, but I have other duties, just as onerous. I have been attached to the commissariat.'

'Is that why you haven't gone with your regiment?'

They passed through the open doors at the back of the building into an enclosed garden. He shut them behind him. 'How did you know my regiment had gone?'

'I didn't particularly, but I thought everyone had gone except the new contingents from England.'

'Mrs Oakingham,' he said slowly. 'You know more than is good for you.'

'I know only what I hear.'

'Then your ears are sharper than most.'

'You are being ridiculous.'

'Am I? Am I now? The trouble is that your ears hear sounds that don't exist, words that are never uttered. In short, my dear Mrs Oakingham, you have a lively imagination.'

'What, in heaven's name, are you hinting at?'

'I am not hinting. You sent me on a fool's errand, and I don't care to be made to look a fool.'

'I didn't ask you to go,' she said, defending herself. 'And I told you nothing that was not true.'

'What else was I supposed to do?' he cried angrily. 'You implied that the Peer was in danger, you said Paul was leading him into a trap. What could a loyal officer do but gallop to the rescue?'

'It wasn't true?' she asked, and she could not keep the note of hope from her voice. 'The Duke wasn't in danger?'

'It hardly seems so does it? The Commander in Chief is directing operations just as masterfully as he always does, and your precious Captain Fourier has his ear. I could not get near them, and when I tried to explain my mission to his adjutant, he laughed in my face. If fact, I've been the butt of the staff officers' jests ever since.'

'I'm sorry,' she said. 'I truly believed . . .'

'Did you?' He seized her roughly by the upper arms and swung her round to face him. 'Isn't it more likely that he caught you in the act of consorting with the French and you decided to turn the tables on him to save yourself?'

She laughed in his face; the idea was so outrageous. 'Why should I consort with the French, as you put it? I have no reason to spy.'

'No? Well, we shall see. Rest assured, someone is going to pay for my humiliation, it will be returned a hundredfold . . .'

'You're mad!' she cried. 'And please let go of my arms, you're hurting me.'

'I will hurt you,' he said grimly, shaking her so that her hair fell from its pins and cascaded round her shoulders. 'If I can't reach him, you will be the one to pay. I will prove you are in league with the enemy. You are a treacherous whore . . .'

'Let me go! Let me go!'

'Whore!' he repeated. 'You will wish you had never made me look a fool.'

As he spoke, he ripped her blouse from her shoulders and stood, holding her at arm's length, looking at her bared breasts. 'A beautiful whore, though,' he said, softly, bending to put his mouth to her nipple.

She shouted and squirmed in his grasp, but no one came to her aid. He held her firmly, imprisoning her arms between their bodies. She was weak and tired from sleepless nights of nursing and he was strong; she could not break free. 'Lovely whore,' he murmured, his face in her neck, one hand holding her shoulders, the other roaming over her, pulling up her skirt. His mouth found hers, his drink-laden breath stifled her, and she thought she would faint.

He let her go so suddenly that she fell to the ground, sprawling on the sun-baked earth, and although she lay panting and unable to move, he did not follow up his advantage. Instead, he looked down on her from what seemed an enormous height, his shadow falling across her like the shadow of evil, and he laughed. 'How are the mighty fallen! You will be humiliated as I have been, but I am in no hurry, we shall resume our sparring match another day. It will be something for you to look forward to, will it not?'

'Never!' she said, finding her voice at last. 'Never in a thousand years! You will never touch me again.'

'My dear lady,' he said easily, while he straightened his tunic and buttoned it again. 'There is only one way to prevent it. Bring me positive proof that Captain Fourier is the spy you say he is.'

'I don't believe he is a spy,' she said. 'I was mistaken.'

'Changed your mind, have you?' he said, sneering. 'Well, I'm afraid it's too late for that. Things have been said which can't be unsaid. I have made certain accusations in high places, and I must substantiate them. I don't care much how it is done . . .'

'You're insane,' she cried scrambling to her feet. 'You're raving mad!'

'No, not mad, but vengeful.' He laughed suddenly. 'I'm also a man who likes to do his wooing slowly, it adds a piquancy to the final act.' She flinched as he put out a hand and calmly adjusted her blouse. 'You know I think I am going to enjoy this conquest.'

He turned towards the building and, because there was no other way out, she was obliged to follow him.

'You didn't say why you came,' he said, as he opened the door with every appearance of gallantry, holding it for her to precede him. 'Why did you?'

There were other officers in the hall, and the regimental clerk still worked at the table in the vestibule. She thought of making a formal complaint against him, but she knew no one would take any notice; an unaccompanied woman was, as far as the authorities were concerned, there for only one purpose and if she got more than she bargained for, it was her look-out. No blame would be attached to the officer.

She spoke calmly, gathering all her strength, though inside she was still shaking. 'I came to ask for help in returning to England.'

'Did you now?' His voice was low. 'Having done your best to wreak havoc with the morale of the men here, having sown your seeds of doubt and mistrust, you are satisfied, is that it? Now you will go to England, and what reports will you make there? Tales of defeat and misery, of spies and plots, enough to demoralise a nation, is that it? Well, you shall not go! I can, as a commissary, see that you don't. I will personally make sure you remain here until victory is won. Then we shall think of a suitable punishment . . .'

She knew from his tone the punishment he had in mind. 'You are talking nonsense! I wish to return because it is obvious that my husband is not to be found and there is no reason to stay . . .'

He laughed aloud, ignoring the curious glances of his fellow officers and the raised eyebrows of the clerk. 'You husband does not exist, madam, except in the imagination of Captain Paul Fourier.'

'Oh, but he does,' said a voice.

Louise swung round to face the lieutenant who had just come in at the door from the street. His red jacket was new and spruce, its gold braid intact, every expensive thread of it, his boots shone like twin mirrors below pristine white trousers; the sword hanging from his belt had never been drawn in anger.

He was smiling openly, amused by her shock. 'Louise,' he said. 'Pray introduce me to your friend and convince him I am bone and flesh and blood.'

She could only murmur 'Dick!' before she fell to the floor in a faint.

CHAPTER NINE

SHE RECOVERED almost immediately, to hear Dick saying, 'Well, what do you expect when a lady sees a husband she thought was lost to her for ever? It is hardly to be wondered at! Bring her to my room.' This last to a couple of infantrymen he had called in off the street.

She felt herself being lifted and carried, but her senses were still reeling, and she could find neither strength to struggle nor voice to protest.

They put her down at the door of a bakery, where Dick took over their burden, picking her up as her legs gave way and she began to crumple towards the paving. He carried her up the stone external stairway and kicked open the door of an upper room. There was another officer there, sprawled on one of the two beds.

'Out!' commanded Dick.

The man looked up in surprise, but seeing Dick's burden, he grinned knowingly, picked up his uniform jacket from a chair and left, saying as he went, 'Being a gentleman of sensibility, I'll leave you, but remember, I want my turn. I'll be back.'

Dick laughed and dropped her unceremoniously on one of the beds, where she bounced once and lay still. Her eyes remained shut but she was aware that he was moving about the room, and still unable to comprehend it was Dick himself, she opened them to make sure. He had taken off his jacket and was sitting on the other bed, pulling off his boots.

'What are you doing here?' she managed at last.

'I am doing my duty as a patriotic Englishman,' he said, his voice heavy with sarcasm.

'But why? I thought . . .' Her voice trailed away.

'You thought I had given you up for dead, didn't you? You thought I would accept you had drowned when your clothes were retrieved from the Thames. You wanted to be free to run away with your lover.'

She scrambled to a sitting position and swung her legs over the side of the bed. 'That is nonsense, and you know it! It was you who wanted me dead. You wanted to marry an heiress . . .' She laughed mirthlessly. 'What happened? Did she discover your deception? Or have you married her and brought her out here? I can tell you she won't enjoy it; it's far from a picnic in the sunshine.'

'If that's the way you found it, it serves you right,' he said, flinging his boots to the other side of the room, where they crashed against the wall. 'Did your fine Captain not look after you? Has he deserted you? I must say it looks very like it.' He looked her up and down, his mouth curled up in an expression of contempt and, for the first time, she became aware of her rough clothes. He had never seen her dressed like that, not even at their poorest, and she realised that she did indeed look abandoned.

'I'll expose you,' she said, refusing to be put on the defensive. 'I'll expose you as a bigamist and an adulterer!'

'As it is, I am neither,' he said, then lay back on the bed and laughed. 'Oh, my dear Louise, you have no call to point the accusing finger at me.' He sat up and leaned forward so that his face was only inches from hers. 'What have you been up to, eh? You have not been the faithful wife, I'll wager. You have not been lonely, not with all these virile men around you, starved of female company.'

'How dare you! How dare you suggest such a thing!'

'Oh, I dare,' he said, equably. 'I'll put it more explicitly, if you like. You are a harlot, a whore, a camp-follower.' He plucked at her skirt. 'Look at this . . . Is this suitable wear for a lady of quality? And it's filthy.'

'It is extremely practical,' she said sharply. 'And if you had walked the miles I have walked, if you had worked as I have worked, you would have kept no cleaner.''

'Oh dear,' he said, smiling. 'I have been put in my place, haven't I? But the small matter of clothes poses no problem. Fortunately, I have been provided with ample funds.'

'By whom?' She was curious in spite of her determination not to give him cause to think she was softening towards him.

'By dear Papa, of course.'

'But what did he ask in return? I can't believe it was unconditional.'

He laughed. 'Louise, my dear, as you think you know me so well, why not guess?'

'That you give up gambling,' she said. 'Gambling has been your downfall.'

'Well, there you are wrong, my pretty! No such promise was extracted from me. Guess again.'

'I'm tired of your silly games! When you arrived, I was making arrangements to return to England. I think I will still do that.'

'Oh no, you don't,' he said, putting his hand on her arm as if to prevent her from carrying out her intention there and then. 'I can't keep my promise to my parents if you do that.'

She did not like the sound of that at all. 'What promise? What have you promised which involves me?'

'Why, to set up home again with my dear wife, to make a model husband in every way . . .'

'But they don't know we are married.' She paused. 'At least, they didn't. Have you told them, after all?'

'No, my dear, believing you were dead, there seemed no point. They learned it from David, through a certain Colonel Fourier . . .'

'Oh.' The fog was beginning to clear. 'Your plans to marry Miss Trent were thwarted, is that it? I'm glad, for her sake. It would have been dreadful for her to wake up one morning to find she wasn't married to the man at her side.'

'She would never have known.'

'But, Dick, I was bound to return to England one day. The war will be won, the army will go home.'

'By that time I expected you to have fallen head over heels with the gallant Captain and not wanted the truth to come to light.'

She blushed scarlet, and he laughed harshly. 'You've done it already, haven't you? You are in love with him.'

'Of course not!' she said, without conviction. 'I don't even know where he is.'

'Good, that will make it easier for us to come to know each other all over again.'

'I'm not at all sure that I want to.'

'You have no choice,' he told her. 'You are my wife and, for better or worse, until death, we are bound to each other.'

It was true; she could not deny it, the fact had to be faced, and only that morning, even before his arrival, she had decided she must face it. But not so soon, not so soon. She wanted to weep, to scream at the unfairness of it all, but her blue eyes remained dry and her voice calm, as she said, 'Very well. I shall behave like a good wife in all but one thing . . .'

'Oh, come on, Louise,' he said, moving across to sit beside her. 'I'm not made of stone, you know.'

'And neither am I. I, too, have feelings, and you have trampled on them for the last time.' Her voice faltered as she added, 'I loved you once . . .'

He put his hand under her chin, pinching it in his long fingers, and turned her head towards him. 'And you will again,' he said. 'I promise.' He bent his head and gently kissed her lips. She felt nothing, she told herself, nothing at all; she was numb from the top of her head to the soles of her feet.

'Your friend will be back,' she said, to distract him.

'Oh, he'll soon find himself another bed! I'll take over these rooms. We'll be quite snug here until we can find something better.'

She laughed suddenly. 'You don't expect to stay here, do you?'

'Why not?'

'Oh, Dick, it's obvious you have only just arrived

from England, and without much preparation either. Here no one stays anywhere for more than a few days at a time—we're either marching north or marching south, advancing or retreating. Nothing stands still. What do you think all that activity in the square is for, all those loaded wagons stretching for miles into the countryside? They're getting ready to move again.'

'I know that,' he said airily. 'But Elvas is a key fortress. Someone has to stay and guard the place.'

'And you don't think troops fresh from England will be wasted in that way, do you? The old campaigners, those who've done their bit and need a rest, they will be left here. You, my dear Dick, will move on wherever the Duke has decided to fight next, I'll take a wager on it.'

He laughed aloud. 'Wager, eh? My dear Louise, *I* am supposed to be the gambler.' He got up and retrieved his boots. 'Now we must do something about clothes for you. Where do the ladies buy their gowns here?'

It was her turn to laugh. Overcome by the absurdity of the whole situation, she dropped her head into her hands and giggled. Here was her handsome husband, dressed in a uniform of such good quality and so well cut that it was more than a general could afford on his pay, let alone a mere lieutenant, with a sword which rightly belonged in a showcase, not on a field of battle—Sir Richard had obviously done his son proud even as he banished him into exile—here was this green officer, so naïve he expected to find gown shops in a fortress preparing for battle. She wondered what he would do when he came face to face with an enemy bent on his destruction. Would he draw his sword and expect the fight to follow the rules laid down by his boyhood fencing-master? He was a joke, a great big joke. Her laughter became shrill and uncontrolled; tears of merriment suddenly turned to tears of anguish and she sobbed as if her heart would break.

Dick's sudden appearance caused a great deal of

gossip and speculation among the few of her earlier
acquaintances who were still in the town. No one had
seriously believed the story of a husband lost on the
plains of Coimbra, and they believed it even less
now. This fellow was fresh from England; he had
never heard a shot fired in anger; Busaco was just a
name on a map to him, if he had even heard of it at
all. It did not need much imagination to deduce that
Louise had run away with Captain Fourier, and that
her husband had followed to reclaim her. There
would be fireworks when the two men met! And their
money was on the veteran campaigner.

Louise was not unaware of their curiosity but,
determined to brave it out, she pretended to be
happy that her lost husband had been found and put
on every appearance of being a loving and dutiful
wife. Her aching heart was hidden behind the façade
of adjusting to a slightly more comfortable way of
life. Miraculously Dick had, by what threats and
bribery she did not know, persuaded one of the
quartermasters, on a trip to Lisbon, to bring back
clothes and toiletries for her, so that she now looked
like an officer's wife and not the camp-follower he
had called her.

Not that she would not rather have been a camp-
follower if it meant being closer to Paul, but Paul had
disappeared, no one knew where; the unkind gossips
said he was running from her husband's wrath. She
wished she knew where he was, wondered if he had
heard of Dick's arrival and what he thought about it.
She longed to see him, to assure him that it made no
difference, that she still loved him. But then, she told
herself sternly, she could not truthfully say that and
she would not be able to bear it—to see him and not
be able to go to him, to have to treat him like a
stranger. Things were different, and she had to accept
it.

She moved about her daily tasks without life, a rag
doll with no stuffing, until about a week later she was
proved right, and Dick received orders to move the
following day.

This time she did not have to walk. From its

hiding-place in someone's backyard Dick produced a mule for her to ride and though she spent more time walking at its head, it did prove useful for carrying some of the women's baggage.

On the second day they stopped on the outskirts of Portalegre, a town built on the steep slope of a hill and whose neat white houses and handsome palaces gleamed in the sun. Louise thought it had once been prosperous; perhaps it still was, if the continually changing line of battle had managed to pass it by.

Dick rode down the lines to find her. 'Come,' he said. 'We have found quarters in the town.'

'Everyone?' she asked, in surprise.

'The officers,' he said, reaching down and taking the mule's rein, while the women retrieved their belongings and Louise mounted. 'The other ranks go to the villages round about.'

He seemed to find it beneath his dignity to have to explain things to the women. Louise bade them goodbye and followed him into the town. The streets were filled with soldiers, most of them officers, vying with each other for the best billets. Dick stopped to speak to the commissary and then led her to one of the many beautiful burgher houses, with a richly decorated façade and ornate iron balcony.

'Here,' he said, jumping down and pushing open the door. 'Home.'

'Home?' she asked, dismounting and following him into the cool hall with its blue and white tiled floor and carved staircase.

'The upper floor. Even in this God-forsaken place, money can buy a little comfort.'

'How long are we going to be here?'

He shrugged. 'Who knows? Does it matter?'

'No,' she said truthfully, as they went upstairs to a small suite of rooms. They were sparsely furnished, and Louise supposed that the owners had taken out their most prized possessions, and she did not blame them. She was grateful for a table to sit at, a bed to sleep in, and a fireplace to cook on.

Here she set up home with her husband, cooked

and cleaned for him and entertained his friends, who repeatedly exclaimed what a lucky fellow he was.

'Lucky,' he said, on one occasion, after two of them had left, full of her good cooking and at least three bottles of red wine. 'Lucky, they call me! What have I got that makes me so lucky?'

'You are not short of money; you have a comfortable room, at least as comfortable as most here, and a great deal better than some. You have your meals cooked for you . . .'

'But I don't get my bed warmed, do I?'

She turned from him to carry on preparing the handful of vegetables she was using to make soup; food was becoming more and more difficult to buy, it was all being snapped up for the supply wagons and there were more of those appearing every day. She knew another move was not far off, but for once the rumours did not agree on the destination, north to face Marmont or south to face Soult, or perhaps a sortie eastward into the heartlands of Spain, even to Madrid itself. Whichever way it was, it would be a long and uncomfortable haul in the heat of midsummer, and she knew Dick would not like it one bit.

'Did you hear me?' he repeated.

'It's too hot to need a bed-warmer,' she said, deliberately choosing to misunderstand him.

He moved across the room, snatched the knife from her hand and threw it down on the table. Then he took her by the shoulders and shook her. 'Damn it, Louise, can't you see what you are doing to me?'

'You do not have to stay,' she said, when he allowed her to speak. 'Why do you?'

He slumped into a chair, with his hands dangling between his knees, and looked up at her like a lost child. 'I don't know.'

'Could it be because Sir Richard will stop your allowance if he hears you have left me?'

'No, damn you!' he shouted.

'Could it be that, like a spoiled child, you always want what you can't have?'

He got up and reached for her, but she had become adept at evading him; she slipped from his grasp, ran out of the room, down the stairs and out into the street.

It was hot: the sun beat down from a cloudless sky and the heat bounced back from the white paving stones and hung in the still air. There were few people about, even the soldiers had retired into whatever shade they could find, only a stray cat stalked along a wall. She hesitated, then turned and crossed the town square to the cathedral.

It was cooler in the cloisters and she walked slowly, trying to make peace with herself, to resign herself to her fate, to recall the words of the nun in Elvas and renew her strength. But it was not the nun who walked and talked beside her, but Paul. Oh, if only he could be real, if only she could be held in his arms again! But it was no good, there was only emptiness, and she knew she should not have come.

'You will find your own penance,' the Reverend Mother had said, and she had been right. There was no escape from it, and she had to face up to the truth. She squared her shoulders and turned to go, then her face lit up with pleasure, for Hetty was coming towards her.

The girl looked haggard, and stumbled as she walked. Her face was red and her lips blistered. Louise ran to her. 'Hetty! Hetty, how pleased I am to see you! But what's wrong? Is it Pringle?' She led the girl to a bench on a near-by terrace. 'Sit down and tell me.'

'If you want to know what hell is like,' the girl said at last, gazing out across the distant landscape, but unappreciative of the magnificent view, 'go to the Caya valley. One week out there is bad enough, but two . . .'

'A battle?' Louise had heard no news of any fresh fighting.

'No, no battle. Worse than that. My Jamie went down with guardiana fever, along with half the battalion. The convent behind the town hall is full to bustin'.' She jerked her head in its direction.

'Oh, I am sorry,' Louise said, thinking of Paul, even as she sympathised with the girl.

'You ain't ever been in heat like it, and there's no
shade, not a tree, nor a house, nor a wall; they've all
been flattened. There's nothing but scorpions and
snakes and creepy-crawly things that bite. We had to
live and sleep out there, and everybody fightin' for an
inch of shade under the supply wagons. It's like bein'
cooked in an oven.'

'What were you doing there?'

'Waitin', just waitin'.' The girl pushed her dark
hair away from her forehead. 'We were expecting an
attack.' She laughed suddenly. 'But that's what the
Frenchies were doin' too . . . Waiting, watchin' . . .'

'Then what happened?'

'Then we started to go down with fever, first one,
then another, then more and more, children and
women too . . .'

'Why didn't the women leave?'

'Some of them did, but I weren't goin' to leave my
Jamie.' She paused. 'You know, 'tweren't only us
sufferin'; the other side was too. They'd each send
out patrols and they'd run into each other and talk.
No one had any fight in 'em.'

'How senseless it all is,' said Louise. 'What a
waste.'

'It was too,' Hetty said, more cheerfully. 'One day
we woke up and they'd disappeared, just upped and
gone in the night . . .'

'Who?'

'The Bluecoats. Turned tail and gone, they had.
We all gave a cheer and set about packin' up
ourselves, and then Jamie went down with fever, just
when I thought we was free of it.'

Louise put out a hand. 'I'm truly sorry, Hetty. Is
there anything I can do to help?'

'No,' the girl said wearily. 'They brought him here
and I've sat by him these three days, but he's better
today and sleeping peacefully, so I thought it would
be safe to leave him for a bit. I knew when he woke
up he'd be hungry . . .'

'There's not much food to be had,' said Louise.
'What there is, is dear. If I can help . . .'

Hetty knew Louise was offering money and she

eyed her keenly. 'If looks tell the truth, your fortunes have changed since I last saw you. That's a fair elegant gown.'

'Yes, my husband turned up.'

Hetty looked at her in surprise; she had not believed the stories either, but she recovered herself quickly. 'I'm pleased for you.' Then she added, 'What did Cap'n Fourier say about it?'

'I don't think he knows. I haven't seen him.'

Louise knew from the expression on Hetty's face that she was doing her share of guessing, but she was managing to control her curiosity. 'Do you know where he is?' she added.

'No, he came with us but he rode out on one o' those mystery trips of his the day before we broke camp. He could be anywhere.' She paused. 'He'll be back, no doubt. Shall I give him a message?'

'Yes,' said Louise, but though she tried to put her thoughts into words suitable for such a message, she could not, and gave up. 'No, Hetty. No message.'

They bade each other goodbye and Louise returned to the house. At least she knew Paul was alive and well, and that had to be enough.

She was relieved to find that Dick had gone out, and set about finishing the preparation for the meal she had begun. There was a scrawny chicken she had bargained for in the market; tomorrow she would take some of it to Hetty to give to Pringle. Dick returned before she had finished; she could hear him whistling cheerfully as he came up the stairs, and wondered what had caused such a marked change in his mood. She waited in some trepidation as he came along the corridor and flung open the door.

'Put those down,' he said. 'We're going out.'

'Out? Where?'

'You'll see. Now put on your best dress, the white one with the Spanish lace down the front. And do your hair up somehow.' He picked up a handful of hair from her neck and held it on top of her head. 'Like that. Here, I've got a present for you.' He turned from her and rooted in his pack, then faced her again, holding out a beautiful Spanish comb with semi-precious stones along its top. 'I really feel we should employ a maid, don't you?'

'It's unnecessary,' she said, taking the comb and turning it over in her hand. Was it a good sign that he was buying her gifts? Did it show a change of heart?

'Oh, it's only a little thing! And you are only a little thing. It will give you stature . . .'

'Thank you. But I meant that a maid is unnecessary. I've no doubt we'll be moving again soon.'

'What difference does that make? You need a maid to fetch and carry for you, to go to market and prepare our meals, look after your clothes.'

Louise smiled, amused by the picture his words conjured up; she could see the long train of men and wagons, the ragged group of women trailing behind and herself in the middle of them, dressed in silk and lace, prancing along empty-handed while some poor girl carried two bundles.

'I think I've found someone,' he said. 'I've told her to report here tomorrow.'

'Who is it?'

'Just a little Portuguese girl, but she speaks very good English.'

'Dick, I wish you had asked me first. I really do not need a servant, but if I did, I would want to choose her myself.'

'You will like this one, I'm sure,' he said. 'Now, let's talk no more of it. I don't want to be rude to our hosts by being late.'

It was no good arguing with him. He would not accept that she did not want to go, did not want company. He loved social occasions, loved dressing up and parading like a turkey-cock; he was never happier than when the centre of attention and did not understand anyone who preferred a quiet existence. She dressed as he asked, still wondering where they were going.

Their destination was only a couple of streets away, rooms very similar to their own but slightly larger and more comfortably furnished. An infantrymen of the 71st Highlanders in kilt and best uniform jacket

answered their knock and showed them into the
reception-room.

'Lieutenant Oakingham, how good of you to come
and bring your lady.'

Louise, in the act of handing her cloak to a servant,
turned in alarm at the sound of the familiar voice.
'And you, Mrs Oakingham. What a pleasure it is to
see you again.' She looked up into the amused eyes
of Humphrey Barton, who held her gaze for some
seconds before turning to his wife. 'Alicia, you
remember Mrs Oakingham, don't you?'

Alicia came forward, both hands outstretched,
smiling. She reminded Louise of a prowling cat, alert
and ready, but with claws sheathed. 'Of course, dear
Louise! I may call you Louise, mayn't I?'

'Of course.'

'You must call me Alicia.' She turned to Dick.
'And this is the husband who was lost and now is
found. My, what a handsome brute he is! How ever
did you come to mislay him, Louise? I'm sure if he
were mine, I'd keep a closer eye on him.'

'Alicia, please,' said Humphrey. 'You are embarras-
sing the young man.'

But it was obvious she was not; Dick was revelling
in the flattery and, taking Alicia's hand, he put it to
his lips, holding it there for several seconds. 'If that
were so,' he said. 'I would take great care not to get
lost.'

She laughed and pulled her hand away, turning
towards the table which, amazingly, had been set
with silver and glass on a snow-white cloth. 'Please
be seated.'

Where the food had come from Louise could only
guess; money could buy most things if you had
enough of it. She picked at the feast without appetite
and fiddled with her glass, now filled with dark red
wine, while the conversation ebbed and flowed around
her, becoming noisier as the evening wore on. She
took no part in it, speaking only when spoken to,
wondering why Humphrey had arranged the meal; it
was unheard of for a major to entertain a junior in
this way, and she ralised there was something more

behind it than mere friendliness. She did not trust
Humphrey, or Dick—nor Alicia, come to that, her
chatter was just a shade to bright, her voice brittle as
cracking ice.

Louise became suddenly aware that they were
talking about Paul.

'My dear fellow,' Humphrey was saying. 'You
cannot let the man get away with stealing your wife.
It's a matter of honour.'

'A gambling debt is a debt of honour, too,' Louise
murmured, but no one paid her any attention.

'He must be punished,' said Alicia. 'And if the law
will not punish him . . .'

'Oh, I mean to make him pay,' Dick said, smiling
silkily at Louise.

'What will you do?' Humphrey asked. 'Call him
out? I should tell you he's a very fine swordsman . . .'
He paused, waiting to see what effect his words
would have, but when no one commented, he added,
'If you do, I will be honoured to act for you.'

'No,' said Louise suddenly. 'I never heard anything
so absurd. You will kill each other!'

'The Frenchman deserves to die,' said Alicia. 'He
is a spy, a traitor.'

'Is that so?' said Dick. 'Why has no one exposed
him?'

'I tried to,' Humphrey explained. 'Unfortunately,
he has the confidence of the Peer himself, and my
accusations were dismissed as nonsense. As it was, I
only just missed being arrested and court-martialled
myself.' He was looking at Louise as he spoke. 'I will
bring him to book, never fear; he will be hanged as
all traitors are hanged. The firing-squad and the blade
are both too good for him.' He turned from Louise
to Dick. 'You see, my friend you are not the only
one with an interest in Captain Paul Fourier.'

'What evidence have you against him?' Dick asked.
'I mean real evidence.'

'Louise has the evidence,' Humphrey said, smiling
mockingly at her. 'She has actually seen him meeting
and talking to a French officer.'

Dick turned to her. 'You didn't tell me this.'

She felt herself colour and wished they would turn
to other subjects for their conversation, but she knew
Humphrey had invited them in order to torment her
and she was determined not to let him see he was
succeeding.

'I told Major Barton what I had seen,' she said
levelly. 'It turned out that I was mistaken, and I am
sorry for the embarrassment it caused him. If Captain
Fourier is not, after all, a spy, then I am glad.'

'He is a spy and you were not mistaken,' said
Humphrey. 'There have been rumours to that effect
ever since he joined this campaign; he seems to have
been on hand, riding that great brute of a horse,
before every major defeat we suffered. Last year,
when the Peer himself was nearly captured by a
French patrol, who was it popped up from nowhere?
Why, the Captain, miles from where he was supposed
to be. He was given the credit for rescuing the Chief,
but it's my belief he hadn't intended anything of the
sort. The French bungled it, and rather than be found
helping them, he did the opposite . . .'

'I never heard such a fairy-tale,' Louise interrupted.

'If it's a fairy-tale, why does the Duke trust him as
he does? Why does he let him wander all over the
countryside instead of staying with his men? Why will
he not listen to anything said against him?' He paused
to fill Dick's glass and then his own. 'I want him,
Oakingham, I want him . . .'

Louise knew with certainty that her husband was
going to be asked to take part in some plot to
discredit Paul, if not to kill him, and she knew Dick
realised it too; he was not slow-witted. If she made a
protest, did anything or said anything to draw
attention to herself, she would be banished from the
room and would hear no more.

'Not just him,' Alicia said, looking at Louise. 'His
accomplices too.'

'Naturally,' said Humphrey. 'Naturally, his accomplices too. It is unlikely he is working alone.'

'A woman,' Alicia smiled. 'The Captain fancies he
has a way with the ladies, doesn't he, Louise?'

'Does he?' she answered dully, trying to shut out

the memory of Paul's kisses and his promise to return. She did not want him to return if he was going to walk into a trap; better to die an honourable death on the field of battle.

'A woman will always put her love before her duty to her country,' Alicia went on. 'She would protect him. You're a woman, Louise, would you not agree?'

'I don't know. I have no experience in such matters,' she murmured ignoring the laughter which followed. 'But I suppose it would depend on the woman and the circumstances . . .'

'Assuming my interest is as great as yours,' Dick said, leaning across Louise to take a cigar from the box Humphrey had just pushed across the table towards him. 'What do you want me to do?'

Humphrey sat back in his chair and watched the young man cut the cigar and light it, then said slowly, 'Do you know where the Captain is?'

'No idea.'

He turned to Louise. 'And you?'

'I do not know where he is. Nor do I wish to know.'

'You are a poor liar,' he said. 'The first may be true; the second most certainly is not.' He held up his hand to stop her protests. 'Be that as it may, I'll wager the gallant Captain has promised to return for you and it is a promise he will keep, especially when he knows your husband has turned up and is bent on revenge for his cuckolding.'

'And that's no lie,' said Dick morosely.

'Put it about more widely,' Humphrey instructed him. 'Make a greater noise about it. We want him to hear of it, don't we?'

'And when he comes looking for me, sword in hand, I'm supposed to cut him down, is that it?' Dick was far from enthusiastic at the prospect. 'You said yourself, he's a good swordsman.'

'That's just the sprat to catch the mackerel. He will come to find Louise, and he will be tried for treason . . .'

'No!' Louise could not keep silent.

They ignored her as Dick went on, 'But you said no one would listen to your accusations . . .'

'Nor they won't, but if he acts suspiciously in the heat of battle, he can be tried there and then and sentence carried out without delay. All we have to do is to make sure he does behave suspiciously.'

'How?'

'Louise will see to it.'

They thought it was a joke, and all three laughed at her shocked bewilderment. It was too much to bear and she got up and ran from the room.

Humphrey caught up with her in the street, grabbing her arm and whirling her round to face him. 'Why such haste to leave, my dear? You have not thanked me for an excellent supper.'

'If that's all,' she said furiously, 'I thank you for your hospitality. Now will you let me go?'

'I told you I would have my revenge,' he said. 'Fourier seduced my wife and made a fool of me. I will have the satisfaction of seeing him hang.'

'Alicia does not behave like a woman deceiving her husband. She is as keen to punish Paul as you are.'

He laughed. 'Alicia is a sensible woman; she knows where her best interests lie. Besides, she is determined that if she can't have him, no one else will.' He bent to kiss her and her body tensed, ready to resist him. 'And that includes you, my dear.'

He stood back and held her at arm's length, gripping her shoulders. 'Such a pity. You are so beautiful. But then I've said that before, haven't I? I wonder if Oakingham realises what he's got.' He smiled and pulled her close to him. 'Someone with such a fiery temper on the outside must also surely have a passion within, isn't that so? Are you passionate? Could you satisfy a man's need? Could your passion rise to meet his? I mean to find out one day.'

'You are a foul-mouthed monster!' she retorted, breaking free. 'You should be locked away from decent society.'

He laughed aloud as Dick came up behind them and took her arm. 'Come, Louise, you are tired. Let us go home.' Then, to Humphrey, 'Goodnight, my dear fellow, our thanks for an excellent repast. Until tomorrow.'

They moved off down the street, arm in arm, but she was aware that Humphrey was still standing in the road, watching them.

'Very enjoyable evening,' Dick said. 'Better than sitting at home, eh?'

She did not answer, and they continued in silence for some time. Then he asked, 'Did you really see Fourier talking to French soldiers?'

'I didn't make it up.'

'What did they say?'

'I don't know. They spoke very low, in French.'

'But you did report it?'

'I told Major Barton.'

He laughed and squeezed her arm. 'Your patriotism does you credit.'

She was not really paying attention; she was miles away in a clearing in a belt of pines above Fuentes d'Onoro. 'Does it?'

'Yes.' He paused. 'You know, there's hope for us yet.'

'What do you mean?'

'You and I. I believe you still love me a little.' And he walked on with a jaunty step, humming tunelessly.

She did not contradict him, not wanting to antagonise him. If he was in a good mood, so much the better.

He stayed downstairs when they arrived back at their own quarters, to join a game of cards, and she went up to bed, for once glad of his gambling. He would not come up until the early hours and, being full of drink, would fall asleep as soon as his head touched the pillow.

She wished she could sleep as easily; her thoughts went round in ever-widening circles, and the questions she asked herself, she could not answer. Her own doubts about Paul had been completely dispelled and she could not let him walk into a trap.

She rose before dawn, dressed silently in the dark so as not to disturb her snoring husband, crept

downstairs and out into the street. It was the
pleasantest time of day, cool and fresh. A cock crew
in a near-by yard as she hurried to her destination,
and a black cat prowled across her path.

She found Hetty at the convent as she had expected,
sitting beside Pringle's mattress, feeding him with a
spoon. The man was emaciated, his skull jaundiced
and his dark eyes bright, but he smiled when he saw
her.

Hetty looked up and said, 'Good morning, Mrs
Oakingham,' and continued with her task. Nothing
could be allowed to interrupt her ministrations and
Louise knew exactly how she felt; she had felt the
same when looking after Paul.

She knelt beside the mattress and took the
Rifleman's hand. It was hot, but dry. 'How are you,
Pringle?'

'On the mend, ma'am, on the mend.' He smiled.
'I'll soon be back on duty, and then old Boney had
better watch out.'

'Perhaps you'll get sent home . . .'

'Then they'd have to send home half the army,' he
assured her. 'And they won't do that, not now we've
got 'em on the run.'

'Have we?'

'We've driven the Frenchies out o' Portugal. Did
Hetty tell you they wouldn't fight?'

'Yes, she did.' She paused. 'Do you know where
the Captain is?'

'No.'

'I don't want you to tell me. Just give him a
message when you see him again.'

'Don't know when that'll be, ma'am.'

She paused before continuing, gathering up her
strength and will-power. 'Tell him,' she said slowly.
'Tell him my husband has arrived to join me. Tell
him we are living together as man and wife and that
he must not come to find me.'

He looked up at her in surprise, causing Hetty
almost to spill the spoonful of broth she had half-way
to his lips.

'Are you sure?' he asked.

IN LOVE AND WAR

'I'm sure.'

'Very well, I'll tell him. But whether he'll believe me or not is another thing . . .'

'You must make him believe you. It's very important.'

She stood up, looking about her at the rows and rows of mattresses with their fever-ridden occupants, some of them dying, some thrashing about in delirium, others, like Pringle, recovering, and wished they could all go home, home to England where the grass was green and the air breathable. She looked down at him, eyes brimming. 'Tell him also to watch out for treachery.'

'What do you mean by that?' Hetty asked.

'I can't tell you. Tell him, please.' She turned to go, then went back. 'I suppose you've heard no rumours about the 77th?'

'77th?' he repeated. 'That's a new regiment, isn't it?'

'Do you know where they're going? Could they be going anywhere with the 95th?'

He tried to laugh, but it was only a croaking sound. The effort made him cough and Hetty gave him a drink from a cup by his side.

'No, he don't know,' Hetty said. 'D'you think he's a spy an' all? You'll just have to wait and see, won't you?'

Louise left the parcel of food she had brought and turned miserably away, envying them their uncomplicated love for each other, and went home to Dick.

When she got there, she found her new servant had arrived in her absence and was preparing their breakfast. It was Maria.

CHAPTER TEN

ONCE SHE HAD overcome her surprise at seeing the girl, Louise greeted her warily. Why did she not trust her? She was young and in love and being carried helplessly along on the tide of war, just as she was. She had no reason to feel threatened.

'How are you?' Louise asked, noticing that the girl looked considerably thinner than when she had last seen her. 'And Tom, how is he? He did go with you, didn't he?'

'He's dead,' the girl said bluntly, tossing something into the pan on the fire and stirring it vigorously, as if to stir away memories.

'Oh, I am sorry. How did it happen?'

'He was caught.' There was no need for her to add to that statement; Louise had been with the army long enough to know what happened when deserters were caught.

'Who is Tom?' asked Dick, looking from one to the other.

'Tom was an English soldier,' Louise said, when it became obvious that Maria would not answer. 'He disobeyed an order not to enter a village and was flogged.'

'That's what to expect if you disobey an order,' he said. 'But he didn't die of the flogging, did he?'

'He deserted,' said Louise.

'He did not!' cried Maria. 'He only meant to stay with me until his back healed . . .' She returned to stirring the pan, giving it all her concentration.

'What have you been doing since then?' Louise asked. 'How did you meet my husband?'

'Never mind what Maria has been doing,' Dick put in suddenly. 'Where have you been? Tell me that.'

'For a walk. The wine we had last night gave me a headache. I needed fresh air.'

'You'll wish you had saved your strength,' he said, putting on his shirt and tucking it into his trousers before reaching for his jacket. 'We have orders to move, and I assume you will wish to accompany me.' He laughed. 'It's no more than you did for the Captain, after all.'

She was hardly surprised at the news, she had been expecting it for days, and as soon as they had eaten their frugal meal, she changed into her old skirt and blouse, now cleaned and mended, and gathered up the necessities for the journey.

Dick said to her as he finished his own dressing, putting on his dark leather belt and sash and strapping on his sword, 'You are not a peasant, so why do you insist on looking and behaving like one? Pack more than that. I'll go and find a conveyance for you.'

As soon as he had gone, the two women looked at each other and laughed.

'We shouldn't laugh at him,' Louise said, trying to be serious. 'He does not understand and he only wants to do his best for me.'

'He is a very fine man,' Maria said wistfully. 'You are fortunate to have the love of two handsome men.'

'Two?'

Maria smiled, picking up her own bundle of belongings which she had dropped into a corner when she arrived. 'Your husband and the rifle Captain.'

'You are mistaken,' Louise said, feeling herself go hot, and thankful that Dick had left. Had he heard Maria's remark, it would have caused more dissent. 'The Captain has no interest in me. I am, after all, a married woman.' She gave a last look round the room which had been her home for so short a time, and added, 'What will you do now?'

'Me? Why, your husband asked me to look after you, and that is what I mean to do.'

'How did you meet him? How did you come to be in Portalegre?'

'Here they shot my Tommy,' the girl said. 'They brought him here and shot him dead . . .'

'You took him away to hide him, didn't you? Did he really want to go?'

'He did at first, after the flogging; it was such a cruel punishment . . .'

'I agree it is, but one every soldier is familiar with. He knew the risks he was taking going into the village to see you. How did he know we were there?'

'My cousin's little boy ran and told him.'

'Where did you go? Afterwards, I mean.'

'Up in the hills.'

'But you couldn't hide there for ever.'

'We would have, but the *guerrilleros* found us. They are animals, barbaric . . .' She shuddered. 'They tormented Tommy, night and day, they kept laughing and calling him a coward and saying he was hiding behind my skirts. Tommy wanted to come back then; he was angry and his back was healed, but I would not let him. I cried, and said that if he left me, the *guerrilleros* would . . .' She paused, allowing Louise's imagination to fill in the details, then went on, 'He stayed to protect me.'

'Couldn't you have left together?'

'We tried to, but that made their chief very angry. You see, the *guerrilleros* make a great deal of trouble for the French, they steal their supply wagons, their guns and horses. They come down from the hills in the middle of the night and disappear again. He said we would give away their hiding-place and he would kill us first. The French would give many 'scudos to know where they hide . . .'

'But you wouldn't want to tell the French anything, would you?' insisted Louise. 'After all, you are Portuguese, and just as oppressed by them as the Spanish.'

'But Tommy ran away . . . They wouldn't let him forget that.'

'What happened? How did you get away?'

'One day the Captain, your Captain'—she emphasised—'rode up to talk to their chief and saw us. The *guerrilleros* delivered Tommy up to him.'

'Paul brought you back here?'

'Yes, and Tommy was shot by a firing-squad.' Her expression became grim. 'I will avenge him . . .'

'You mustn't talk like that,' Louise soothed her, wondering, as she did so, if Paul was near at hand. If only she could see him! 'Revenge won't bring Tommy back, and the Captain was only doing his duty.'

'Duty!' The girl spat.

'You are young and lovely; you will fall in love again.'

Maria laughed a little wildly. 'Perhaps when the black hate has gone from my heart; there is no room for both love and hate in it.'

'And when did you meet my husband?'

'Two days ago. I was begging in the street and he stopped to talk to me. He asked me if I would be a servant to you, and I said yes. He is a kind man.'

Louise, remembering Dick's frustration, doubted his motives, but she said nothing. If the girl saw him as a knight in shining armour, it would not hurt anyone. 'Things have changed now,' she said. 'You do not have to stay with me.'

'That is for Lieutenant Oakingham to say,' Maria said complacently. 'He has promised to pay me well, and I must earn money for food.'

Louise could not bring herself to turn the girl away after that and so they went together to where the army was mustering on the slopes below the town. Once again a long column of troops, on horseback and on foot, set off with guns and baggage train behind them and the women bringing up the rear.

It stretched for miles along the hot white road, climbing hills, descending into valleys, twisting and turning, stirring up a dust which hung in the air above them, advertising their presence if the sound of their coming did not. To Louise it was the same as the other marches she had followed, but with a subtle difference. This was an army with the smell of victory in its nostrils; reinforced with new contingents from England, revictualled and rested, they were off northwards to drive old Boney out of Spain and back across the Pyrenees. And so they sang.

Whenever they stopped, they were joined by more battalions, more supply trains, more guns, more horses, mules and wagons. From the surrounding hills they came, company by company, English, Scots, Welsh, the stoically brave Portuguese, the flamboyant Spanish, disciplined German Hussars. To Louise it seemed the whole army of the Peninsula was there— all except one man, and although she scanned the lines, especially for green uniforms and black horses, she could not pick him out.

'You could stay behind,' Dick said on the third evening, for the first time showing concern for her. They had stopped outside a small walled town, and the camp fires twinkled like a mirror image of the stars above them. The air was filled with the scent of burning rosemary and thyme, the smell of cooking-oil and strong tobacco, as the men found what rest they could in the short hours of darkness. 'I could find you rooms in the village here. It would be cooler.'

She looked at him in surprise. 'I thought you wanted me to follow you. You said . . .'

'I know what I said, but I didn't know it would be as hot and uncomfortable as this. There is no need for you to endure it.'

'It's only hot during the day,' she said, too weary to smile. 'What did you expect? It is August, after all. Did you think it would be a pleasant stroll?'

'No, of course not. Sometimes, Louise, you try my patience sorely! You know very well I did not intend you to walk. If I had managed to find a carriage or even a riding horse, it would have been different.'

'I will not be left behind.' She did not know why she was so adamant; it was not as though there was anything pleasant to look forward to at their journey's end. She was being driven by her own stubbornness, an obstinacy which had governed most of her actions in the last four months.

'Do as you please,' he said huffily. 'But don't come to me later and complain that the sun has ruined your looks.'

She did manage to laugh then. 'The damage has

already been done,' she said. 'You forget that I have done this journey before.'

She should not have reminded him. He turned away without another word and went to join his fellow officers in the kitchen of a near-by farmhouse, where they were taking advantage of the farmer's forced hospitality, drinking his wine and playing cards. She wandered away by herself and stood looking up at the star-filled sky, wondering where Paul was. Somehow she felt he was near, but she could not explain why.

Alicia had returned to Lisbon and she had seen nothing of Humphrey, whose battalion marched near the head of the column of infantrymen, three miles in front, and Dick had said nothing more about setting traps and catching spies; she hoped he had abandoned the idea.

It was just as well she had not seen Paul on the march, she told herself sternly. She had to put him from her mind. Her future lay with her husband, and she ought to be making the best of it instead of goading him as she so often did. That was her penance, and if nothing more were asked of her, it was hard enough.

She returned to Maria, who was crouched over one of the fires, cooking a meal. Louise sat down to eat without enquiring too closely what it was or where Maria had obtained the ingredients; better not to know. She was glad of the girl's company, because Hetty was far too busy looking after Pringle to spare her much time. The Rifleman was judged fit enough to march, but he was still weak and so Hetty carried his pack and fussed round him, expending all her considerable energy, and there was none left for anyone else. Tonight, Maria's scavenging had produced enough for four, and so Hetty and Jamie joined them, squatting on capes or blankets round the fire.

'We're in for a real battle this time,' Pringle said, enjoying the food and not caring what it was. 'I heard there's a siege train been landed on the Douro and they're bringing it up over the mountains. When that gets here, it'll make old Boney sit up . . .'

'What's a siege train?' asked Louise.

'Battering-rams, explosives, big guns, all we need to storm Rodrigo.'

'Rodrigo?' Hetty asked. 'You mean Ciudad Rodrigo? But that's impossible! We tried it before, and failed.'

'Well, we ain't goin' to fail this time. When the stuff gets here . . .'

'When will that be?' asked Maria, pouring more wine for them all.

He shrugged. 'Depends. It'll take some shiftin', but I heard it's already on its way.'

'And when it gets here?'

'Then you'll see some action, and no mistake!'

'I wish you wouldn't talk like that,' said Hetty. 'Anyone would think you enjoyed fighting.'

'I enjoy winning,' he said confidently. 'And this time we will win; old Hooknose has seen to that. While we've been restin', he was preparing the ground, hidin' away supplies and ammunition, making fascines and gabions . . .'

'What are they?' Louise asked.

'Fascines is brushwood tied into faggots, and gabions are wicker baskets filled with earth. They're used to fill ditches or hide guns, things like that . . .'

Louise had a mental picture of the General actually going out and doing these things himself, and she suppressed a smile. It was the loyal way the men always thought of their Commander in Chief, and they would not have been surprised to see him on foot with a bundle of brushwood in his arms.

'They're piled up now, ready to bring out when the time comes.' Then, emptying his mug and holding it out to be refilled, he added, 'That's a good drop o' vino, Maria. Where did you find it?'

'The farmer sold it to me.'

'He swore he hadn't got any when we asked,' said Pringle. 'Just shows what a difference a pretty face makes!'

'I am Portuguese.'

No one spoke for some minutes, each immersed in private thoughts. Then Maria, stacking the empty plates, continued, 'I do not see how the Duke can know where he is going to need these things . . .'

'He knows,' said Pringle. 'He is clever, is old Hooknose; he will make the French fight where he wants them . . .'

Hetty seemed uncomfortable and ill at ease and twice during the conversation had endeavoured to attract her husband's attention, but he was too busy talking and enjoying his meal to notice. Now she said, 'Jamie, you are not completely well yet; it is time you rested. Tomorrow will be no easier than today.'

She was right. The next day began even hotter, and Louise almost wished she had accepted Dick's suggestion to stay behind. The ambulance wagons were filled with men who had dropped from heat exhaustion, and when there was no room for more, they were given rides on the supply carts, until their combined weight threatened to topple them or the poor horse could pull no longer. The luxury of riding was denied the women who were, after all, not expected to fight at the end of the journey; they were left to catch up as best they could.

But as they climbed into the hills to find the passes, a cool breeze played about their faces and the heat became less intense. If she had not been intent on keeping up with the march, Louise would have stopped to admire the scenery, mountain streams cutting deep gorges through craggy rocks, clear lakes and dark forests, all spread out below her. The dust-bowl of the south was left behind. She was acutely aware that the forests and rocky outcrops provided ample cover for an enemy, and if they were attacked on the march, there was little they could do about it; they would all be slaughtered. Even knowing that scouts were being sent out frequently, she felt nervous, and unconsciously quickened her pace.

Then Maria started to limp and fall behind, and Louise, feeling sorry for her, stayed to help her along, putting the girl's arm round her shoulders and taking some of her weight. 'What happened?'

'I twisted my ankle on a stone,' Maria said,

grimacing as she tried to put her foot to the ground. 'You go on, I will follow.'

'No, I won't leave you.' She looked up at the hills, scanning the skyline, but it was empty. She looked down at the steep slopes below them, where the trees met the road. 'You never know, the French might be close.'

Maria managed a smile. 'They are miles away! And what could you do?'

But Louise would not abandon her and they stumbled on painfully slowly, while the column disappeared from view. The road dipped into a hollow where a clear stream ran into a small lake surrounded by pines, and Louise guided Maria over to the water and sat her down at its edge.

'There! If you bathe your ankle, I will bind it up. There's a bandage in my bundle.'

'No, please . . .'

'Come on, take your shoe off. Let me see it.'

Maria was reluctant, but under Louise's persuasion, she had no choice. There was no swelling or bruising that Louise could see, and she was puzzled that the girl seemed in such pain. 'Where does it hurt?'

'There.' The girl reached out and winced and then allowed Louise to bind it up.

Louise, looking up from her task to reassure the girl, found her gazing up towards the hilltop.

'What's the matter? Did you see someone?'

'No, it was only a goat.'

'All the same, let's be on our way. The sooner we catch up with the others the better, it's creepy here.'

Louise stood up, helped Maria to her feet and, when she looked up towards the road, she found their way blocked by a goatherd. Heavily bearded, he was wearing rough peasant clothes with a cloak made of straw and a felt hat pulled down over his ears. She stopped, not daring to go on. Then he stood to one side to allow them to pass and Louise, relieved he obviously meant no harm, looked up at him to thank him.

She found herself looking into eyes almost as familiar to her as her own and stopped in her tracks, too shocked to move. Before she could utter his name, a slight narrowing of those expressive eyes, and a quick glance at Maria, warned her to remain silent. As she moved on past him, their hands touched and he gripped hers, putting everything he wanted to say into the pressure of his fingers. Maria seemed unaware of the contact and they continued on their way. Once Louise looked back and he was still standing there, watching them.

From then until they struggled into the women's camp, two hours after everyone else, Louise could think of nothing else, not the limping Maria who leaned more and more heavily on her, not the danger from enemy patrols, nor the heat, not even Dick; her thoughts were full of Paul. What was he doing, dressed up like that? Could he possibly be a spy after all? If Humphrey and Dick had not forgotten about the trap they meant to set for him, here was the opportunity they had been waiting for, because Paul's behaviour was certainly suspicious. But how would they find out? Who would tell them? Perhaps Maria, but Maria had given no indication she had recognised him.

'Where have you been?' Dick greeted her. 'Don't you know better than to lag behind? Anything could have happened.'

She was too exhausted to notice that he seemed really concerned. 'I had to help Maria. We were quite safe.'

'We were watched over by a goatherd,' Maria said and laughed, as both girls sank to the ground near the fire Hetty had made.

Louise looked at her sharply, but her expression was bland and gave nothing away.

'Another time,' Dick said, standing over her, feet apart and hand on sword-hilt, 'if anyone falls behind, they must be left. We're getting too close to the French lines for comfort.'

Maria looked up at him, smiling. 'I did tell her to go on, Lieutenant, I really did.'

'As no harm has been done, we'll say no more. I

have work to do, preparations to make for tomorrow. I'll stay in the men's lines tonight.'

'Very well,' said Louise, without showing her relief. She was too tired for the usual arguments and did not feel like conversation, afraid that she would give herself away. 'I'm going to bed soon, anyway.'

Bed. She smiled as she said it, because bed was the hard earth, her bundle a pillow, her wool cape a blanket, and that was little enough covering; now the sun had gone down, it was bitterly cold. They curled up as close to their fire as they dared, and slept.

When Louise awoke, Maria had gone. It took her several minutes of searching and asking those around her before she realised that, for the second time, Maria had left without saying a word; she had just got up and gone while everyone was still asleep, taking her belongings with her.

'But she was in pain,' Louise said to Hetty, when the truth finally dawned. 'Yesterday, she could hardly walk.'

'She's devious, that one,' said Hetty. 'I never trusted her, and I don't believe she had a bad ankle at all . . .'

'But why pretend?'

Hetty shrugged. 'Like I said, she's devious. I wish now Jamie hadn't kept talking about our plans the other night. Wouldn't surprise me if she's gone to meet the Frenchies . . .'

'Oh, no, I can't believe that!' Louise's thoughts immediately jumped to their meeting with Paul on the road. Had it been planned? Had the twisted ankle been a ruse to fall behind? But Maria had shown no sign of recognising the goatherd and, even if she had, what did it prove? She knew she would not rest until she had spoken to Paul.

'What's done is done,' said Hetty. 'We've wasted enough time already. I heard the call to muster half an hour ago.'

Louise continued to follow the now familiar pattern of days; it had become automatic, and she had learned how to husband her strength so that she had

enough energy left in the evening to take her part in
making the camp fires, cooking, putting up shelters
where they could, looking after the sick, and she had
learned to sleep on the hard ground but to be
instantly awake if an unusual sound disturbed her. It
seemed as if she had been doing the same thing for
years and years.

She sang as she marched and recited poetry aloud,
teaching it to the others as they walked, and every
night, when they stopped, Jamie would come back to
Hetty, and Dick would ride up. After a few minutes'
conversation, he would leave again to drink and play
cards with the other officers of his regiment, who
usually managed to find quarters under a roof, be it
farmhouse, barn or pigsty. She had long since given
up minding about that, and was surprised that he
even troubled to enquire about her welfare each night
before joining his friends.

Her spirits rose immeasurably two days later when
they stopped outside the little village of Sabugal, and
Paul reappeared. Once again in uniform and riding
his own black horse, he cantered up to the battalion
command-post which had been set up in an outlying
farmhouse and reported briefly, then rejoined his
men at their bivouac, just as if he had never been
absent.

'He's back,' Dick said, without naming him. 'Seems
he can take his leave just when he fancies and come
back fresh as a daisy, without a speck of dust on his
boots and full of jest. What makes him think he is
special?'

He is special, Louise thought. He is special, and his
men know it, and I know it. And nothing can change
what I feel for him.

'We'll have him,' Dick said. 'I'll repay him for
what he did to me.'

'What he did to you?'

He stared at her. 'You know what I mean! He
stole my wife from me, and even though I've got her
back, she's no wife . . .'

'Oh, Dick, it wasn't like that at all, and you know
it.'

'Wasn't it? That's the way I see it; that's the way the whole regiment sees it; and I have to bring him to book if I'm going to hold my head up with honour. Would you have my fellow officers think I don't care for you?'

She laughed. 'You have told that tale so many times that you have come to believe it yourself. The truth, if it were known, is that you were glad to be rid of me, and if your criminal plans had not gone awry, you would never have given me a second thought.'

'That's not so! I believed you were dead, I told you so. How could I not think of you? You are my wife.'

He was behaving like a jealous lover, and if she had not known differently, she might have softened towards him. As it was, she gave up arguing; it would only lead to angry words and bitter recriminations and there was no point to that because, whatever happened, they were man and wife and they had to make some sort of life together after the war was over and they returned to England. It was not something she looked forward to, but she accepted it, and so did her best not to provoke him any more than she could help.

'I'm glad to hear it,' she said. 'And if it is so, then I can see nothing to be gained by seeking revenge. Leave it be. It is enough that I am here with you of my own free will and have had nothing to do with him since you arrived.'

'There has been no opportunity,' he said sulkily. 'He was away, but he's back now.'

'It will make no difference,' she said quietly. 'I shall not forget I am your wife.'

For one brief moment she almost did forget—she forgot everything, because Paul contrived to find her alone when she was returning from the lake with a full water-bottle. They were among trees, out of sight of the camp, and he was on foot. She ran into his arms and he held her tight against his chest, not speaking.

'Oh, my love,' he said at last. 'The past weeks have been torment! Are you well? Are you happy?'

'I am now.'

They kissed each other with all the longing a forced separation could bring about, clinging to each other, murmuring words of love.

She lifted her head suddenly to look into his eyes. 'Did you receive my message?'

He smiled. 'The one telling me not to come to you? Did you expect me to obey it?'

'I wanted you to.'

'Why? Shall I leave now?' He drew away from her as if to go, but knowing the answer, turned back as soon as she cried out.

'No. No! It's just that everyone seems to be plotting against you, and I'm afraid.'

'Don't be, my little one; petty jealousy won't hurt me.' He paused to look at her face, searching it for something, she could not tell what. 'Is he good to you, that husband of yours?'

'He treats me well, better than before,' she said truthfully.

'Do you love him?'

'Oh, Paul, how can you ask? I love only you.'

'Then when this war is over, we'll . . .'

She put a hand up to cover his lips. 'Please don't say it, Paul! Please don't. I couldn't bear it. I promised Dick I would not forget I am his wife . . .'

He pulled her close to him, almost forcing the breath from her body. 'What a foolish promise, my little one. Did you mean it?'

'Yes.'

He took her face in both his hands and looked into her eyes. 'What can I do? Dear God, what can I do?'

'Nothing.' She pulled away and looked at him with eyes that sparkled with unshed tears. 'Nothing, Paul, nothing at all. We must endure . . .'

He did not answer, and she left him standing there, gazing after her, as she dragged leaden feet back to the camp, where Hetty demanded to know why she had taken so long to fetch a canteen of water, and what had she done with it anyway.

In the next two days Louise noticed a different
atmosphere in the lines, a sort of eagerness, a
suppressed excitement; riders came and went, patrols
were despatched, and a great deal of activity centred
on the guns and ammunition wagons. The countryside
into which they were marching became familiar to
many of them, including Louise, who realised they
had returned to the plain round Fuentes d'Onoro,
just over the border from the Spanish stronghold of
Ciudad Rodrigo, still held securely by the French. It
became apparent to the more seasoned campaigners
that Wellington was planning an assault on the hitherto
impregnable town before the French, marching from
far behind their lines, could relieve it with fresh
supplies of food and ammunition. It was the thought
of such a victory that sustained the British forces and
made them more than usually cheerful.

But it was not to be; they had advanced to the
border itself when Pringle, always the harbinger of
news, let it drop that the assault had been cancelled.
'Seems the Bluecoats have made up their minds we
shan't have the prize,' he said. 'They're bringing up
everything they've got.'

'How do you know this?' Louise asked.

'The French johnnies aren't the only ones with
spies,' he said, chuckling. 'Old Hooknose knows the
disposition of the enemy down to the last man, and
he won't risk any of ours on a hopeless battle.'

'I'm glad to hear it! What is going to happen now?'

Pringle, as ever, was well informed, and they
retreated next day to the safety of the craggy hills
around Sabugal and made camp. Disappointment
made the men irritable and quarrelsome and the
women fretful, but, resourceful as always, they found
a way to relieve the tedium. Wine was brought out of
concealment and consumed in extraordinary quantities,
considering it was against the rules for the men to
carry it in their canteens.

Louise, sitting by herself, leaning against the trunk
of a pine, watched with a kind of detachment, as the
fires burned late into the night and sounds of
merrymaking rose on the air. What would happen if

they were surprised, she wondered, as if she were not part of the scene, for the sentries themselves seemed to be drawn inwards and were more interested in what was going on inside the perimeter of the camp than the darkness which surrounded it. Would the men be capable of putting up a fight?

Hetty, coming to see why she sat alone, laughed at her fears. 'They know there'll be no fight tonight, nor tomorrow neither. The Bluecoats are far away on the other side of the mountains.'

'How can you be sure?'

Hetty shrugged. 'Pringle says so.'

For Hetty that was enough, and trust in her husband allowed her to sleep peacefully. Louise sat on for some time after the fires had died and a stillness settled over the camp, contemplating the stars with heavy eyelids, too lethargic to go to bed.

The man crept up behind her silently. She did not hear a sound until a hand was put across her mouth and she was dragged backwards into the copse behind her. She was so surprised that she did not struggle at first, and by the time she became alive to her danger, her single assailant had become two and they were trussing her up and gagging her. She wriggled and tried to scream, but they were too quick, and having finished their task, they picked her up, carried her to a waiting mule and sat her on it.

Neither of them spoke and she had no idea who they were, or even their nationality. It was only when they mounted horses and, leading the mule, crossed the rough road and started up a narrow mountain trail where the moon highlighted the rocky terrain, that she realised they wore French uniforms.

Dick was sitting half-dressed in the yard of the farm where he had spent the night when Hetty came to him in great distress to tell him that Louise had disappeared.

'She wouldn't leave of her own accord,' she said. 'I know she wouldn't! She'd have nowhere to go, and besides, she left all her things behind.'

'When did you last see her?'

'Last night, just before I went to sleep. She was sitting by herself . . .'

'What was she doing?'

'Nothing, just sitting. I thought she would move nearer the fire to go to sleep, so I didn't call her. Oh, I wish I had! I wish I'd made her come. But she looked so sad, as if she wanted to be alone, so I didn't disturb her . . .'

'Don't distress yourself,' he said, refusing to be ruffled. 'It wasn't your fault. Louise can be difficult at times. Are you sure she isn't hiding?'

'Of course I'm sure!' Hetty was becoming exasperated with him. 'Why would she hide? Besides, there's hoof-marks near where she was sitting.'

'They could have been there before.'

'So they could. But what are we going to do? Who would take her? You don't suppose it was the Frenchies?'

'No, I don't!' He snapped at her, then as an apparent afterthought, 'Fourier!'

'The Captain?' said Hetty, in surprise.

'Wouldn't surprise me if he is missing, too.'

'He isn't!' said Hetty indignantly. 'He sent for Jamie this morning, and they're together now.'

'Where?'

'Wherever the 95th lines are. Forward a bit, I think.'

Dick left her, went into the farm kitchen to retrieve the remainder of his clothes, found his own mount and rode off towards where he knew the forward battalions had made camp.

It was not difficult to find the Captain, who had mustered his men for rifle practice, setting up targets among the rocks. He turned from them as Dick approached.

Sensing trouble, he greeted him warily, then added, nodding towards his men, 'They need something to occupy them. What are yours doing?'

'They aren't wasting ball and powder,' Dick retorted, dismounting. 'And I didn't come to discuss the men.'

'No?'

'Louise has disappeared.'

Paul's eyebrows rose a fraction and, for a fleeting moment, Dick thought he saw alarm on his face, but it was quickly gone, and he sounded cool as he said, 'If she has decided she has had enough of trudging about, you can hardly blame her!'

'Hetty says she didn't go of her own free will; there are signs of horses.' He paused, then added, 'But then that's how it was meant to look, wasn't it?'

'What do you mean?' He turned and ordered his sergeant to continue with the drill, and the two men walked over to a ruined stone wall that had once marked a grazing boundary, and stood leaning on it, surveying the mountainous country around them.

'She wanted me to think she had been taken by force.'

'But you don't believe it?'

'No, that's why I came straight to you.'

Paul was carefully nonchalant. 'My dear fellow, what do you expect of me?'

'If you know where she is, if you have spirited her away, meaning to meet her later . . .'

Paul laughed. 'Why should I do that?'

'You may think you have a right . . .'

'Oh, that gambler's debt. I absolve you. Besides, I would never hold a woman against her will, and she has made her choice.'

'Then the French have taken her.'

'For what possible reason?'

'I don't know. For goodness sake, man, do something.'

'Me? You expect me to do something?'

'Yes. You know the French, you speak the language, you know where to find them and get her back.'

'My dear Lieutenant,' Paul said, moving away from the wall and taking a step or two back towards his men. 'If the French have got her, which I doubt, I haven't the least idea where to look for her. Contrary to your belief, I am not privy to the movements of Napoleon's army.'

'You mean you'll just let her disappear? You'll do nothing?'

'She's your wife,' Paul said, striding over to join his sergeant. 'You look for her.'

Dick, remounting, muttered, 'I thought you loved her. How wrong I was!' Then he cantered away, not back to the lines of the 77th where he belonged, but towards the 71st, where Major Humphrey Barton stood witnessing a flogging of one of his Highlanders.

CHAPTER ELEVEN

ALL THROUGH THE darkness of the night, Louise's captors climbed higher into the mountains, one in front, the other behind her on the narrow path. She supposed they had found a pass unknown to the British forces, which led to the French lines. Even in her fright, she tried to remember the route so that she could find her way back if she managed to escape. But the landscape was barren; heather spread like a carpet on either side and provided no landmark. There were no buildings, no people. Now and again a goat, disturbed by their coming, scrambled over the rocks to safety, bleating as it went, and the silence which followed was more dense than before.

No one spoke.

Although Louise's legs were free and she was sitting astride the mule, her hands were tied behind her; she dared not risk kicking it into a run because the path was uneven and stony and, if she fell, she would undoubtedly be hurt and she felt she needed all her wits about her. She managed to wriggle her foot out of one of her shoes, which she let drop to the ground. The men did not appear to hear it fall, and a few minutes later she rid herself of the other; someone following might see and recognise them.

Her skirt caught on a gorse bush, scattering the petals, and the tearing sound made the first man stop and turn. The one behind leaned from his horse and ripped the skirt free, slapping the rump of the mule to get it going again. Neither men seemed to care that a fragment of material blew on the bush for all the world like a battle-scarred pennant. Having abducted her, in such secrecy, they seemed to have become very careless.

She began to squirm and grunt, and eventually the bigger of the two men drew alongside her and looked down on her from the greater height of his mount. His eyes shone steely in the moonlight.

'What ails you?' he asked in English. 'Like all women, you don't care to be silenced, is that it?' He laughed and, leaning forward, pulled the gag from her mouth, jerking her neck painfully as he did so. 'Is that better?'

'You're English,' she said, shocked to find herself the prisoner of her own people. 'Why are you dressed like that? What do you want with me?'

He laughed again. 'There are Englishmen you could take for French, and Frenchmen you could take for English . . .'

'Which are you?'

'Now that would be giving away our little secret, wouldn't it?'

'What do you want with me?'

The smaller man, who had been leading the way, turned, and for the first time Louise had a proper look at him, realising with surprise that he was very young, hardly more than a boy. 'Keep silent,' he said. 'Do not ask questions and you will not be hurt.'

'I will not be silent. I shall scream!' She opened her mouth to suit action to words, but was prevented from doing so by the older man's hand under her chin, forcing her jaw upwards.

'Be quiet! Do you want both armies down on our heads? These hills make every sound reverberate; it carries for miles.' He released her and steadied his horse, which, unlike the plodding mule, was spirited and restless. 'Now, forward, if you please.'

They found the pass as dawn lightened the sky and began a descent into a gorge. Its steep bank was tree-lined on the side where they were riding, but the far side was bare, precipitous cliff. They were almost down to the treeline when the leader turned off the track. The horses picked their way delicately over the rough ground while the sure-footed mule, carrying Louise, continued to plod. Five minutes later they came across a cave mouth, and there they dismounted.

'Home,' the older one said. 'At least for a time.'

'Until?' prompted Louise.

'Until what we expect to happen, has happened.'

'And what is that?'

'You ask too many questions,' the older man said, tethering his horse to a bush and ducking into the cave mouth.

The young one came and helped her off the mule, steadying her as she put her shoeless feet to the ground.

'Where's your shoes?'

She shrugged. 'I wasn't wearing any.'

He did not believe her, and called to his companion. 'Hey, Sergeant, she's lost her shoes on the way.'

The other, whose uniform gave no indication of his rank, emerged from the cave, laughing. 'How very resourceful of you, my dear! Now all you have to wish for is that someone thinks enough of you to come looking.' He paused, and eyed her up and down. 'Do you think they will?'

'Of course!'

'Good.' He moved towards her, taking a knife from his belt. She tensed with anxiety, but all he did was to slice through her bonds. 'You may go freely about this camp, but don't try to leave it.'

'If I do?'

He shrugged. 'I have a pistol and my knife, and young Billy here has his musket. You will not get far.'

'You would kill me?'

'If necessary. But, rest assured, that is not our intention. If you do as we ask, no harm will come to you and in the fullness of time you will be restored to your loving husband.'

'You know who he is?' she asked in surprise, rubbing her wrists and hands to restore the circulation. Until then she had imagined she had been picked at random to be used as a hostage, that any woman from the English lines would have served their purpose, and she had been unlucky because she had been sitting apart from the others.

'Yes, Mrs Oakingham, we know who he is.'

'And you expect him to pay a ransom for me, is that it?'

'No, not him,' the boy said.

'Then who . . .' Her voice trailed away. Paul. did they mean Paul? 'You must be mad!' she said. 'What possible use am I to you?'

'Oh, a great deal of use,' the Sergeant said, fetching his saddlebag and taking it to the cave mouth. 'The sprat to catch the mackerel.' He laughed suddenly. 'A very beautiful sprat, I'm bound to say.'

Her thoughts went back to a conversation over a supper table not so long before; they had been talking of sprats and mackerels then, and she was beginning to fear that this was the much-talked-of trap. She stood looking about her, wondering which way to run if the opportunity arose to make a dash for freedom— downhill towards the trees and river, where there was cover, or up over the mountain the way she had come. There was nowhere to hide that way, but it did have the merit of leading back to the British lines, whereas she was not sure who held the valley. It could very well be French, especially if her captors intended to barter her with one side against the other.

'I don't know what you mean,' she said.

'All will become clear,' the Sergeant told her amiably, delving into his bag to pull out bread, cold cooked mutton and a skin of goat's milk. 'But not just yet. The sun is barely up, and reveille hardly done with. Later, we can expect a visitor.'

'Who?'

He handed her food, and poured some of the milk into the mug he took from his belt. 'Here, eat and drink. We must deliver you in good condition.'

Louise sat down and took the food, pretending to eat, but her mind was full of possibilities which whirled about in her head, making her dizzy. They expected Paul to come, she was sure of it; they thought he would drop everything to rescue her. Perhaps he would. The idea raised her spirits, but they quickly sank again when she thought of the

implications. A trap had been set and she was the
bait, but what then?

'If I am the sprat, who is the mackerel?' she asked.
'It won't do any harm to tell me, for what can I do to
prevent his coming?'

'True, true,' he said, and smiled. 'The man we are
expecting is a spy, and we are going to prove it.'

'How?'

'When he realises you have been taken by French
soldiers, he will go to his French friends and enlist
their help to free you. He will give himself away.'

'He won't need help to overcome the two of you,'
she retorted. 'He's man enough to beat ten.'

'Oh, so you do know who it is?'

She blushed in confusion.

'No matter. When he comes looking for you, which
we have been assured he will, he'll be followed and
arrested, and there will be evidence enough to hang
him, you can be sure.'

'And what do you hope to gain?'

The Sergeant laughed. 'A voyage home and a nice
little pension, awarded by a grateful country.'

'And supposing he—the one you want—doesn't go
to the French?'

'Oh, but he will,' said the young soldier, laughing
and pointing to his borrowed blue uniform.

'Can you speak French? Enough to convince a
Frenchman?'

'Don't have to,' he said complacently. 'He only has
to be seen talking to us from a distance. It will be
enough for anyone coming up behind him; specially
when it secures your release.' He sounded as if he
was repeating a drill, for the words did not seem
natural to him at all.

'Then what?'

'The Frenchmen disappear, back to their own lines,
and are never seen again . . .' He pointed to himself
and his companion to make his meaning clear.

'The whole idea is outrageous!' she cried. 'Who
thought of it first? I'll wager it wasn't either of you.'

'We'll leave you to guess that,' the Sergeant said,

jumping up on a rock to survey their surroundings.
'No sign of him yet.'

Louise felt both relieved and despondent. What
had happened when it was discovered that she was
missing? What did Dick do? Had he engineered the
whole thing? Had Humphrey? They had said she
would help them to catch Paul, and now she had
unwittingly done just that. But perhaps Paul had
realised what was happening and refused to be drawn
into it. The practical, common-sense side of her
nature, the realist in her, hoped that was so, but the
other side, the side which ached for love of him, the
side that would give almost anything to be held in his
arms again, longed for him to come.

The two men prowled about the camp, taking it in
turns to keep watch, but, as the day progressed, they
became impatient and irritable and at last the
Sergeant, who had been sitting near Louise, drinking
from his canteen, threw it down and scrambled to his
feet.

'I'm going to see if he's coming,' he said to the
boy. 'Watch her well.'

He took his horse, mounted, and was soon lost to
sight among the rocks.

Louise, left with only one guard and that hardly
more than a boy, realised that if she was going to try
to escape, now was the time to do it. If she could
reach either Paul or whoever was following him,
before the Sergeant, their so-called evidence would
not stand examination and the plot would fail. She
began moving slowly away from the cave mouth,
keeping her eye on the boy, who was lying in the
shade with his eyes shut. She hoped he was asleep,
but she couldn't be sure. Once clear, she turned and
began to run.

It was no good staying on the path if she was going
to outmanoeuvre the Sergeant on his horse; she
would have to strike across the side of the mountain
slope to get in front of him. The going was rough,
and loose stones, becoming dislodged, rattled down
towards the valley. She hardly noticed that her
shoeless feet were bleeding, as she pressed on. Once

she paused, when she heard shots down in the tree-lined ravine behind her, but they were a long way off and she supposed a French and British patrol had met, or someone was firing at animals. She would not let it deflect her from her purpose, but stumbled on.

Suddenly she found herself on a promontory, and although she could clearly see the path she wanted, winding between the rocks ahead of her, she could not reach it; between the spot where she stood and the track was a deep gorge. In the distance, too far away to recognise, was a group of horsemen riding upwards. They would not hear her if she shouted. She turned to look for another way; higher up the slope, the Sergeant sat on his horse, watching the approaching party.

Unable to go forward, or sideways, she turned to retrace her steps and came face to face with Billy, who stood with feet apart, blocking her path.

'Thought I was asleep, did you?' he said. 'Well, Billy don' sleep. Not when he's on duty, he don't. Now let's have you back and there'll be no more runnin' away, to be sure . . .'

He reached out towards her; involuntarily she shrugged off his hand and stepped back. Her feet slid, her hand clutched the empty air as she began to fall. Her shrieks echoed round the mountain and the split second it took for Billy to grab her arm and hold her seemed an eternity. He said nothing as he hauled her to safety.

She sat on the ground, shaking and panting for breath, unable to speak or stand, until he bent to help her up. 'Come,' he said gently. 'Let's go back.'

'Thank you.'

He helped her to hobble back to the cave, where they arrived at the same time as the Sergeant. 'What happened?' he demanded. 'I told you to watch her!'

'So I did, so I did.' The boy laughed suddenly. 'Now her friends have seen her with her French captors, they'll be more convinced she needs rescu-ing . . .'

The Sergeant grunted. 'She made enough noise to rouse the whole French army . . .'

'They're miles away.'

'Don't you believe it. I've got the smell of 'em in me nostrils.'

'So what do we do?'

'Wait.'

'What about that patrol we saw?'

'They got here afore the fellow they're supposed to be followin'. I waved 'em back.'

Louise, still shaking, had dropped to the ground, and was sitting with her arms round her knees, resting her forehead on them. She looked up and laughed nervously. 'See,' she said. 'See what a senseless idea it was. Your plot has failed, and if we stay here much longer, we'll be captured by the real French and what will those uniforms do for you then? Tell me that.'

'She's right,' Billy said.

'Take me back, and no more will be said. If I put in a word for you and tell them how you were duped . . .'

'Duped!' the Sergeant repeated. 'Who says we've been duped? I ain't givin' up yet. We've got food and drink for another day, and there's still time for the traitor to turn up. And when he does . . .' He drew his hand across his throat and laughed.

'And if he doesn't?'

'We'll leave you to the wolves,' the boy said, with a grin.

'You wouldn't,' she gasped, wondering if he meant it. 'My husband . . .'

'Be good, then,' the Sergeant said. 'No more runnin' away; it ain't worth your effort.' He looked down at her bloodstained feet. 'Though it seems to me you've hobbled y'self. Be sure, the Frenchman will come.'

Louise prayed that he would not. If nothing happened by nightfall, they would surely give up and take her back to the horsemen who were lying in wait half-way up the mountain. Dick and Humphrey were probably not with them, but would have detailed others; whoever they were, they would be duty bound to escort her back to her own camp. She kept her courage up by fuelling her anger planning what she

would say to her husband and Major Barton when
she saw them again. Sprat, indeed! Mackerel! Not
that Dick was entirely to blame; Humphrey was using
him, and although he was a willing accomplice, she
did not think he really appreciated the depth of
Humphrey's hate for Paul.

The long day dragged on, hot, uncomfortable,
silent except for the occasional cry of a bird or bleat
of a goat. Once they heard more shots, and both men
scrambled to a vantage-point to search the landscape.
But there was nothing to be seen.

'Gives me the jitters,' the boy said, returning to the
cave. 'I'd as lief pack up and go back.'

'That's the most sensible thing you've said all day,'
said Louise.' 'Why don't we all go back to the British
lines?'

'We wait,' the Sergeant said. 'We wait until I say
otherwise, d'you hear?'

When darkness fell, they gave up watching and
withdrew into the cave. Louise had been dreading the
moment all day, fearing they might try and rape her,
and prepared to defend herself in whatever way she
could. If they both fell asleep, she would try to leave,
but they were not so stupid; one watched while the
other slept. Neither made any move to touch her,
and she was grateful to whoever had hired them; they
had obviously been given orders they dare not
disobey. She wrapped herself in the old blanket they
had given her, too grateful for its warmth to wonder
if there were any livestock in it and, after wriggling
about to make herself comfortable, she finally went
to sleep.

They were all startled into wakefulness at dawn by
a sound just below the hill, the sound of stones
plummeting downwards. Billy sat up, eyes wide, and
reached for his musket. 'What was that?'

The Sergeant stirred, and Louise realised they had
both been fast asleep and she had missed her
opportunity. 'How should I know?' he said, irritable
at being woken. 'Go and see.'

The young man crawled cautiously forward and out

into the light of dawn. He peered over the ledge, looking down, then scuttled back in great haste.

'It's *guerrilleros*! If they see us in these jackets . . .' He began feverishly to divest himself of the incriminating uniform.

'Shut up and keep still!' the Sergeant commanded. 'They might go by.' He crept out on all fours to confirm what the boy had said. The hill was alive with men dressed in rough wide trousers tucked into their boots, and linen shirts. They wore scarves knotted round their heads, and their leather bandoliers were bulging with ammunition. Every one carried a musket.

The Sergeant retreated into the back of the cave, tugging at the boy's sleeve and motioning Louise to follow. Then he picked up the only musket they had and loaded it, tamping down the powder and pushing the ball down on top, ready to fire.

'Don't do that,' the boy whispered hoarsely. 'There's hundreds of hundreds of 'em.'

'You can reload while I use my pistol.' The Sergeant was determined to make a fight of it. 'We'll get one or two afore we go.'

'But they're on our side!' Louise cried in horror. 'You can't kill your own allies.'

'They'll think we're Frenchies,' the Sergeant said. 'They won't stop to ask first.'

'We could shout and tell them.'

'They don't understand English . . .'

'Don't you know any Spanish?' Louise asked, as the sounds of boots scrambling over rocks came closer.

They held their breaths; nothing happened. They sat and waited, the sounds outside ceased and still nothing happened. Daylight increased, and the sun climbed up the cobalt sky, outlining the mouth of the cave. Outside was all white light and heat, inside, gloom and chill. But though they waited, hardly daring to move, no one came.

'They've gone,' Billy whispered at last.

'Are you sure?' Louise, remembering Maria's tales

of the *guerrilleros*, was no more ready to fall into their hands than were the two men.

The boy crept forward, first putting his head out of the cave and peering round, then crawling right out and dashing for the cover of a near-by rock. Silence. A hawk swooped, a vulture hovered, a goat bleated, jumping from crag to crag; the wind stirred the trees. They could hear the rush of water down in the bottom of the gorge, but on the mountain, there was silence.

'They've gone!' Billy shouted. 'Come on out.'

The Sergeant went cautiously, pausing at the mouth of the cave to look and listen before striding out to join his companion, who laughed aloud now that his fears had been dispelled.

Louise, following, had only just emerged into the sunlight when a *guerrilla* rose above the rock behind the men and pounced on the Sergeant, followed by another who toppled the boy. Before she could cry a warning, yet another had crept round behind her and clapped a hand over her mouth.

The whole thing had been done in an efficient silence, and even now it was over, no one spoke. The two men were trussed up and thrown sideways over their horses, while Louise was guided firmly to the mule and helped to mount. She was terrified, unsure whether she had been rescued or had just exchanged one captivity for another, but she was determined not to show her fear and held her head high as she was led down the mountain path, surrounded by a band of about twenty men. They were in jubilant mood, as if the capture of two insignificant soldiers and one frightened woman was cause for celebration.

There were more men in the camp among the trees on the lower slopes, and some women, dressed as the men were, in trousers and shirts; all were busy, some cooking, others cleaning weapons, some standing about a captured field gun, stroking it possessively as they would the woman they loved. Still more were stacking ammunition in piles, counting it; one was weighing out powder and pouring it into little leather pouches. It seemed they had recently made a

successful raid and taken over a camp which, until
the previous day, had been held by the French. It
accounted for the shooting they had heard, and
Louise felt the rise of fear in her throat at the
thought of how near they had been. Now the
Spaniards were sorting out the spoils.

When they rode in, a tall man in a heavy cloak
detached himself from the crowd round the gun and
walked towards them, throwing the cloak from his
shoulders, so that it hung down his back from its ties.

'Paul!' The exclamation was out before she could
stop it, and she slid from the mule and stood
hesitantly facing him, still afraid of her captors. Was
he a prisoner too? It certainly did not seem like it.
Was he angry? But he was grinning like a schoolboy.
She could only stand and stare at him, repeating his
name. 'Paul. Paul!'

'Louise, my love, you're safe!' He held his hands
wide and she ran forward to be enfolded into the
protection of his arms. He stood holding her, his big
frame her security, her hiding-place from the torments
of the world. She was trembling, unable to keep her
body still, and she did not know why. The danger
was past, she was safe, so why shake?

She looked up at him with tears wet on her lashes.
'Oh, Paul.'

'It's all over, my darling,' he said gently. 'All over.
You are safe now, praise God.' He led her to a log a
little apart from the bustle of the camp and sat,
drawing her down beside him. 'I'm sorry I left you so
long, but I had to throw my followers off the trail
while I went to fetch help.' He laughed suddenly.
'Help that wasn't French.'

'You guessed it was a trap?' Some of his strength
had flowed into her, and she was feeling better.

'Yes.' He paused to kiss her, and it was some time
before he went on. 'You know Dick put on a very
good show of being the distraught husband? I was
almost ready to believe he really cared . . .'

'Then?'

'I saw him ride over to talk to Major Barton
instead of returning to his own lines; if he was really

as concerned as he pretended to be, he would have
gone back to help search for you. It was when I saw
them talking together and laughing that I began to
think all was not as it seemed.'

'They say you are a French spy.'

He laughed and rumpled her hair. 'Humphrey
Barton knows I am not.'

'Then why?'

'He had his reasons . . . Personal reasons, nothing
to do with the war.'

'Oh.' She looked up into his eyes, wanting
reassurance, and it was there in the tender look he
gave her. 'He thought Alicia . . .' She paused. 'Was
he right to think that?'

He laughed and bent to kiss the tip of her nose,
making her giggle. 'Alicia Barton would like to think
so. She had openly boasted of her conquests, not just
of me, but of others. No one but Humphrey takes
her seriously.'

'He's just a jealous husband?'

'Yes. He is older than Alicia and terrified of losing
her. He seized the opportunity to involve your
husband in seeking revenge, but whether Dick told
him the true story of how you came to be with me, I
don't know.'

She took his hand and put the palm to her cheek.
'Dick needed no urging. He imagines he has a score
to settle, too.'

He chuckled. 'Oh, that impossible gamble! I never
expected him to let me take you.'

'Why did you do it then?'

'Because I could see the danger you were in and
wanted to buy you a little time to escape.' He paused,
smiling. 'Besides, I think I had already begun to love
you even then.'

'Truly?' she asked, in surprise. 'And did you cheat
in order to win?'

He bent his head to kiss her again. 'I didn't need
to, my love. Your husband is such a poor player that
a child could have beaten him!'

'So you didn't intend to bring me out to Portugal?'

'No, of course not! I had no intention of subjecting

you to the hardships and danger of a military campaign. I thought you could stay at my home until your husband came to his senses.' He laughed suddenly. 'I should have known someone as spirited as you would have her own ideas about that. Events took charge; fate, if you like. Before I knew what had happened, we were on board that ship. But, even then, I thought you would stay safely in Lisbon.'

She laughed, leaning away from him, so that she could look up into his face. 'You bargained without me . . .'

'Yes, my love, and you have endured far worse than I intended, walking with the women and working with the surgeon . . .'

'It was my choice,' she said simply.

'You saved my life.'

'Nonsense! You weren't badly wounded at all.'

'But you stayed by me. Why did you do that?'

'Because . . .' She paused, then added in a rush, 'Oh, Paul, I'm so sorry, so very, very sorry! I told Humphrey I thought you were spying . . . I made it so much more difficult for you. I've been tormented by it ever since. Please say you forgive me? I have never regretted anything so much in my whole life. In the hospital, when you were ill, then I knew . . .'

'You loved me?' He finished for her. 'You know, I still can't believe my good fortune.'

'But . . .'

He tilted her face up to his and kissed her lips, silencing her. 'I knew what you had done,' he said. 'Pringle told me.'

'Pringle?' she repeated. 'But how?'

He grinned. 'Pringle knows everything, or almost everything. You'd be surprised at the depth of his knowledge! And what he doesn't know, Hetty does, or guesses, with a woman's intuition.'

'Oh.' She suddenly felt very small and ashamed. Then, 'What will happen now?'

'I wish I knew.' His eyes looked troubled and he no longer smiled. 'I wish I knew.'

One of the *guerrilleros* came over and offered Louise a plate of hot food, which she accepted gratefully. He spoke in Spanish and pointed to a group of partisans who were questioning the two bogus Frenchmen and treating them none too gently. Paul left to remonstrate with them, and although he was back at her side, the feeling of euphoria had vanished and they were back in the harsh world of reality.

'Those two will have to be taken back to our lines or they will be branded deserters,' he said. 'It answers your question, doesn't it?'

She did not want to reply, to have to face the truth. She was a married woman; she was not free to fall in love, and her duty was clear. She had told him that before and made him accept it; it was almost as if he wanted to hurt her by reminding her of it. With vision blurred by tears, she looked round the busy scene as if to find the solution to her heartbreak in her surroundings.

'These men,' she said, changing the subject abruptly and indicating the *guerrilleros*, who were striking camp and preparing to move the big gun. 'Are they your friends?'

'I don't know if you could call them friends,' he said, smiling again. 'They are certainly allies. That murderous-looking fellow over there is their leader, Don Julian Sanchez; he and his band of cut-throats have succeeded in isolating Ciudad Rodrigo from the outside world for weeks. The inmates were on the point of starving to death when the French commanders decided it had to be relieved at all costs. It took them a great multitude of men—60,000, so I am told—one hundred and thirty field guns and a thousand supply wagons . . .'

'Who told you?'

'I have my informers,' he said. 'That's why we were ordered to retreat into the hills . . .'

'So Rifleman Pringle said.'

'Pringle talks a great deal more than he should.'

'The day after he told us that, Maria disappeared.'

'Maria?'

'Yes. The girl whose soldier lover deserted.'

'Oh, that young lady! When did you see her?'

'She has been travelling with me. Dick employed her as a servant.'

'I asked Mrs Pringle to do that.'

'Hetty is more concerned with looking after her husband, and I certainly don't blame her for that. And I didn't really need a servant anyway, but I felt sorry for her. She needed to earn a living after the soldier was executed . . .'

'He deserted in the face of the enemy; there can be only one punishment.'

'I know that, but she is very bitter.' She paused to search his face for a clue to what he was thinking. 'She has been making threats against you. I am afraid for you . . .'

He laughed. 'What can she possibly do to me that your husband and his friends have not already attempted—and failed—to do? No one can prove me a French spy because I am not one, and what else is there? Do not worry, my darling. Think no more about her.'

He became suddenly serious and pressed her closer to his side, kissing the top of her head as it rested on his shoulder, and stroking her hair. 'We must think of you. However much it breaks my heart, I must return you to the British lines . . .'

'Can't we have just a little more time together?'

'If I had my way, it would be the rest of our lives, but I, too, have my duty.' He got up and stood looking down at her with that amused smile of his which she had come to know so well; it was a smile meant to be slightly cynical, meant to hide his true feelings, and she understood that now. 'The war cannot wait.' He bent to take her hand and draw her to her feet beside him.

'And I must return to my husband.' She faltered on the last word, but recovering herself, added with a poor attempt at a joke, 'But how can I do it without shoes? You know those silly men said they had orders to return me in good condition, just as if I were a piece of furniture. I dropped them on purpose; I thought they would be angry when they found out, but they didn't seem to care.'

'No, because they wanted me to follow.' He nodded towards the *guerrilleros*, who had completed their packing and were manhandling the gun on to the mountain trail with a great deal of shouting and grunting. 'Wait here, my love.' He strode over to Don Sanchez, who spoke to one of his men, who laughed suddenly and went to a spot near where the fire had been kicked out, and, from beside a tree stump, produced Louise's shoes.

'There,' Paul said, returning with them. 'One wife in good condition.'

She sat down to put them on, swallowing and blinking to prevent the tears. How was she going to continue living without him? How could she possibly be a good wife to Dick when her heart ached for someone else? How could she endure his inconsiderate behaviour and his gambling, when she knew that not far away was someone who would treat her with tenderness?

He bent to help her to stand. 'Louise . . .'

She looked up into his brown eyes, and her own filled and overflowed. 'Yes?'

He turned away suddenly as if he could not bear to look at her. 'Nothing. When you go back . . . Later . . . if life becomes too intolerable . . .'

'I know.' She followed him to where his own horse and another had been tethered, and they mounted in silence.

The rest of the band had gone, leaving Louise, Paul, and the two English soldiers already on their horses.

'On your way,' Paul said, indicating they should precede him. 'Back to our lines.'

They rode slowly out of the encampment and turned up towards the mountain pass. It was a silent ride; Louise and Paul were too emotionally full to speak and the two soldiers too dejected and humiliated. They had been tricked into believing they were helping to catch a French spy, responsible for the deaths of untold soldiers, someone whose traitorous activities were prolonging the war by months, even years, and it was not true. None of it.

And if a word ever reached ears senior to Major
Barton and Lieutenant Oakingham, they would be in
dire trouble for leaving their posts. If the grim look
on Captain Fourier's face was any indication, that
seemed likely, and they were in for a flogging at the
very least.

They topped the rise in the middle of the morning
and found themselves on a high ridge with magnificent
views of the surrounding country spread out below
them. Behind them was the gorge, to one side the
mountain pass and the rough path which led back to
the British lines; on the other side, hundreds of feet
below them, rolling plains of farmland, dissected by a
narrow road. In the distance, shining in the heat,
were the walls of a town.

Paul reined in and pointed at it. 'That's the place
that's been causing all the trouble! That's Ciudad
Rodrigo, and while the French hold it, we can't
advance.'

'Pringle says there's a siege train on the way,' said
Louise. 'Is that why we hold back?'

'It's one of the reasons . . .' His voice trailed away
as his attention was distracted by something he saw
across the plain. He reached down into his saddlebag
for his telescope, and trained it on the distant town.

'What is it?' she asked.

'I thought I saw a movement.'

'And a signal,' the Sergeant said. 'Look! A flash of
light coming from the battlements.

Paul picked it out and then swung himself round in
the saddle to search the cliff top on the other side of
the gorge. There was a distinct flash, as if the sun
had caught something shining. 'There's someone up
there,' he said. 'Whoever it is, he is signalling to the
French.'

'Look! Look!' cried the boy excitedly. 'Oh, look at
that for an army.'

They sat unbelievingly as squadron after squadron
of cavalry rode out of the fortress and set off along
the road towards Portugal and the British lines, their
swords and accoutrements flashing in the sun. After
them came battalions of infantry, marching confidently

forward, plumed heads held high, muskets at the trail, and the eagles, which served them as banners, held aloft. This was no skirmish party, no patrol, but an army going into battle.

'God in heaven!' Paul exclaimed. 'There must be . . .' He paused to make a swift calculation. 'Four brigades of cavalry, and . . .' he put the telescope to his eye again, 'at least eight thousand infantry.'

'More, I should say,' said the Sergeant. 'They're making for El Bodon.'

'And our lines are strung out for sixteen miles. We're totally unprepared.'

'Do they know that?' asked Louise, unable to take her eyes off the spectacle.

'I doubt if they'd attempt it otherwise,' said Paul.

'Spies,' said the Sergeant. 'The Major weren't so far wrong, after all.'

'We're safe enough up here,' Billy said happily. 'And we'll be able to see it all.'

'You would stand by and see your countrymen slaughtered?' Paul turned on him. 'Besides, if there is a battle and you are not at your post, that makes you a deserter.'

The boy's smile faded. 'We didn't know it was going to happen, did we? It ain't our fault. We had a special mission.'

'You have certainly got one now,' said Paul. 'Sergeant, take your man and ride hell for leather for General Picton's position! Tell him he'll be over-run if he doesn't fall back.' He pointed. 'Go that way, it's quicker.'

'It's quicker, and that's a fact,' Billy said, looking down the slope which fell almost precipitously to the plain. 'We'll go head over heels before we get half-way.'

'Sergeant?' Paul raised an eyebrow, as if daring either of them to defy him.

'Yes, sir!' The Sergeant said, nodding to his subordinate and, digging his heels into his mare's flanks, he urged her slowly downwards, picking his way carefully over the uneven ground. Billy followed reluctantly.

They had no sooner started than Paul turned his attention once more to the columns of French troops, then across to the other side of the gorge, looking for the signals. There was nothing to be seen at first and then he saw it, a short flash of light, followed by another. 'Whoever is there must be stopped,' he said. 'My guess is that they can see over to the British positions.' He turned to Louise, reaching across and taking her hand. 'Do you think you can continue alone?'

'Yes, of course. What are you going to do?'

'I must get over there somehow, go down into the valley and climb the cliff. He did it; so can I.'

'He?'

'Whoever it is doing the signalling.' He lifted her hand to his lips. 'Now, ride as fast as you dare. You may meet the patrol sent to follow me, still waiting.' He smiled ruefully at the thought. 'But, if not, find the Commander in Chief, and tell him what we've seen.'

'Wellington?' she asked.

'Or his aide. Now go, my love, and God take care of you.'

Before she could reply, he had left her. Stifling her inclination to watch him go, she turned her horse to the mountain path along which she had been led two nights before.

Once she had negotiated the steeper slopes, she set her horse to a trot, and as soon as she reached the dusty white road, to a gallop. There was no sign of the horsemen who had been standing by for her bogus rescue; they had obviously tired of waiting and returned to the lines, but she hardly spared them a thought as she spurred the horse on.

She had only a vague idea where the British headquarters were, but if her two abductors could alert General Picton and if she could reach the main positions in time for reinforcements to be sent, tragedy might yet be averted. Paul had to reach the signaller too, if any new moves were not to be communicated to the enemy. Oh, there were so many ifs, and as the ground rushed by under the galloping hooves, she prayed they would all be in time.

Set against the defeat of an army and the slaughter of thousands of men, her own problems seemed infinitesimal, and she had no time to spare for them. Her whole mind was fully occupied with riding and willing the beast beneath her to go even faster.

It was well into the afternoon when a forward sentry stepped into the road from the shade of a eucalyptus and raised his musket to challenge her. Louise pulled on the reins, and the sweating horse came to a halt in a flurry of white dust.

'I must speak to the Duke of Wellington,' she said. 'At once.'

He laughed, taking the bridle and steadying the horse. 'There's many as'd like to do that, but he's got more important things to do than talk to the likes o' you.'

'How dare you!' she snapped, then realising that, in her dishevelled state, with torn skirt and loose hair, she did look like the kind of camp-follower he took her for. She could hardly expect an audience of the Commander in Chief in that state. She softened her voice to try persuasion. 'I've ridden hard to bring him an important message, and it must be delivered without delay . . .'

'Important message?' He seemed interested at last, though still disinclined to allow her to continue; his hand still held the bridle.

'The French are marching on El Bodon in force.'

He laughed, showing uneven black teeth. 'How long have you been out here, miss? Don't you know a patrol when you see one?'

'Course I do! This is no patrol . . . There are three thousand horse and eight thousand infantry . . .'

'How come you can say it so accurate?' he asked, becoming suspicious. 'You been in among 'em and counted 'em?'

'No, but I saw them from the ridge.' She jerked her head back the way she had come. 'Captain Fourier estimated their numbers, and he sent me to tell the Duke . . .'

'Well, I can't go to old Hooknose, can I? I've got to stop here 'til I'm relieved.'

Exasperated, she jerked the leather from his hand and kicked her heels into the poor horse. The sentry, reluctant to shoot her, fired above her head, shouting to her to stop. By the time he had reloaded to fire at her in earnest, she had gone from his sight. A few minutes later she entered the little frontier town.

She was undecided where to go, when she came upon a group of Highlanders and, recognising the uniform of the 71st, pulled up sharply and dismounted.

'Where is Major Barton? I must speak to him.'

One of them came forward and pointed to a house whose blue front door gave directly on to the street. 'In there, miss.'

She handed him the reins. 'Look after the horse, please, he's had a hard ride.'

'He has that,' the soldier said, as she left him. 'Look at the poor beast.'

She knocked at the blue door but, receiving no immediate reply, pushed it open to reveal a dim cool hall.

'Is anyone there?' she called. 'Major Barton?'

He came out from one of the rooms and stood staring at her in surprise. 'Louise, is it really you?'

'Of course it is!' she snapped, suddenly remembering he had been one of the instigators of her abduction and was hardly expecting her to return by herself. 'I have an urgent message which must be conveyed to the Duke . . .'

'Come in, my dear,' he said. 'Come and sit down and have some refreshment. I'm sure we can sort this out without troubling the Peer . . .'

'Sort what out?' Why was there all this delay? First the sentry and now Humphrey. Why couldn't they see how urgent it was?

'I'm sorry, Louise. You have obviously been through a great deal of discomfort, and that was not our intention . . .'

'Oh, that,' said Louise. 'There will be time for explanations and apologies later. Now it is more important to tell the Duke that the French are marching on El Bodon; I've seen them from the ridge. We all saw them . . .'

'All?'

'The two men you ordered to take me to the mountains and Captain Fourier . . .'

'He came then, did he? I knew he would.'

'That need not concern us now,' she said, resisting the urge to slap him. 'It's far more important to deliver that message. I can hardly go to the Duke looking like this! He wouldn't listen to me, but if you went . . .'

'You've sent me on wild-goose chases before . . .'

'For goodness' sake, this is serious!'

'You really mean it? There is a large force marching on our positions?'

'Yes, cavalry and infantry, ten or eleven thousand all told, Paul said.'

'Paul?' His eyes narrowed. 'Where is he now?'

'We saw someone signalling to the enemy. He went to stop them . . .'

He laughed suddenly. 'Alone? Oh, my innocent sweet girl, he has slipped through our fingers after all. Now he's gone back to join his countrymen.'

'You are wasting time,' she said. 'If you won't go, tell me where Dick is. Perhaps he will . . .'

'He was ordered to El Bodon yesterday.'

'Oh, no!' She felt the colour drain from her face. 'There's going to be a massacre if we don't do something. He'll be killed!'

'Here, come and sit down.' He led her into the room he had just left, and guided her to a chair. 'Have no fear. Your husband has the gift of self-preservation, you must have realised that. Have you at last come to realise he means more to you than the traitor?'

'Please go,' she said, coldly, refusing to be drawn. 'Please go and report what I've told you, otherwise you will have the deaths of thousands of brave men on your conscience.'

'Very well,' he said, realising she was in earnest. 'You can make yourself comfortable here until I return.' He clapped his hands and shouted, 'Pedro!'

When the elderly owner of the house shuffled in he turned to him and said, 'Find the lady water to wash, food to eat and something to wear. She may use this room.'

'*Si, señor.*'

The man left, and Humphrey turned back to her. 'I am not altogether convinced this is not a ruse to make me look a fool again . . .'

'I promise you it is not!'

'If it is, I will see that you pay dearly. And if that traitorous Frenchman has enlisted you as one of his band of spies, I will see that the full penalty of the law is exacted, do you understand?' He laughed harshly and looked her up and down, taking in her dusty torn clothes and untidy hair, the tired blue eyes and cracked lips. 'Make yourself beautiful again while I'm gone; then I might be more inclined to mercy.'

He turned to the door as the Spaniard came in bearing a bowl of warm water, soap, towel and hairbrush and, thrown over his shoulder, a bright red woollen skirt embroidered in traditional pattern. He put the bowl and toilet articles on a table, and the skirt on the bed. 'It belonged to my wife,' he said, crossing himself. 'God rest her soul.' He turned to the door. 'Food is more difficult. I will see what I can find . . .'

'I'm not hungry,' Louise said truthfully. 'Please don't inconvenience yourself.'

He shrugged, accepting what she said, and left them. Louise stood up and took two or three paces towards Humphrey. 'Oh, please make haste,' she entreated. 'Please go now.'

'Very well. When I come back, we shall have a nice long talk.' He took his jacket from a peg behind the door and put it on, taking his time doing up the rows of buttons, while Louise fidgeted impatiently. He put on his belt and sword and the sash which denoted his rank, and turned to look for his shako. She picked it up from a chair and took it to him, trying to hasten his departure. 'Hurry,' she said. 'And pray you are in time.'

She continued to pray after he had gone, falling to

her knees beside the bed, pleading that Humphrey should be believed, that Dick should be unhurt, that the two soldiers Paul had sent to El Bodon would be in time, that he would scale the cliff without falling to his death, that the real French spy, whoever he was, should be uncovered . . . But, above all, that there should be peace—peace in the world and in her own tumultous heart.

At last she rose and, pushing aside the overwhelming temptation to stretch out on the bed, washed and dressed and brushed the tangles from her hair. Once more refreshed, she was eager to know what was happening; she could hear booted feet running over the paving stones, shouts, galloping horses, guns being dragged along, but when she went to the door, it would not budge. Humphrey had locked her in.

CHAPTER TWELVE

THE NOISE IN the street died down, the town became quiet, although away in the distance Louise could hear the guns and the battle-cries of the men, rising and falling like waves upon a sloping shore. She paced the room as it went on and on, offering a prayer with every step.

'Let the slaughter stop,' she said aloud. 'Dear God, let it stop. Keep Paul safe, make Dick stop gambling, help Humphrey to scour the hate from his heart.' And then, as an added inducement, 'I will be a dutiful wife. Let them all come back safe.'

Although she tried, it was impossible from the noise to distinguish one side from the other, the victor from the vanquished. She went to the small barred window, but there was nothing to see but puffs of smoke over the hills to the east. She went to the door and banged on it, demanding to be let out, but no one heard her or, if they did, they had been given orders to ignore her. She lay down on the bed and shut her eyes, but sleep did not release her from her anxiety.

She sat up suddenly as she heard a horse and then boots on the street, followed by the sound of someone coming along the hall. The door was unlocked, and Humphrey came in.

'Why did you lock me in?' she demanded immediately, then, 'What happened? Were you in time?'

'No. They had seen the columns for themselves only minutes before I arrived.'

'What about those two soldiers? Didn't they reach them, either?'

'They were mistaken for French skirmishers,' he said, throwing off his hat and belt. 'They were shot.'

'By their own comrades?'

'Yes.' He sat down on the bed to pull off his boots, and at once she scrambled to her feet and moved to the other side of the room. 'They were in French uniforms.'

'And who put them in French uniforms?' she cried. 'You did.'

'We had to catch the spy.'

'You are obsessed with spies! Can't you think of anything else? What is happening? Have we been defeated?'

'No, just withdrawing, falling back . . .'

'Dick? Did you see Dick?' He was her husband and she had loved him once; she could not be indifferent to his fate.

He grinned a little lop-sidedly. 'In the thick of it. You know, Louise, he has the makings of a good soldier . . .'

'But he is safe?'

'He was when I last saw him an hour or so since.'

'And Captain Fourier?' She had to ask.

'I told you, we've seen the last of him. He's either dead or he means us to believe he's dead. His horse was seen galloping riderless along the ridge. It'll stop when it runs out of wind, but I doubt anyone will risk going out to try and catch it.'

'But he could be lying injured somewhere,' she cried, thinking of the cliff he had intended to climb. 'Can't we go and look for him?'

He laughed harshly. 'That ground is in the hands of the enemy, and he is back where he belongs, injured or no.' He stood up and came towards her; she backed away. 'But just because he has escaped, it doesn't mean his accomplices go free. Men have died today, died needlessly and bravely, and it would make their comrades feel a great deal easier if someone were to pay for that.'

'I don't know what you mean.' She was frightened by the steely look of hate in his eyes. Surely he had not locked her in the room in order to come back and murder her? 'I came to warn you . . .'

'Too late, too late.'

'I nearly broke my neck to get here,' she said, as he advanced and she retreated. 'You were slow in leaving.'

'How did the Bluecoats know our lines were stretched?' he demanded. 'How did they know when and where to strike?'

'I don't know. Perhaps the signaller on the cliff.'

'If such a one exists. I have other theories.' She had her back to the wall now, and he put his hand on it above her head, so that he was leaning over her. 'Now you . . .'

'Me?' she said, in surprise. 'You can't possibly suggest such a thing!'

'Why not? You heard Rifleman Pringle speaking out of turn, and very soon afterwards you left the camp in the company of two French soldiers . . .'

'That's preposterous,' she interrupted sharply. 'You know those two weren't French.'

He laughed. 'Difficult to gainsay now, isn't it? They're dead.' He paused. 'And you met and spoke to Captain Fourier, a Frenchman born and bred, and your lover to boot.'

'That's not true!' she cried.

'What isn't true? That Captain Fourier is French or that he is your lover?'

'I will not allow you to question me in this fashion,' she said angrily. 'Please take your hand away and let me go.'

'I'm afraid I can't do that,' he returned. 'Let you go, I mean. You are a material witness, and I ought to arrest you. Treason is punishable by death, you know.'

She stared at him, wondering if he meant what he said, but she could not tell from his expression; he was smiling confidently.

'You can't mean that!'

'There is a way. If you denounce Paul Fourier and give us the evidence we need.'

'I can't do that! You know I can't! There isn't any evidence.'

'Why are you so sure?' He grabbed her hand and pulled her over to the bed where he pushed her so that she sat down heavily. 'He is a spy, an adulterer, a liar, surely you cannot condone such things?'

'I don't believe them.'

He sighed dramatically. 'Ah me, there is no one as stubborn as a woman in love, but I assure you your love is misplaced.' He paused, watching her face intently. 'Now if you were to place your affections elsewhere, then suspicion would be lifted from you. I am sure you understand.'

She understood; understood only too well. 'I have a husband. Have you forgotten that?'

'Dick?' He stooped to put his hand under her chin and forced her to look up at him. 'Dick let you go once; he will do so again. That is if he survives this day, though if the manner in which he is conducting himself is anything to go by, it is unlikely.'

'What do you mean?'

'Reckless,' he said. 'Reckless to the point of heroism.'

'Earlier today you said he had the gift of self-preservation.'

'So I did, but since then he has been foolishly trying to prove his invulnerability.'

She tried to look away from his hard grey eyes, but he held her chin firmly. 'I mean to survive,' he said. 'Of the three of us, I shall be the one to survive. I intend to live to be an old, old man, the others . . . .' He shrugged. 'Days, maybe weeks, if they're lucky.'

'You're drunk!' she said suddenly, as he bent low over her and put his mouth to hers.

She squirmed away. He laughed and reached for her again. She scrambled on hands and knees across the bed and off the other side. He dodged round the foot of it and grabbed her, still laughing like a child playing a game. Only it was no game; he was in earnest, and she was terrified. Neither heard the door open.

Suddenly she felt him being wrenched from her, as

Dick strode across the room, pulled him round and delivered a blow to the point of his jaw. Humphrey reeled back and sprawled across the bed.

Louise felt almost tempted to laugh, Humphrey looked so taken aback, but she was completely taken by surprise too. She knew Dick had a temper, but she had never seen him land a blow like that before, or even attempt it.

'Come along,' he said, taking her hand. 'Let's go.'

'It's a court-martial for you,' Humphrey called after them. 'Striking a superior officer isn't tolerated in this army.'

'He's right,' Louise said, as they stepped out into the street. It was no longer deserted but filled with weary dust-covered soldiers and sweat-lathered horses. 'Why did you do it?'

He stopped to look down at her. 'Did you wish I hadn't?'

'No, no, I'm very grateful.'

'He won't risk reporting it,' he said. 'Drunk on duty, away from his post, being offensive to a brother officer's wife.' He laughed suddenly. 'Besides, if the news reaches Alicia's ears, she will give him hell.' Still holding her hand, he began to push his way through the crowd filling the small town, looking for his own company.

The tattered remains, only a handful of men, were resting in the shade of an olive grove. They were filthy and blood-spattered, their faces blackened by powder burns, their clothing torn. Too weary to choose a comfortable place to lie, they were stretched out on the hard ground in whatever position they had dropped. It was only then, looking up at Dick, that Louise realised he was in little better condition.

'It's terrible,' she said. 'Humphrey said we hadn't been defeated; he said it was just a withdrawal.'

'So it was, but we were caught too far forward.' He grinned suddenly, and through the dust caking his face, his teeth gleamed white and strong. 'But you don't want to hear about that, do you?'

'Yes, I do. I saw the beginning of it from the ridge;

I saw the French march out of Ciudad Rodrigo, and I
tried to warn the Duke.'

'I know. Humphrey came to tell us, but we were
already in the thick of it.'

The women were coming out from wherever they
had been waiting, coming to succour their men,
bustling round lighting fires, cooking, nagging them
out of their lethargy, making them clean themselves
up. Louise and Dick threaded their way between
them and up the slope to a quiet spot near a tiny
stream which ran sparkling down towards the camp,
where the women were already sullying it with their
washing.

Dick threw down his shako, unstrapped his sword
and sank wearily to the ground, leaning against a tree
trunk and shutting his eyes. 'Humphrey told me what
you had done. He said it strengthened our case
against Fourier . . .'

'Dick,' she said, sitting beside him. 'Paul is not a
spy, I am sure of it. Humphrey is seeking revenge
only because he believes he has been cuckolded . . .'

'I know. And to be honest, my motives were the
same, but after today . . .'

'I swear you have no cause to believe that,' she
cried. 'You know why I left with the Captain; it was
not of my own free will.'

He opened his eyes and smiled at her. 'No?'

She hesitated only a second, but then decided there
was nothing to be gained by trying to explain how
she felt about Paul; she had to bury that love if there
was to be any future with the man who was her
husband. 'No,' she said firmly.

'You know, Louise, my dear,' he said, reaching out
to take her hand. 'That was the biggest gamble of all
and it went against the grain, I can tell you.'

'What do you mean?'

'Why deliberately setting out to lose a wager.' He
laughed suddenly. 'I had such a good hand, too.'

'Lose?' she echoed, withdrawing her hand from
his. 'You wanted to lose?'

'Well, you don't think Black and Fletcher would

have allowed you to live if I had won, do you? By
losing, I saved your life . . .'

'I find that difficult to swallow.'

'Nevertheless, it's true. I had to appear to agree to
their plans, for both our sakes. I was gambling on
finding you a few days later and fetching you back.'
He smiled ruefully. 'That was another gamble I lost.
You disappeared, and then Black brought me evidence
you had drowned . . .'

'And you believed him?'

'I had no reason not to.'

She did not know whether to believe him; it would
make her future life with him so much more tolerable
if she could. Tolerable, perhaps, but not happy,
because her happiness lay with someone else. 'So you
decided to go ahead with your plans to marry again?'

'Why not?'

She smiled. 'You were ever an opportunist.'

He put his head back against the tree and shut his
eyes. He looked immeasurably weary, his energy
sapped, his emotion drained, and she found herself
feeling sorry for him.

'Was it very bad out there?' she asked.

'Hell,' he murmured. 'We were overwhelmed by
the French cavalry, caught on an open plain. They
captured the Portuguese guns we had with us and
made straight for us.' He smiled. 'There's no one so
angry as a British infantrymen when taken by surprise.
We rallied and formed squares and recaptured the
guns. Then Humphrey arrived bringing orders, we
were to hold on until we had gathered in the scattered
units and could withdraw in good order. That was the
bad part, really bad. The French horses kept coming
at us, cutting us down with their flashing sabres and it
wasn't long before they flashed no more; they were
covered in blood, the blood of our brave soldiers . . .'

'Humphrey said you were being brave too. Reckless,
he said.'

He grinned. 'You know me! I have to be as good
as the next man, or better.'

'He said you had the gift of survival.'

'So I have, so I have, but every soldier has to

believe that, otherwise he couldn't go on. He has to
be convinced on his own invulnerability.'

'He said you were putting it to the test.'

'I didn't have time to think of such things. When
the battalions formed squares, we brought up the
rear. The French cavalry kept riding furiously round
the square, trying to break it. At one time we were
attacked on three sides at once; you couldn't see
anything but dust and smoke, and we couldn't tell if
we'd broken or not . . .'

'But you hadn't?' She had no difficulty in picturing
the scene, the colours flying in the square above the
smoke, the smashing and crashing and shouting, the
flash of steel, the thunder of guns, men and horses
falling. She had seen it before, she knew what it was
like, but for Dick it was the first time. His sheltered
upbringing, his wealthy background had not prepared
him for the reality, but for all that he had acquitted
himself well. Today he had become a man, a man
able to lead men and not be led by them. His fault
had always been weakness; she had to make herself
believe that if she were going to go on living with
him.

'No,' he said. 'Six miles we retreated like that, six
miles walking backwards over open country and still
they came at us.' His blue eyes held the far-away
look of remembrance. 'The Bluecoats tired at last
and the main force turned to march, leaving only us
in square. The cavalry couldn't break us, so they
brought up the artillery and fired into our flanks . . .'
His voice trailed away as he put a hand through his
hair, caked with dust and grime. 'We were nearly
back safe when the devils decided to make a last
charge, galloping right up to the points of the men's
bayonets before backing off. It takes a special sort of
man to stand firm without flinching when a horse is
galloping right at him and its rider is brandishing a
sabre and hallooing like a madman, but my men
didn't waver, and Picton just sat his horse and stared
at them as if he meant to frighten them off with a
look.' He chuckled at the memory. 'With the French
only yards away, he said, "It is but a ruse to frighten

us, but it won't do." I don't know about anyone else,
but I was terrified out of my life . . .'

'But you did well! Humphrey said so, and he
wouldn't give such praise lightly. I detected a grudging
admiration for you.'

'I think I did,' he said slowly. 'I hope I did. But,
you know, I wasn't cut out to be a soldier.'

'No?'

'No. I think I'll write to my father and suggest
resigning my commission.'

'But will he allow you to go back to England?'

'He will if you put in a word, if you tell him I'm a
reformed character . . .'

'Are you?'

'I think so,' he said. 'Yes, I know so. Louise, my
dear, do you think we could start again, pretend last
year never happened. We loved each other once . . .'

She did not know what to say because he had
taken her by surprise. For the first time since their
wedding day, he sounded sincere. Did he mean it?
Could she believe him? And was that what she really
wanted?

She ached for news of Paul, just to hear whether
he was alive or dead would be something to hold on
to and though she scolded herself for her thoughts,
she kept remembering the times they had had
together, times too brief, too heart-breaking to dwell
on. She told herself over and over again that he had
gone for good, but she could not make herself believe
it. If she took Dick up on his promise, could she
forget? Would the ache in her heart diminish? Would
she ever look back and imagine it had all been
fantasy, dreams mixed with nightmares?

'And are you prepared to face everyone if we go
back home—your father and mother, David, Miss
Trent? Miss Trent most of all.'

'I can if you are by my side, you are so strong.
Besides, I have reason to believe Miss Trent was not
entirely heart-broken; before I left England, she had
become betrothed to David.'

'David Marriott?' She remembered Dick's cousin
with affection, and wished him happiness.

'Who else? She won't get the title her father craved for her, but she will get a good husband.'

'And the man you killed; Fletcher, wasn't it?'

He looked up, startled. 'How did you know about that?'

'It doesn't matter how I know. Tell me what happened.'

'He tried to blackmail me and when I refused, there was a fight. He picked up a paper-knife and I had to defend myself. I didn't mean to kill him . . .' He paused, leaning forward, watching her face. 'It's God's truth, Louise. Everyone else believes it.'

'Perhaps everyone doesn't know you as I do.'

'You don't know me at all,' he said. 'Not as I am now. I've changed. Coming out here and seeing men kill each other in battle, seeing them cut to pieces and blown up, seeing their terrible injuries, has made me realise that life itself is a gamble, and that should be enough for any man. It made me see how unimportant I am in the scheme of things. I can't explain, Louise, but I need you to understand . . .'

'I'll try,' she said. She would try, she really would.

His whole body seemed to relax and he leaned back against the tree and shut his eyes. 'Good,' he murmured. 'I'll go and see the Colonel tomorrow. The sooner he lets me go, the better. We'll go home, my dear, home to England where the meadows are green and the rain is gentle. Home . . .'

He looked so boyish sprawled against the tree, dirty, dishevelled, exhausted, his fair hair falling over his forehead, it was difficult to recall that he had treated her abominably and would possibly do so again when he felt more like his old self. She was under no illusions. He had fallen asleep and was snoring gently.

She rose, shook out the lovely skirt the man at the cottage had given her and, taking his empty canteen, went down to the camp fires. When he woke, he would be hungry and thirsty, and she must do as all soldiers' wives did; she must look after her man.

When night fell, instead of settling down to the usual routine of evening, they were ordered to leave

their fires burning to deceive the enemy and, under
cover of darkness, moved back once more. For the
remainder of the night and all next day they marched,
while the French, waking up to the ruse too late to
prevent it, followed cautiously.

'Shall we be forever retreating?' asked the girl who
walked beside Louise. She was very young, not much
more than a child, and she had not been long in the
Peninsula; her husband had come out with Dick's
regiment, and to her it was all new and strange.
Louise felt like an old campaigner beside her, though
it had been only five short months since she had
herself arrived. It seemed a lifetime ago, a lifetime
when she had soared to the heights of happiness and
plumbed the depths of misery, where she had learned
the value of friendship. She missed Hetty and the
other women she had known; they were with their
husbands' regiments and marching, just as she was
marching, somewhere over to their right.

'No,' she said. 'But the Duke won't risk his men
unnecessarily. He'll want to fight on ground of his
own choosing. You saw what happened yesterday
when they were caught unprepared.'

She was right. By the next evening, the whole
army of 45,000 men were stationed in the positions
Wellington had chosen and prepared, and the enemy,
realising they had been out-manoeuvred, withdrew.
Everyone relaxed; someone killed a wild pig, others
found a few chickens in a farmyard, and before long
the camp around Dick's section smelled of roast pork.
Wine was produced, seemingly from the empty air,
flutes, Portuguese pipes and even a guitar were
brought out from kitbags. Withdrawal it had been,
but as Paul had explained to her not so long ago, a
withdrawal was not necessarily a retreat, they were
far from defeated.

Dick joined his fellow officers in a game of cards,
and Louise, unwilling to take part in the jollity, went
off by herself. She walked up on to the road and
stood looking down it; the moon was throwing deep
shadows across it from the pines and outcrops of
rock, but it was empty of life. She turned and went

back to the spot she had chosen for her bed and sat down, hugging her knees and gazing at the revellers with eyes that did not see.

While there was no news of Paul, either good or bad, she could not rest. It was all very well to promise herself she would forget him, it was easier said than done and she was only deceiving herself when she told herself that once she knew he was safe, she could bear the pain of parting.

When she went to the little near-by village next morning to bargain for vegetables, she saw the well-loved figure on the big black horse riding in, with Maria up behind him. Louise turned from the woman who was offering the produce and stared as if she had seen a ghost. Her prayers had been answered, he was alive and seemingly well, but she was far from feeling better. She found she was shaking, and her heart was thumping so fast that she thought she would faint.

'Señora,' the woman said. 'You no like this fine pumpkin?'

Louise half turned, accepted the pumpkin and paid for it without taking her eyes from the man on the horse. He rode up to one of the burgher houses which had become a divisional headquarters, set Maria down and dismounted, throwing the reins to an orderly. It was then he noticed Louise. For a moment their glances met and held, then he raised one hand in a signal of acknowledgment and turned to escort Maria into the building. Louise took a step towards him, her own arm upraised, but then she dropped it and turned to go. What purpose would it serve to speak to him? None. It would only be twisting the knife in the wound, still so very raw. She turned her back on him, on the village, on her love, and returned to the camp site with leaden feet.

Dick was very late in coming for his supper, and when he did return, he was in jubilant mood, picking her up and swinging her round as if she weighed no more than a feather. 'We're going home,' he said. 'We're going home!'

'Home?'

'Yes, back to England. I've spoken to the Colonel, and we leave tomorrow.'

'Everyone?'

'No silly, you and I.' He paused, watching her face, then added, 'I have been given a job to do, a special job . . .'

She was not really listening, because her thoughts had flown to Paul and the last glimpse she had had of him, the slightly mocking smile, the hand raised . . . was it in goodbye? But then she suddenly became aware that he was saying something important and forced herself to pay attention.

'Did you hear me? I said they have captured the spy. I'm to escort her back to Lisbon; then we embark for home.'

Paul? No, he had said 'her'. 'The spy?'

'Yes, it was Maria all along. Fourier has just brought her in, and she has confessed. She's to be taken back to Lisbon, for her own people to deal with as they think fit. It's all political, of course, but providential for us.'

'Why?' she asked dully.

'Because when I first requested leave, the Colonel was ill-disposed to grant it, but needing someone to escort the prisoner, he changed his mind.' He laughed. 'Pack your things, we're off at first light.'

They were provided with a gaily-painted mule cart for travelling and Louise, who had walked everywhere during her stay in the Peninsula, found it the height of luxury. It was driven by a fiercely loyal Spanish boy who looked daggers of hate at Maria and who did nothing to help her, while being excessively attentive to Louise. Dick rode beside them, enjoying his role hugely and smiling benignly at both women. It was almost as if he had already shrugged off the war and was out for an afternoon's pleasure. Maria, sullen, pulled her shawl close about her shoulders and refused to speak.

Louise would have liked to draw her out, to find out exactly what she had done, to ask about Paul and how he had caught up with her, but in the face of a wall of silence, she gave up.

They made a good pace along the main road for a full day, but on the second, their driver suggested a short cut over the hills.

'Is it safe?' queried Louise.

'*Sı, señora*. The mule, she go well over the mountains.'

'No, I meant from the French.'

'We're miles behind our own lines,' Dick said, then turning to the boy, 'You are sure you know the way?'

'*Sı, señor.*'

'Then off you go. The sooner we get to Lisbon, the sooner we can go home.'

Louise said nothing, but she remembered seeing Frenchmen well behind the English lines before, and she had been with Maria on that occasion too. She glanced at the girl, who was looking straight ahead, her expression stony. It was just beginning to rain as they turned off the road on to a mountain track and began to climb, the first rain Louise had seen during that long, hot summer.

It happened when they were least expecting it, a volley of shots which toppled the Spanish boy and panicked the mule into a crazy gallop. Louise clung on as they hurtled off the track and into a copse of trees. The boy fell from his seat and the reins flew out and across the mule's rump. She tried to reach forward to pick them up as the cart careered over the uneven ground, bumping and jolting its two occupants. She could hear Dick pounding after them, shouting instructions. There were more shots, and then Dick's riderless horse overtook them. She looked back. Her husband was nowhere to be seen, but four French horsemen were bearing down on them. She turned to make another effort to reach the reins, just as a wheel caught in a tree root and the cart overturned.

The breath was forced from her body as she hit the ground and lay still. Miraculously she was not hurt, and looked round for Maria. The girl was unconscious, pinned beneath the overturned cart, while the mule was struggling to stand up.

Another shot was fired, and Louise looked up to see a Frenchman fall. Dick was limping after them,

pistol in hand. He had brought one down, could he
load and fire again before they turned on him? She
knew it was impossible. But the enemy had wasted
their shots in the pursuit, and now two of them
turned and galloped at Dick with drawn swords,
while the other dismounted and ran to the aid of
Maria. What was it he had said only a few days
before? 'It takes a special sort of man to stand firm
when a horse is galloping straight at him.' He was
standing there now, in the pouring rain, re-priming
his pistol, and he had no infantry square to protect
him. He did not stand a chance.

She screamed at him to take cover, but he could
not have heard her. They were within yards of him
before he managed to reload, but his hand was steady
as he raised his arm and fired. One fell. The other
wheeled and lashed out with his sword at the now
defenceless man. Again and again he struck, as Dick
tried to draw his own weapon. He fell at last under
the rain of blows and, regardless of her own safety,
Louise ran towards him.

The horseman, his sword dripping blood—Dick's
blood, she realised with horror—turned and cantered
past her to help his compatriot to free Maria. For the
moment they were not interested in Louise.

She knelt on the wet ground beside her husband
and opened his jacket. One of his many wounds was
deep and bleeding profusely. When she lifted her
skirt to tear a strip from her petticoat to stanch it, he
said, 'Don't.'

'Why not? You'll bleed to death if I don't stop it.'

'I'll bleed to death anyway. Leave me be. Save
yourself.' There was blood in his mouth as he spoke,
and she was appalled. She took his canteen from its
holder and put her arm under his head to help him to
drink.

'Oh, why did you have to be so foolish?' she cried.
'So foolish and so brave.'

He grinned lop-sidedly. 'I gambled and I lost . . .'
His head dropped on her arm. For a moment she sat
there, numb, unable to believe he was dead, unable
to think.

Slowly, through the mists of her mind, sounds penetrated. The Frenchmen had succeeded in righting the little cart and calming the mule; now they were lifting Maria, conscious and apparently unhurt, into it. In a moment they would turn their attention to her, and she had better be ready.

Gently she withdrew her arm from under Dick's head and laid him down, took off his ammunition pouch and powder bag and crawled over to where he had dropped his pistol, thankful it had landed in a dry spot. She had managed to load and prime it by the time they turned towards her. But even if her hand was steady and her aim true, she could hit only one of them. Then what? She glanced at her husband, lying so pale and still in death, and an anger welled up in her and overflowed. She moved over to him and drew his sword. She would die with honour as he had done, and she would welcome death when it came.

They came towards her on foot, confident, relaxed, unprepared. Coolly she waited until they were close, then raised her arm and fired. The man's look of surprise as he fell was almost comical, but there was no time to be amused; the other, in anger, was drawing his sword and she had no doubt that he would use it. She could hear Maria in the mule cart, screaming encouragement at him as he advanced warily, like someone trying to corner a wild animal. She backed away, feeling for a tree behind her, Dick's sword heavy in her hand; time seemed to stop as the Frenchman circled her, coming nearer, poised to strike the weapon from her hand as soon as she made a move to use it. He was breathing heavily and her heart was thumping in her ears; she heard nothing until the shot rang out and he crumpled at her feet.

She stood rooted to the spot, staring down at him. He twitched once and then lay still. She looked towards Dick, half expecting to see him sitting up with a smoking pistol in his hand and a wide grin on his face, but he had not moved. The puddle at his side was pink with blood. She glanced up as a horse galloped through the trees towards them. The rider dismounted and ran towards her. Then she fainted.

'Oh, Louise, my brave, brave girl!' His voice came to her through a fog. 'I was miles away when I heard the first shots.' Her eyes flickered open and met his, then closed again. 'Why were you so far from the road?'

'The silly fool of a driver decided to take a short cut,' Maria called in answer, apparently fully recovered. 'It made no difference; we were followed just the same.'

The shrill voice brought Louise to her senses. She wriggled in Paul's arms and sat up. 'You saved me,' she said. 'Another minute . . .' She looked over towards her husband. 'He is dead. He died very bravely. There were four of them.' She did not need to tell him that, for all the bodies were sprawled over the rain-soaked ground where they had fallen. And a little further off was the body of the little Spanish boy, killed by the first shot.

'It's all over,' he said gently. 'You are quite safe now.'

'Where did they come from?' she asked. 'What did they want with us?'

'They have been with us all the time,' Maria said, bringing the cart up to where they sat on the ground. 'They were waiting for a chance to free me . . .' She laughed suddenly. 'They did not die in vain.' And she slapped the reins on the mule's back and whipped it into a fast run, making for the road.

Paul started up, but he had not reloaded his pistol and she was well away before he could do anything. He sat down beside Louise and put his arms about her shoulders. Her face was the colour of parchment and she was shaking with shock. Now it was all over and the heat of her anger had cooled, she was trembling with fear.

'You're safe now,' he said, again and again. 'Safe with me.'

They sat together in silence for some minutes until she felt more composed, then he kissed the top of her head and pulled himself away from her. She felt

too drained, too lethargic, to move, and watched
with half-veiled eyes as he buried Dick's body in a
shallow grave, fashioned a small cross above it and
then left the clearing. She sat up in alarm, terrified of
being left alone, but he was soon back, leading Dick's
horse.

'Come, my love,' he said, holding out his hand to
help her up. 'Time to go.'

'How did you know where to find us?' she asked,
much later, as they approached a small village in the
gathering twilight.

'I didn't, but I guessed there might be some
treachery afoot when I heard that Major Barton had
persuaded the Colonel to detail your husband to take
the prisoner to Lisbon, and without an escort. It was
highly irregular and invited trouble. The girl had vital
secrets; the French were bound to try and reclaim
her . . .'

'But what did Humphrey hope would happen?'

'Exactly what did happen, my darling, except that
you survived . . .'

'Does he hate me that much?'

'Humphrey hates everything he can't have.'

'Maria really was a spy?'

'No doubt of it! I caught her sending messages to
the garrison at Ciudad Rodrigo with a looking-glass.'

'It was she on the cliff?'

'Yes, but she led me a dance before I caught her,
and by that time the French had over-run our position
and my horse had bolted.' He smiled at the memory.
'I was in something of a pickle, and she was being as
difficult as she could, but I managed to bring her
in . . .'

'I know. I saw you.'

'I wanted to come to you,' he said, reaching across
and taking her hand. 'But then I thought it would not
be fair to you, not if you had decided to stay with
Dick . . .'

'I had to. We had made vows before God, and I
don't take such things lightly.' She paused. 'And he
was trying to behave himself . . .'

'That's why I thought it best to stay away. But it was hard, my love. You'll never know how hard.'

They stopped outside a small single-storey cottage nestling in a valley beside an olive grove, and he dismounted and knocked at the door. It was opened by a middle-aged woman in a black skirt and colourful apron, whose face lit up when she saw him. She greeted him in Portuguese, and he hugged her and answered in a mixture of French and Portuguese, which was apparently understood.

Paul turned and helped Louise down, then led her into the house, as the woman's husband, calling a greeting, passed them to go and look after the horses.

'The *Señora* asks would you prefer to eat first or sleep or take a bath?' Paul said, smiling at Louise. 'Which is it to be?'

'A bath?' Louise repeated. 'Oh, yes, please, a bath.'

He smiled and spoke to the woman again and she led Louise down a hall to a back room. It was obviously the main bedroom of the house, filled with sturdy carved furniture, and the bed itself was covered in a beautifully patterned bedspread. Louise stood admiring it, while the woman and her husband brought a tub indoors and filled it with pan after pan of warm water. Then she was handed some clean clothes and a towel and left to herself.

Slowly, as if in a dream, Louise stripped off all her clothes and stepped into the water. This was the ultimate in luxury and she revelled in it, washing away the blood and grime which clung to her; it was almost as if she were washing away her past, peeling it from her like an outer skin and discarding it. The past was gone, the future lay ahead, clean and sparkling.

At last she stirred herself, rubbed herself dry and dressed in the voluminous skirt and blouse she had been given. They were much too big, and she laughed as she caught sight of herself in a mirror. But she could not put her own clothes back on, they were caked with mud and blood, and so she left the room and went down the corridor to find Paul, with a light step.

She could hear him before she had gone half-way down the hall, speaking in rapid French and then being answered by another man, also in French. For one heart-stopping moment her doubts returned, and her hand shook as she lifted the latch of the door where the voices were coming from. They turned to face her as she went in, Paul and his companion, the French Captain with the same name.

CHAPTER THIRTEEN

SHE MUST HAVE looked as startled as she felt, because they both laughed. 'Louise,' Paul said, coming forward to take her hand. 'Come and meet my cousin, Henri.'

'We have already met, do you not remember?' Henri said, taking her hand and putting it to his lips. 'I most certainly have not forgotten a pleasant hour or two in the midst of war.'

'Cousin?' repeated Louise, finding her voice at last.

'Yes,' Paul said. 'Henri is my cousin. Although he chose to stay in Europe when the rest of the family moved to England, his sister Jeannette came with us. But she was never strong and died very young . . .'

'Your mother told me about her,' Louise murmured. 'She gave me one of her gowns . . .'

'So she did.'

She looked from one to the other. 'Are you on opposite sides in this terrible war?'

'No.' Paul led her to the table where a simple meal had been laid out for them. 'Sit down and eat; you must be hungry.'

She was still too keyed up from the events of that day to eat and sat picking at her food, but her eyes were bright and her cheeks a rosy pink.

'Henri has good reason to hate the French,' Paul began.

'No, not the French,' Henri corrected him. 'Not the French people, nor even the French soldier, just the régime, Napoleon Bonaparte and his insane idea to conquer Europe.'

'You are a spy?' she asked.

Paul laughed. 'Yes, he is. We both are. That's why I couldn't deny it when you accused me and I couldn't, at that time, tell you the truth. I am on the side of the British, always have been.'

'I saw Henri on the mountain the day before Maria and I joined the column,' she said. 'The day after that, we were bombarded. I thought he was responsible.'

'No, I was there to keep a rendezvous with Paul,' said Henri. 'I didn't see the gun until it was too late, and I couldn't stop it immediately because, after all, I was supposed to be a French officer.'

She turned to Paul. 'Is that why you rode off? You went to meet your cousin?'

'Yes. And we had to silence that gun, but we had to make it look as though the *guerrilleros* had done it, otherwise our secret would have come to light. We couldn't risk that; there was too much at stake, too much work still to do.'

'Is that why you often used to ride off by yourself? Is that how the rumours started?'

'Yes, but it never bothered me until you came along.' He smiled, and she felt warm and comfortable and happy. 'I hated keeping the secret from you. You don't know how many times I nearly blurted it out!'

'Did Pringle and Hetty know?'

'No, but they trusted me.'

'And I didn't,' she said, bitterly ashamed. 'I am so sorry, Paul, truly sorry I ever doubted you.'

'You should never doubt your heart,' said Henri. 'No matter how bad things look.'

'What are we going to do now?' she asked. 'Are we going back to the battalion?'

'We?' Paul repeated.

'Yes,' she told him. 'We. I am your camp-follower, don't forget.'

He laughed. 'I suppose you are. Well, tomorrow morning, my darling camp-follower, we ride to Portalegre with a message from the Peer to General Hill; this time we've got those Bluecoats stretched out from their base, scouring the countryside for food, and if we move secretly and swiftly, we can

turn the tables on them.' He paused. 'After that, my
love, you and I are going to find a priest.'

She was so surprised at this unexpected proposal
that she could only say, 'Oh, Paul!'

'You do want that, don't you?'

'Oh, yes. Yes!'

'I feel a shade *de trop*,' Henri said, rising. 'I'll
leave you two love-birds to talk. Besides, I must
return before I'm missed.' He went to Louise and
took her hand. '*Au revoir, ma chère.* When this war
is over, I will come to England to visit you. Expect
me.' He bent to kiss her cheek, then went to Paul
and clapped his hand on his cousin's shoulder,
gripping it firmly. 'Take care,' he said. 'Take care.'
And then he was gone.

Paul stood up and went to the window to watch
him ride off. When the clatter of hooves had died, he
turned and held out his arms to Louise. She went to
him at once and he held her close, murmuring her
name. In his arms she felt safe and loved; nothing
and no one could harm her now, not the French, nor
Humphrey, nor Reuben Black, no one. And it would
always be the same. In her turn she would give him
her love and devotion to the end of time.

At last he drew away and held her at arm's length,
looking at her with his head on one side and smiling.
'The *Señora* us a mite larger than you are!'

'I know. I look like a sack tied in the middle.'

'You look beautiful, as always,' he said, kissing
her. 'It is of no consequence to me what you wear. In
fact . . .' He stopped speaking and took her hand,
leading her along the corridor to the bedroom where
she had bathed. It had been tidied, the bath had
gone, and her own clothes, clean and pressed, were
hanging over a chair. He kicked the door shut, picked
her up and carried her over to the bed.

She submitted, as he slowly removed the overlarge
blouse and skirt and began untying her underwear,
stopping frequently to kiss her and murmur her name.

There was a brief moment when she felt she ought
to resist, ought to stop him, but the beating of her
heart and the tingling of her body told her otherwise.

She wanted him, wanted this fulfilment of their love
with every nerve and sinew. What had Henri said?
'Never doubt your heart.' Her heart was telling her
what to do now.

She smiled up at him. 'Paul?'

'Mm.'

She reached up and began unbuttoning his shirt. 'I
love you.'

It was some time before she learned the full extent of
Paul's contribution to the war, and it was the Duke
of Wellington himself who told her. It was at a
glittering reception held to celebrate the capture of
Salamanca, that beautiful Spanish city which, together
with Ciudad Rodrigo, had stood so long in the way of
the British advance.

The city had been badly damaged during the
fighting and parts of it deliberately demolished by the
French when constructing their defences, but even so,
much of its grandeur remained and now, crowded
with British troops bent on celebration, it was bright
and noisy. No less so than in the splendid reception-
room of one of its many palaces, where the Spanish
nobility entertained their liberators.

The inhabitants of Salamanca had been hungry as
all French-occupied towns were, but now it was in
hands of the British the supplies were coming in; the
tables were laden. Not to be outdone, the Spanish
people had raided their hidden cellars and produced
wine in abundance with which to toast the victory.

The men's uniforms embraced all the colours of the
spectrum, while the ladies, from trunks and supply
wagons, from hidden closets, from little shops still
managing to trade, had found gowns of unbelievable
richness. Even Louise, who hated ostentation, was
wearing a deep blue silk tunic trimmed with pearls
and tiny white feathers. On her auburn curls she
wore the antique circlet Paul had bought her in
Portalegre as a wedding gift.

Everyone of any importance seemed to be there,
all the senior officers and their wives, Spanish,
Portuguese, German, and a few people invited at the

special request of the Duke, Captain Paul Fourier
among them. Major Barton and Alicia were there
too, because he had been instrumental in recapturing
Maria; the girl had been tried and executed, in spite
of an attempt by Louise to intercede for her.
Humphrey had not been pleased by that, but realising
it would be imprudent to show any animosity to the
wife of one of the Duke's favourites, he had wisely
called a truce. And because Louise no longer walked
behind the army, she had been freed from the
necessity to be more than civil to him and polite to
his wife. They were on the other side of the room
now, enjoying the evening, as she was doing.

But it was not the end of the war, rather the
beginning of the advance, And Louise was all too
aware that this was only a brief respite, that there
was more fighting to come. And, for the first time,
she was really afraid; she had so much more to lose.

She had only to shut her eyes and the noise of the
revellers became the tumult of battle, the thunder of
guns, the clashing of swords; the laughter became the
cries of wounded and dying men. She could see again
the dust and smoke, the bright red uniforms, the
dark green jackets of the riflemen, mud-caked, blood-
spattered. Her memory ranged back over her fifteen
months in Portugal, the people and the ever-changing
scenery, the long marches and, at the end of the day,
the myriads of fires glowing through the night. She
could almost smell the aromatic woodsmoke, the
roasting pig. The heat from a thousand chandeliers
became the heat of the sun beating down on her
head, the splashing of the waterfall in the courtyard
became torrential rain.

The rain which had begun on the day Dick died
had gone on and on. It had been raining when they
rode into Portalegre, raining when Paul had left her
to join General Hill, still raining over two weeks
later, when he returned. It had been the longest
fortnight of her life, and her joy at seeing him safely
back was tinged with concern for the condition he
was in. Soaked through, bedraggled and exhausted,

he had fallen on the bed in the room he had taken for her, and slept for twenty-four hours.

She had sat and watched over him, knowing that every time he left her in the future, part of her would die until he returned, and she made up her mind that she would not be left behind again, not ever. She was his camp-follower, and she would follow him, come what may. The decision had precipitated an argument.

'There are times when it is just not sensible for you to come,' he said. 'In summer when the march is not forced . . .'

'I've been on forced marches before.'

'Not like this one. Five days we marched in torrential rain and icy winds, five nights we bivouaced without fires and hot food, just to beat the enemy to Arroyo dos Molinos.' He laughed suddenly. 'It was worth it though, just to see General Giraud, when he realised he had been tricked and we had taken the town. He ran out of his house, threw his cocked hat on the ground and stamped up and down on it in a rage.'

'You are smiling, Mrs Fourier. Will you tell me the joke?'

Startled, Louise turned to find the Duke of Wellington standing beside her, for once in full-dress uniform. He was not a handsome man but he had a commanding presence which, she realised, was hardly surprising, but his eyes were gentle and his manner relaxed, and she found it easy to understand the affection and loyalty in which he was held.

'I was remembering Paul's tale of General Giraud and his cocked hat,' she said, not in the least overawed by the great man.

'Oh, that! Yes, he has told it to me.' He paused as they watched Paul making his way towards them with two very full glasses. He was smiling at Louise in that special way of his which still made her heart turn over. 'Your husband makes light of his adventures,' the Duke said, smiling. 'But he is a very brave officer and a fine man.'

'I know that, my lord.'

'He has been of immeasurable service to me at great risk to himself.'

She smiled but did not answer, unsure of just how much she was supposed to know.

The Duke sighed. 'Now everyone knows it, too, and he is no use to me any more.' He smiled at her expression of indignation. 'I think,' he went on slowly, 'he should have a rest. Indeed, I am ordering him to return to England.' He watched her face light up with pleasure. 'It will do him good to go back to rearing horses. And children.'

'You know?'

'Yes, my dear, I know. I would not wish your child to be born out here. He must be a son of England, and then one day he may make as good a soldier as his father.'

Louise was not at all sure she wanted her son, if her child turned out to be a boy, to join the army, but she judged it prudent not to say so. It was enough that they were going home, home to England, home together, she and her beloved husband.

YOU'RE INVITED TO ACCEPT
2 MASQUERADE ROMANCES
AND A DIAMOND ZIRCONIA NECKLACE
FREE!

Acceptance card

| NO STAMP NEEDED | Post to: Reader Service, FREEPOST, P.O. Box 236, Croydon, Surrey. CR9 9EL |

Please note readers in Southern Africa write to:
Independant Book Services P.T.Y., Postbag X3010, Randburg 2125, S. Africa

YES! Please send me 2 free Masquerade Romances
and my free diamond zirconia necklace – and
reserve a Reader Service Subscription for me. If I decide to
subscribe I shall receive 4 new Masquerade Romances every
other month as soon as they come off the presses for £6.00
together with a FREE newsletter including information on top
authors and special offers, exclusively for Reader Service
subscribers. There are no postage and packing charges, and I
understand I may cancel or suspend my subscription at any
time. If I decide not to subscribe I shall write to you within 10
days. Even If I decide not to subscribe the 2 free novels and the
necklace are mine to keep forever.
I am over 18 years of age   EP22M

NAME _____
                                                    (CAPITALS PLEASE)

ADDRESS _____

_____

_____ POSTCODE _____